A.

S

DREAM ON

DREAM ON

Anthea Cohen

Chivers Press   G.K. Hall & Co.
Bath, England   Thorndike, Maine USA

This Large Print edition is published by Chivers Press, England, and by G.K. Hall & Co., USA.

Published in 2000 in the U.K. by arrangement with Severn House Publishers Ltd.

Published in 2000 in the U.S. by arrangement with Vanessa Holt Limited.

U.K. Hardcover   ISBN 0-7540-4299-5   (Chivers Large Print)
U.K. Softcover   ISBN 0-7540-4300-2   (Camden Large Print)
U.S. Softcover   ISBN 0-7838-9258-6   (Nightingale Series Edition)

The text of this Large Print edition is unabridged.
Other aspects of the book may vary from the original edition.

Set in 16 pt. New Times Roman.

Printed in Great Britain on acid-free paper.

British Library Cataloguing in Publication Data available

Library of Congress Cataloging-in-Publication Data

    Cohen, Anthea.
     Dream on / Anthea Cohen.
       p.   cm.
     ISBN 0-7838-9258-6 (lg. print : sc : alk. paper)
     1. Mothers and daughters—Fiction. 2. Extortion—Fiction.
     3. Arson—Fiction. 4. Large type books. I. Title.
    PR6053.O34 D74 2000
    823'.914—dc21   00-059676

CHAPTER ONE

'Where's Neeny?' Henry Mason called out as soon as he entered the front door.

Elizabeth, his wife, wished, as she always did, that he wouldn't persist in calling their daughter 'Neeny'. Her name was Nina, the name he had chosen when she was born. The nickname irritated Elizabeth.

'She's taken Polly into the field for a walk.' She spoke with some difficulty as she was holding a paint brush in her mouth, not wanting to put the brush down and waste the paint on it, which she had just managed to mix to the right shade.

'What?' Her husband poked his head round the kitchen door.

Elizabeth took the brush out of her mouth. 'She's taken Polly for a walk in the field.'

'Oh.' Henry came into the kitchen, opened the refrigerator door and took out a can of beer. 'How long since she went out, then?'

Elizabeth looked at him. He pulled a face as he opened the can and it made the usual swishing sound and the fine spray rose to his face. 'Bit early for that, isn't it?' she said.

He shrugged. 'Thirsty,' he said and repeated his question.

'Oh, I don't know, Henry, twenty minutes, maybe longer—what time is it?'

'Twenty past five.'

Elizabeth looked mildly surprised. 'She went out at tea time, we had a cup of tea before she went out.'

Her husband finished his beer. 'You don't keep tabs on her, not enough. She's fifteen now, getting too independent, too self-willed.'

Elizabeth nodded in agreement but did not speak. Henry moved across the kitchen and, in doing so, knocked the corner of the table. An orange rolled off the pile of fruit in the pottery bowl.

'Don't do that. Put the orange back on the top, where it was. It's for my still life, for the painting class.'

Henry put the fruit back. He wandered over and looked at the painting his wife was working on, then turned round and looked at the fruit and the glass bottle beside it. 'You haven't done the bottle very well.'

'You try painting glass!' Elizabeth almost snapped at him.

Henry dropped the empty beer can in the bin. 'Was it four o'clock when you had tea with Neeny?'

Elizabeth had resumed her painting. She was short-sighted and hated wearing her glasses, so she had to peer rather closely at the picture, leaning slightly forward. 'I expect so. We usually have a cup of tea when she's not in school.'

'Well, it's half-past five now, she should be

2

back.'

Elizabeth straightened her back, stretched a little, then rubbed the back of her neck. 'Maybe Polly's being naughty again and has chased off after a rabbit. Don't go on so, Henry, you worry too much.'

He walked out of the kitchen. 'You'd do better with your glasses.' His parting shot.

Elizabeth decided he had destroyed her painting mood and cleared away her easel and paints. Supper was a beef casserole, cooking slowly in the oven, getting ready to be served about seven. She felt Henry, as usual, was being obsessive about Nina. At fifteen she should surely be trusted to take her dog for a walk, and Polly was her dog.

The field where Nina had gone was a fairly big park-like space in the middle of the estate. Houses, bungalows, regulation cut lawns, flowering cherry trees in spring. Henry loved the neat, tidy arrangement of it all; in Elizabeth's opinion it was suburbia at its worst. Not what she had hoped for when they moved from town to what Henry called the 'country'. Admittedly it was useful for the short run to Nina's school and the shops were not far away, but she had imagined they would find a stone-built cottage with small windows and a thatched roof. That she realised now was all a fantasy. She had tried for it. Several estate agents had sent them brochures of such places, but Henry's remarks had been pretty well the same about all of them: 'Needs a lot doing to it.' 'Dark inside.' 'Probably damp.' Hopeless.

'Elizabeth!' Henry's voice, urgent and loud.

'What is it?' She made her way across the kitchen to the back door. Henry's voice had come from the garden. The path ran between two lawns, from the back door where Elizabeth now stood, to the back gate which led out into the field. The gate was slightly ajar. Trotting up the path, fawn and white coat gleaming in the evening sun, undocked tail wagging, her new blue collar and metal disc in place, was Polly. No lead, no Nina. The dog went straight into the kitchen and to her water bowl. Elizabeth could hear her drinking thirstily.

'Where's Neeny? She always puts the lead on to bring her home, she knows to do that.'

Elizabeth forced herself to be patient, pleasant, reassuring. 'Henry, Polly's done this before, you know, chased off and come home alone. Nina's probably looking for her.'

'But it's nearly two hours.' He looked distractedly at his watch. 'I'm going to call the police.' He started for the house.

'Hello, Mum, I've had such a time.' Nina pushed open the gate and came in.

Henry turned. 'Where have you been? We were worried sick.'

Nina looked surprised. 'Worried? What about? I met this man and we—'

'Man? What man?'

4

Nina's lower lip thrust out as it always did when she was displeased. She was a compact girl, dark-haired, not pretty. Her brown heavy-lidded eyes made her look slightly sly. She looked at her mother now and raised her eyebrows at Elizabeth.

'Your father really was worried, Nina.'

'Well, cool it, Dad. I was just helping this man, see?'

At the mention of 'this man' Henry became even more incensed.

Apparently 'this man', as her parents learned while Nina helped herself to a glass of orangeade from the fridge, was with his son, aged about five. Together they were flying a blue kite. The kite had got stuck in the branch of a tree, just too high to get at. 'The man' had suggested using Polly's extending nylon lead to throw over the tree branch and dislodge the kite. 'Polly shouldn't have run off home, but we were rather a long time.'

'You should have run off home too,' Henry said, banging his fist on the table.

'Why, Dad? He was hardly going to rape me with his five-year-old there. Don't worry, for God's sake.' She left the kitchen carrying the glass of orangeade; the door banged after her.

Henry, as Elizabeth expected, blew his top. 'How many times have we told her not to speak to strange men? How many?'

'No harm done, the man had his little son with him and they were flying a kite, and

5

they'd—'

'That's not the point, he could have been a rapist, a child abuser.'

Elizabeth sighed. She sighed a lot when talking to her husband. 'Like a whisky, dear?' she asked.

'Yes, I need one. You don't seem to understand, nowadays . . .' He didn't finish the sentence, or if he did the door banged behind him and obliterated his last words.

She went to the oven, opened it and looked at the gently bubbling casserole. Time to put the vegetables on. Supper would be a familiar meal. Nina would sulk. Maybe the casserole would not suit her, she was leaning towards vegetarianism these days. She fed Polly, tail-wagging and pleasant Polly, who attacked her meal with gusto then made for the back door. Elizabeth closed the back gate latch and turned the key in its lock. No more tradesmen would come this evening. Polly, replete with her favourite dog food, rolled on the grass. How much easier, pleasanter, better companions animals were than humans, Elizabeth thought. She realised that her daughter was not pleasant, not lovable—a terrible thing for a mother to think. Not lovable. Henry must find her lovable, he worried about her enough. Nina preferred her father to her, Elizabeth knew that, accepted that he spoiled her.

Supper that evening was as Elizabeth

suspected it would be, uncomfortable, cool and full of instructions from Henry about 'strange men'. It culminated in Nina throwing her knife and fork on to her plate, sending a little splash of gravy over the clean tablecloth, and leaving the room, once again crashing the door behind her. Her departing words, 'Oh, sod off,' did even more to inflame her father's anger.

'Where would she learn language like that at her age, unless she was ganging up with some . . .'

Elizabeth got up. 'Baked apple, Henry?' she asked, but he had left the kitchen and was calling, 'Neeny, Neeny, come and finish your meal.' His voice was pleading.

Elizabeth brought her plate with the apple on to the table, poured some cream over it, especially bought as a little treat during today's shopping. She wildly felt she would like to run away, walk out, pack a bag and do a Shirley Valentine, leave these two hateful quarrelsome people behind.

Henry came back to the table after his fruitless calling at the foot of the stairs. He accepted the apple, poured cream over it and ate in complete silence. Directly he had finished he got up. 'I'll try again,' he said.

Elizabeth shrugged her shoulders. 'There's an apple here if she wants it,' she said. She knew her husband would go upstairs, knock on Nina's door and make placatory noises. He could not bear being at odds with his daughter.

'I don't think she will do it again.' He came back into the kitchen, shook his head when Elizabeth offered him Nina's baked apple.

She got up and took her plate to the sink. 'Coffee?' she asked.

He nodded abstractedly and went on. 'It was the kite and the child with the man. Gave her a false sense of security.' He was excusing her, he always did.

Elizabeth suddenly, perhaps because of her scorned apple and cream, lost her temper. 'That teenager, what was his name, Alistair, he didn't have a child with him or a kite.' She knew she was snapping but she just did not care.

'Ah, well, that boy was different. I went to see his parents, you remember.'

Justification again, Elizabeth thought. 'How different? No sense of security then, though, was there, and Nina saw him again.'

The argument went on and on until Elizabeth had finished making two cups of coffee and had taken them through to the sitting-room, switched on the television. Henry sipped his coffee and watched in silence, which was broken by a loud bang, the front door shutting, a man's voice.

Nina had defied all the rules and gone out with a boyfriend, a biker. They heard her footsteps, the sudden roar of a motor-bike engine, then the television's voice was allowed

8

to be heard again.

'She's never done that before.' Elizabeth sipped her coffee, too aware she did not care a rap. She spoke to the air however. Henry had obviously pelted down the front garden path and she knew he would be looking up and down the road, perhaps even calling 'Nina!' He was stupid enough.

He came back into the room, his face quite white. 'What shall we do?' He looked helpless, almost pitiful.

Elizabeth thought, What will *I* do? but she answered, 'Do what I want to do, go to the doctor and get her put on the pill.'

Henry looked agonised. 'Not my little girl!' he said, sitting down on the settee and putting his hands over his face.

'Yes, your little girl. It's time. She's fifteen, nearly sixteen.'

'I could take the car and go and look for her.'

'You could, if you were silly enough.' Elizabeth realised that her impatience was making her appear more indifferent than she really felt. She tried to make herself sound more caring. 'She's just showing off, dear. She'll be back once she's succeeded in making us anxious.'

'Yes, but—'

'She's probably forgotten her key, we shall soon hear the bell.' She pulled back the curtain and peered out into the road, well lit and empty. As she held the curtain back a solitary car, red lights gleaming as it turned into a driveway, stopped, switched off. The bang of a door, a car door. Then a front door, and silence again. 'It's a fine night and warm. She'll ride around a bit, call in and see Margaret, then come home.'

'At this time of night? What would Margaret's parents think of her coming round at this time of night?'

'Perhaps they are out. Margaret's sixteen.'

The rest of the evening was pure hell as Elizabeth knew it would be. At ten o'clock Henry rang the police. They were not as helpful as he had hoped. 'How long has your daughter been missing, sir? Two hours? Give her a little more time, sir.'

He told Elizabeth what their answer had been. She agreed with them. 'That's right, Henry. She just flounced out, she will be back.'

She was—at ten thirty. The bell rang. The old routine: 'Where have you been?' 'I'm not telling you. You treat me like a child. If you go on like this, Dad, I'll move out, I will.' In tears, she stomped up the stairs, her bedroom door crashed shut.

'A happy evening was had by all,' Elizabeth said. 'Shall we look at the news?' She switched it on. They watched it in silence.

Twin beds. Elizabeth could hear her husband tossing and turning, but did not feel like comforting him, reassuring him about his wayward daughter. She lay still, gazing at the lighted window. The estate was well lit all night; through the curtains the window shape was visible and the rest of the room was dimly lit. Henry, when they had first moved into this house, had complained that the light kept him awake. He had talked about a dark blind being hung, but nothing had come of it. Elizabeth usually slept well but tonight the new, rather more worrying behaviour on Nina's part had disturbed her, made her think—not so much of her daughter's failings, but of her own.

Nina had been a late baby. She and Henry had given up all thoughts of having a child. She believed that to Henry it had been a great though well-concealed disappointment, but to her it had seemed of no importance whatsoever. Early in her marriage she had come to realise that her maternal instincts were practically non-existent and when, at forty, she had become pregnant the anxiety that she would give birth to a disabled, deformed child, perhaps not even carry it to full term, had swamped any joy in her condition. She had loathed being pregnant. Hated her swollen belly, enlarged and sometimes painful breasts. Admiring babies in other people's prams had never been one of her preoccupations. During her pregnancy she had looked curiously at children, asking how old they were—two weeks, two months, six months. She tried to guess what she would

11

have to put up with—nappies, puking, wailing, sleepless nights.

Henry had been so different—full of plans. He wanted a daughter. He cosseted his wife, buying her flowers, insisting on weekend breaks. Often in bed, a double bed then. Putting his hand on the child, beaming when he felt it kick or move. Henry insisted all would be well and he was right.

Elizabeth's pregnancy, in spite of her age, had been quite uneventful. She had gone into hospital, given birth to a daughter, a rather large, eight pound daughter, eight pounds two ounces.

Elizabeth turned on her side, her eyes still fixed on the lighted square of the window. The name Nina had been chosen by Henry. Why Nina? Elizabeth had never understood his insistence on that name. Nobody in his family was called Nina. Elizabeth had never understood and he had never explained, only saying it was such a nice name, one that no one could alter or shorten, then he himself had promptly turned it into Neeny. Perhaps, she thought, he had once had a girlfriend called Nina, a lost girlfriend, way back in his youth, though by the time Nina was born he was forty-five. Fixed in his ways, and though they had made a baby together, Elizabeth was bored with Henry, in bed and out of bed, and she suspected he was bored with her. She knew too that the birth of their child had not drawn them closer together, rather forced them further apart.

Elizabeth felt she had tried, tried really hard to be a good, loving, tolerant mother. Nina had been an almost model baby. Sleeping all night, taking her feeds, seldom crying. Smiling and gurgling when friends or relatives cooed into her pram or cot. But Elizabeth had always felt—no, not just felt, been certain—that the baby, then the toddler, then the child, then the schoolgirl, had never really liked her. She had tried to communicate, explain this feeling to Henry, but he had laughed at her. 'Don't be ridiculous, Elizabeth, all children love their mothers,' but Elizabeth knew that in her case, this wasn't true.

When she called for her daughter at the school gates, the other children would rush out to their respective mothers or fathers, throw their arms round them, or show pictures painted in class that day, screaming, 'Look, that's Daddy and that's you.' Then Nina would walk slowly towards her, a sulky-looking child, dark hair cut in a straight fringe across her forehead, her brown eyes pebble-hard, her lower lip thrust forward. If she carried a painting, it was always clutched against her for Daddy to see first.

So it went on. Elizabeth gradually and guiltily accepted the fact that there was no love lost between her and her dark-eyed daughter. It became more subtly expressed, but it was there. They even went shopping together. Elizabeth would suggest a dress, shoes. Whatever it was, it was always wrong. 'You would pick that, Mum, you just would, you don't care how I look, do you? You don't understand. You're so old-fashioned.' Then Elizabeth would give way, let her have the dress that half exposed her daughter's budding breasts, reached her thighs. She would put it on to show to Daddy. 'Dear God, you can't wear that, Neeny.' 'Mum said I could. She chose it.' Oh, she was clever, Nina. Clever as paint.

It was paint or painting that did a lot to rescue Elizabeth from the rows and arguments. She picked up a leaflet in the local library. A painting class, weekly, two hours from seven to nine in the evenings. She arranged the evening meal to suit. Henry agreed and she started, found the class of fourteen to sixteen—it varied from week to week—composed of pleasant people: some lonely, some like herself wanting to get away from the household chores, usually more women than men. Still life, watercolours, a pause for coffee and an appraisal from the teacher, a grey-haired man who exhibited and sold his paintings locally.

She made one friend in the painting class, a rather pretty woman of about her own age. She went to coffee with her one morning. It had been a particularly unpleasant evening at home the day before. Henry and Nina had ganged up against her about some trivial thing, or had it been so trivial? Elizabeth hardly remembered how the whole thing had started or finished. Mary Hughes apparently had a rather difficult son. She tried to convince Elizabeth that her feelings for Nina were just because the girl was going through, as she put it, 'a difficult teenage phase'.

Elizabeth had tried to explain. 'You don't understand, Mary. She's always hated me, when she was little, even as a baby.'

Mary had shaken her head, disbelievingly. 'I love my son, Elizabeth, even though he can be awful to me sometimes. Sometimes I think he's taking drugs. He's so difficult and irritable. Won't eat, won't come home at night. Bill and I get worried of course, but he loves us really, I'm sure he does.'

Elizabeth had felt an almost hysterical wish to convince Mary it was not the same. She hated Nina and Nina hated her. 'Well, I'm not wrong about my child and I hate her.' Suddenly she had burst into tears, realising for the first time how much the situation at home was really getting to her, wearing her down. Mary had been concerned about her outburst. Elizabeth had managed to regain control of herself, feeling foolish and vowing that no matter how Nina behaved, she would never try to consult anyone, ask advice, even talk to anybody about her again. She managed to drink her cup of coffee and eat a slice of Mary's rather dry and tasteless sponge cake and left.

So it went on. Nina developed more and more into the rebellious teenager she had earlier started to be. 'It's growing up, turning from a child to a young woman,' Henry would say, excusing one of Nina's sudden tantrums or late nights. Elizabeth's tart reply was that their daughter seemed to be making heavier weather of this change than most of her friends.

Nina stayed out till twelve thirty one night. Elizabeth was almost sorry for her husband. He got into such a state that he was furious when Nina eventually arrived home, almost raved at the girl. She was wearing the briefest of skirts and a short white top showing her midriff.

'Oh, Daddy, for heaven's sake stop ranting, everyone wears these tops.'

'Well, not you, my girl.'

Nina had flounced upstairs and as usual the crash of her bedroom door had shaken the house. They had retired to bed, but not before Henry had downed a stiff whisky. Maybe the spirit helped, because after about ten minutes he seemed to drop off to sleep. Elizabeth was glad; she was sure their daughter's behaviour really disturbed him. She closed her eyes but couldn't sleep, so decided to read for a little while. She put on her bedside lamp, hung a brown transparent headscarf on the shade which shielded the light from Henry's bed but gave her enough light to read. After a couple of pages she sniffed the bedroom air. She was sure she could smell burning. Had she left something on the stove? Had Henry left a cigarette? He had gone back to smoking lately, a habit they had both given up some five years ago.

She got out of bed. They had two smoke alarms, one upstairs and one downstairs in the hall. Neither had gone off. She almost decided to go back to bed and put the whole thing down to her imagination, but when she opened their bedroom door, the smell was stronger. Nina's light was on—the strip of light from under her door lit the hall dimly. Elizabeth crossed the landing and opened the door.

Nina was naked, sitting on the side of her bed, both hands clasped between her knees, completely still. She was watching her metal waste-paper bin, which was placed in the middle of her bedside rug and from which flames about two inches higher than the rim and spirals of smoke, were belching out. She looked up as her mother came into the room. 'Don't worry, it's only my skirt and top. It won't hurt. I've done it before—burnt things, I mean.' Her eyes, those hard brown eyes, gazed at Elizabeth, large and vacant. She looked tired and much older than her nearing sixteen years.

Elizabeth said nothing, went out of the room, crossed to the bathroom and came back with two tooth mugs full of water. She hesitated, looking at her daughter. Nina's thin, naked shoulders rose in a shrug. One glass of water was enough. Steam took the place of smoke—a hissing noise.

Elizabeth sat down on the bed and watched as the vapour subsided. The hissing stopped. Nina turned to her. 'Well, if he doesn't like what I wear, I'll bin it', she said, shrugging into her dressing-gown. Elizabeth could think of nothing to say. The vacant look in her daughter's eyes disappeared. 'I like the flames. It's nice to get rid of things.'

'You could set fire to the house!'

'Yep, I know, but I'm careful. I burnt that dress you chose for me—remember? The flowered one? Yuk.' She almost laughed then. 'Don't tell Daddy, will you? You know what he's like.'

Elizabeth shook her head. 'No, I won't tell him this time, Nina, but if you ever do it again . . .' She got up, picked up the metal waste bin and took it through to the lavatory. She emptied the black half-burned contents down the pan, pulled the chain and took the bin back into her daughter's room. The girl had shed her dresssing-gown, which lay on the floor by her bed. She had put on a nightdress and climbed into bed.

Elizabeth pointed to the round stain on the

18

bedside rug. 'I'll put that in the washing machine tomorrow.'

'Fine'. Nina cuddled down in her bed. Polly appeared—she had pushed open the door—and leapt on to the bed. A real look of love and caring came over Nina's face. She cuddled the dog. 'She can stay, can't she?'

Elizabeth nodded, half moved toward the bed to touch or kiss the girl—but she couldn't. Perhaps this little incident had drawn them closer together? She wasn't sure. Back in her own bed she lay for a long time, staring at the ceiling. What kind of child had they made between them? At last, as dawn was beginning to light the square of the bedroom window, she fell asleep.

In the morning Nina had eaten her breakfast in complete silence, now and again glancing at her mother. Henry said little. In her school uniform Nina looked demure. She had not, Elizabeth noticed, done her usual trick of hoisting the skirt of her school uniform as high as possible. It was left at its recommended length of three inches above the knee. She did not speak to her father until she was leaving the kitchen to put on her coat.

'Sorry about the clothes, Daddy. I won't wear them again if you don't like them.'

Apologies were unusual and this one, Elizabeth could see, completely disarmed Henry. 'Oh well, Neeny . . .' He stopped and looked rather helplessly at his wife. Nina left the room without waiting for a reply.

Maybe the fire incident had been useful if a little frightening. Maybe Nina would watch her behaviour a little more carefully.

CHAPTER TWO

The painting classes were becoming more and more of an escape for Elizabeth. She hated driving in the dark and an acquaintance who lived in the same estate, Mrs Albright, Mabel, picked her up and brought her home. This arrangement had at first been comfortable, then things changed a little. Some of the painters suggested a visit to the local pub, the Black Horse. Mabel Albright did not like visiting a pub, so Elizabeth either relied on someone else or mostly called a taxi for the journey home. This meant she could have a couple, or even three, glasses of her favourite drink—red wine—and not have to drive home. About half a dozen of the painters met in the Black Horse. They never talked about personal things; mostly their chat was about art, or their particular favourite artists both old and new, or what they thought of their own and each other's progress in the class. Elizabeth enjoyed it so much she made the visit to the pub last as long as possible. It was convivial, unlike the rest of her life. No arguments, no undercurrents, no wondering what row was going to start next and what about, where Nina was, how she was dressed. God, how she hated it all.

However, this evening was a particularly enjoyable one. Argument and banter were passing to and fro. Elizabeth was on her third glass of wine when she noticed Stanley Wiltshire. She, of course, did not know his name then, but she liked the look of this man sitting by himself at the end of the bar, one hand supporting his chin, his elbow on the bar, the other hand twisting a half-pint lager glass. He looked vaguely miserable, but interestingly he was gazing directly at her, or so she thought. His eyes dropped. Had he really been looking at her—or through her? He was about seven feet away. She had immediately registered that his eyes were cornflower blue; his hair surprisingly—he looked too young— was wavy and silvery white. He looked up again and this time he smiled at her, a tentative smile. Elizabeth smiled back, just as tentatively, then turned to her friends, feeling for some reason, she told herself, ridiculous that her heart had quickened its beat at his smile.

As they broke up one of the girls from the class offered her a lift, so the taxi was not after all needed. Elizabeth was surprised and pleased at the offer of the lift home. As she passed the white-haired man at the end of the bar, he spoke. 'Good-night—perhaps see you tomorrow?'

Elizabeth shook her head. 'No, not until next week,' she said and hurried out, rather frightened by her remark.

In the car her fellow painter, Brenda, looked at her with a trace of amusement. 'He liked the look of you, Liz,' she said, then, 'Oh, bugger,' as she missed the gear and the car made a protesting grating noise. 'I always do that. My boyfriend says I'll mess up the clutch or gearbox or something. I haven't so far though, so sucks to him.'

The car moved off. It was slightly out of Brenda's way but only a couple of streets. At her door, Elizabeth swung her legs out of the car and thanked her companion for the lift. 'Nice of you,' she said.

'OK—you're welcome.' Brenda pushed back her long frizzy hair, glanced in the mirror, then grimaced as she punished the gears again. The car drew away and disappeared along the deserted road. It had rained during the pub visit and the road gleamed black, the grass and trees smelled sweet and fresh. Elizabeth stood there for a moment, savouring her own loneliness, wishing for a moment she was back in the Black Horse, talking with the crowd of painters, smiling, perhaps more positively, at the blue-eyed, white-haired man at the end of the bar.

She turned and walked up the short garden

path, feeling strange, different, younger. In that pause before she put her key in the lock, she made a little resolution. She must take more trouble with her make-up, use mascara again, eye shadow, maybe get her hair done more often. Use that moisturising cream someone had given her for Christmas and which had so far sat on a bathroom shelf, gathering dust, never used.

As she entered the house all those feelings blew into the back of her mind and she returned to now, here. Tomorrow's meals, shopping . . . She called out, 'I'm home.' The door shut behind her.

Nina came into the kitchen, chewing. 'You smell of drink and I can't find my white blouse. Did you wash it?'

Elizabeth had a great longing sweep over her to go out again into the sweet-smelling darkness and run away, but where could she go? 'It's in the linen cupboard, Nina.'

'Well, why didn't you tell me?'

Elizabeth watched her daughter walk into the sitting-room and slump down on the settee next to her father. He looked up at his wife and said, over the man chatting on television, 'We had the meal you left early and now Neeny's hungry again.'

'Why didn't she make a snack then? There's plenty in the kitchen.'

Nina stuck out her lower lip. 'What, me? Why should I? I'm not old enough to make

23

snacks, not if I'm not old enough to stay out after ten.'

Elizabeth went upstairs, took off her headscarf and coat. 'Oh, bloody hell,' she said to her reflection in the dressing-table mirror. She sat down and looked at herself. Mousy hair—it normally had a slight wave, but the scarf had flattened it. Tired-looking skin, no visible trace of make-up though she had put lipstick on before she started out. No make-up. She seldom put much make-up on for the painting class, but she would in future.

Did many women feel like this, she wondered? Hate their offspring and feel bored with their husbands? Downstairs again she went into the kitchen and made herself a cup of tea, using a one-cup teabag. Next week she would really give herself a makeover. Of course, he might not be there, but it would make her feel better, make the painting lesson a more exciting place to go. She found herself looking forward to it, but she was rather surprised at her own reaction, that it was not the painting class that was causing the little rush of excitement she felt.

In the sitting-room she sat down in an armchair, slightly askew to the television screen.

'There's rather a good play later,' Henry said.

Elizabeth did not reply, not out of rudeness but her thoughts were far away.

'Did you make a cup for us?' Nina asked, not looking towards her mother, keeping her eyes fixed on the screen.

'No, I didn't.' Elizabeth felt a feeling of satisfaction she couldn't quite account for.

'You look like the cat that swallowed the cream,' Henry said. 'Good painting evening?'

'Yes, yes. Very.'

'Did they like your still life?' he asked.

She tried to drag her mind back to the class. 'Yes, they did, especially the glass bottle.' She lied glibly and felt slightly ashamed at doing so.

'Who brought you home?' Henry didn't sound terribly interested. His eyes remained fixed on the screen.

'This terribly dishy man. Max, his name is, he's about my age and . . .' Elizabeth paused as Henry looked up at her. '. . . and I really think he fancies me.'

Henry's eyes returned to the screen. Nina looked up, her full lips almost sneering. 'Dream on,' she said and got up and flounced out of the room.

'Little bitch,' Elizabeth said under her breath. 'Little bitch.'

'What?' Henry asked.

Elizabeth didn't reply at once, then, 'Brenda brought me home, kind of her.' She sat down and opened the local paper.

Nina came back carrying a cup of coffee.

'Oh, thank you, Nina. How nice, how

thoughtful of you.'

The sarcasm in her voice spilled over even to Henry. Nina sat down and sipped. 'You could have made your mother and me one, Neeny,' he said with just a shade of reproach.

'Well, I didn't.'

Elizabeth left the room, went into the kitchen, made herself another cup of tea and sat at the kitchen table. For some absurd reason she felt tears pricking behind her eyes. 'Family life,' she said aloud. 'Bloody family life.' She thought of Margaret Sands, Nina's friend. They had been to the Sands' house, all three of them, to a meal a few evenings ago. Nina and Margaret had retired upstairs after the meal and loud music had been all that had been heard of them for the rest of the evening. Once Margaret's father had gone half-way up the stairs and called out, 'Turn it down a bit, girls.' For a few minutes, perhaps twenty, the music had lessened, then the noise had come up to an even greater level and Margaret's parents had shrugged it off with 'What can you do?' What can you do indeed, Elizabeth had thought. Be like Henry, spoil, bribe, placate, overlook, worry. Nobody seemed to think of discipline, plain good old-fashioned discipline. We are afraid of them, these young ones, afraid of them.

*　　　*　　　*

The week until Elizabeth's next painting lesson went slowly. Henry was trying to get on with a new and seemingly rather arrogant addition to the firm, a young, good-looking, recently chartered accountant. Every evening he had long and bitter harangues about this young man. 'Oh shut up, Daddy. It's just because he's younger than you. Why don't you ask him to dinner? Is he married?'

Henry had shaken his head—not a good idea, it was obvious to Elizabeth what her husband was thinking. A little devil in her made her say, 'Yes, let's do that. He probably would like a good dinner. Is he in digs or is he living at home?'

Henry had to admit the young man was in digs and looking for a flat.

'Goody, goody, he'll be flattered if you ask him to come, Daddy.'

Henry's expression changed, smoothed out. 'Perhaps he would, we'll see.'

Elizabeth, for the hundredth time, felt slight disgust at how easily her daughter could handle her father. For the moment the subject was dropped, but Elizabeth knew her daughter. The seed had been sown and she wondered how soon it would be brought up again—by Nina, of course.

Her daughter's attitude to men, boys, sexual matters generally, was almost completely unknown to her. Once or twice she had tentatively approached the subject.

Contraception, boyfriends, the pill. She wondered about Margaret's mother. What did she say to her daughter? The two girls seemed to be close, intimate, giggled together a lot, dressed, or attempted to dress, in the same way, were obviously equally rebellious. Should she ask her? Yes, she would do that.

Now the painting class loomed and the man at the end of the bar. Perhaps if he was there this evening she would find out his name. Was he there every evening? But how could she do that—and anyway, he probably wouldn't be there. After all, the encounter had been a week ago and so brief. But he had said . . . Elizabeth admonished herself. What could he possibly see in her? Fifty-six, not all that well preserved. Still, she had made a hair appointment for the day of the class, bought some new foundation, a new lipstick and eye shadow. All for what? She realised with some resentment that both Henry and Nina had done a lot to reduce her self-esteem to nearly zero. The girl's comment 'Dream on' still rankled. As she applied the eye shadow, foundation, a touch of blusher, she really felt different, glamorous in fact.

She slid out of the house, purposely avoiding Nina. Easily done, she was upstairs playing 'Please Release Me, Let Me Go'. God, had that come back? Henry was glued to the television, the news. She called out as she left: 'Won't be late.' Mrs Albright was outside,

28

engine running. Elizabeth got into the car. If Mrs Albright noticed a difference in her companion's appearance she said nothing, but she did remark, 'Nice perfume.'

'Thank you. Henry bought it for me, a little present.' Elizabeth lied automatically and wondered why. She was not normally a liar. Maybe she wanted to let Mrs Albright think she had an ideal marriage, that Henry was an attentive, loving husband. Well, so he was. He didn't apparently lust after other women. Come to that, he didn't lust after her either. She couldn't remember when they had last made love. Anyway, it was a boring ritual. Perhaps he did lust, but not for her.

As Mrs Albright's car got mixed up with home-going traffic and she had to concentrate on the driving, Elizabeth avoided talking so she could think more. 'Boring.' How many times had she told her daughter off for using that word? School was boring, television was boring, the clothes she had to wear to school were boring. Maybe she was beginning to feel the same. Henry was boring and his routine taste in food, his clothes, his unexciting, infrequent love-making. 'Boring is the word.'

Mrs Albright, having negotiated the traffic and pulled up outside the hall where the painting class took place, turned to her. 'I beg your pardon, what did you say—I didn't quite catch . . . ?'

'Oh, nothing, nothing. I was just thinking

aloud.' She scrambled out of the car, lumping together her bag of painting equipment and her easel. The latter was a great nuisance but there were not enough to go round and Elizabeth had offered to bring her own as had several of the others. An easel is an unwieldy thing, and once she had snagged her tights on the back strut. She was anxious not to do this tonight because of that white-haired, pleasant-looking man at the bar in the Black Horse. How stupid can you get? she thought. Nevertheless, she was hopeful that he would be there.

As she entered the hall she could sense an air of excitement and anticipation. Mary Hughes came up to her. 'What do you think? No more fruit and bottles and cubes and pyramids! We've got a real live model.'

'Really? What . . . ?'

'An elderly lady—well, not terribly elderly.'

'What, naked?' Elizabeth asked.

Mary shook her head laughing. 'No, dressed.'

Elizabeth put up her easel and prepared her paints. The model appeared, sat on the throne, the chair, over which was thrown a brightly coloured blanket. She was neatly dressed and sat slightly sideward, giving the class a view of her profile rather than full face. This posture was arranged by the art teacher, who gave a talk to the class. This evening it was slightly longer than his usual address.

'This is, for many of you, a first attempt at a live model. Draw her as you see her. You will all see her differently. Don't worry about how your next-door neighbour is drawing her.'

Mary, next to Elizabeth, nudged her and winked. 'You won't want to copy mine,' she giggled.

Elizabeth smiled back at her, listened to the rest of the talk, then, when they were told to start, looked with some doubt at the large blank white sheet on her easel. She decided to do an outline of the chair and cover, and fill the figure in later. Probably quite the wrong way to cope, but she made some bold strokes and as the shape of the blanket-covered chair started to appear, she began to enjoy herself. The outline of the model's face and hair gave her some trouble. The art teacher came round, looked over Elizabeth's shoulder at her efforts. 'Try to be more positive, do the nose and mouth and notice the reflected light.' Elizabeth listened to his comments when he moved along to her friend Mary. 'Oh, quite good. You've got movement, flow there.' He went on.

Mary turned round and gave Elizabeth her familiar wink. 'What about that then! I've got movement!' she whispered, grimacing. 'Can't see it myself.' She looked pleased though.

After an hour the coffee was made and the whole class collected around the little table at which it was served. The presence of a live model had animated the class and one rather waggish elderly man asked their teacher, 'When do we get the naked one then?'

Everyone laughed and another man replied, 'In your dreams, Jim.' The words brought back to Elizabeth her daughter Nina's contemptuous 'Dream on' and she felt, as she had felt then, hurt, resentful of her daughter's youth, self-assurance and the number of years she had in front of her to spend as she wished.

Still, one can't be sure, she told herself as she sipped her coffee. She could get run over, die of one those diseases that the young can die of, nobody could be sure. The thought comforted, then shocked her. What would anyone think of a mother thinking such thoughts? But, she argued, she wasn't, of course she wasn't wishing any such dire mishap on Nina, just trying to be reasonable. Come to terms with the fact that no one can bank on living any number of years. In some ways, youth was just as vulnerable as age. 'Hateful little cow,' she muttered, putting her cup and saucer down with a little clatter.

'Who is?' Mary turned round from chatting with someone else.

'Who is what?' Elizabeth was unaware she had spoken loudly enough to be heard.

'You said "hateful little cow",' Mary said.

Elizabeth shook her head. 'No, I said, let's get on now.'

Mary shrugged. 'Must be getting deaf in my

old age,' she said cheerfully.

They walked back to their easels and the model resumed her position. Elizabeth was aware that Mary gave her a rather curious look before she resumed her drawing. It was obvious she did not believe Elizabeth's hastily amended sentence and had heard 'Hateful little cow.' Well, so she was, daughter or not. That had been a catty and hurtful thing to say to her mother.

The end of the painting class was always signalled by the arrival of an elderly man, jangling a bunch of keys. He did not actually say, 'Time, gentlemen, please,' but his manner did. He always appeared at five minutes to nine and the painting stopped. When the classes had first started the pupils had not automatically downed brushes but an irate word from the key jangler to the teacher had effectively seen to that and now, at the first jangle, painting stopped. Brushes were hastily washed and put away, easels folded, those belonging to the class neatly stacked against the wall and the others, belonging to the would-be artists themselves, carried out to waiting cars. It always amused Elizabeth that the mere appearance of the 'jangler' was enough to do the trick and clear the hall.

This evening though, things were a little different. The model got up, folded the throwover from the chair and approached Mark Evans, the teacher, who handed her what was obviously her fee. She turned to the class and waved a hand in farewell. She was a pleasant-looking woman with a fresh round face, rosy-cheeked, homely, topped however by a very obviously dyed head of rather brassy blonde hair. As she left, Mary turned to Elizabeth. 'That hair's going to be difficult. Wish it were brown, or darker anyway.'

'Probably will be by next week,' the man whose easel was next to Mary's said with a bit of a sarcastic twist to his mouth.

Mary laughed, as did Elizabeth, but she thought the remark bitchy. She realised that she was feeling over-sensitive at the moment, and was anxious to get to the Black Horse to see if the man who had spoken to her was there.

'Are you going to the pub?' asked Mary. 'I thought I'd join you this week—I could give you a lift home afterwards if you like.'

'That would be lovely—thank you, Mary. I must spend a penny first though, wait for me.'

They were out of the painting room now and the 'jangler' had departed. The Ladies was just off the corridor. Elizabeth closed the outer door behind her. Spending a penny was not her objective. She went towards the row of white handbasins, touched up her lipstick and powdered her nose. The blusher she had used at home seemed to have completely disappeared. The harsh neon lighting in the lavatories made her, Elizabeth told herself, look like a corpse. Her hair looked nice though. Even the ghastly light could not dull its shine, and the waves, natural and curling round her forehead and ears, had so far retained their reddish brown with, as yet, no hint of grey. Half satisfied, half dismayed by her appearance, she switched off the light and joined Mary. Together they made their way along the street to the pub. It looked cheerful and welcoming.

Inside they joined eight or nine of their classmates, slightly more than usual. The live model had made them feel closer together, Elizabeth could sense the feeling. Glass bottles and apples and oranges were all very well, but a live model was harder, more vital, different.

Her friends, or fellow would-be artists, surrounded her. One man, a fat jolly fellow, buttonholed her almost as she entered the bar. 'What do you think, she gets eight pounds an hour for just sitting there! Sixteen pounds! I'd do it for less and take all my gear off!' He had already managed to get a pint of beer and as he threw back his head and laughed some of the liquid spilled out of the glass. He hastily put the dripping glass to his lips and drank, then looked up. 'Mustn't waste it, eh?' he chuckled. Elizabeth moved past him and nearer to the bar.

There he was, the same white-haired, young-faced man, sitting there, just the same as last week. Her heart quickened. Her eyes met his. He smiled, she smiled, then felt a quick feeling of despair, of inadequacy. A look, a smile, but what then? What could she do, what could he do? Neither were young things who could say, 'Hi, there. You were here a week ago. I really fancied you.' God, she thought, how lovely to be young, uninhibited, casual, laid back, easy. Yet, were they right? Was Henry right, in saying the transition from child to woman was a difficult and traumatic experience? The fat man and his still dripping glass moved and the space beside her was open. Then it happened. The white-haired man got up and came over to their group, still smiling at Elizabeth, but passed her.

'Mary Hughes, what are you doing here?'

Mary turned and greeted the man with a wide smile. 'Hello, Stanley. Nice to see you.' She took his hand, did not unclasp it, as one would after the normal handshake. Then Mary continued: 'So sorry to hear . . .' She paused and gave a quick glance at Elizabeth and finished her sentence. 'About everything, so sorry.'

'Thank you. Won't you introduce me to your friend?'

'Oh, of course. This is Elizabeth Mason, a fellow painter, we . . .' She gestured at the people around her. The Black Horse was pretty full. 'Well, about eight of us are trying very hard at watercolours. Elizabeth, Stanley Wiltshire.'

Those blue eyes, bluer now they were closer, smiled as his lips smiled. 'How do you do, Elizabeth. I saw you last week, didn't I?'

Mary answered for her. 'Yes, it's once a week, our lesson. Tonight we had a live model, first time. I've got movement and flow, haven't I, Elizabeth?'

No answer from Elizabeth. For some reason, her natural shyness when meeting new people seemed even worse than usual. She longed to say something clever, amusing, so that this attractive smiling man would remember her, think her worth getting to know better. As it was, she suspected he would just think her a big bore and take off as soon as he could. She was wrong. Mary was called away by another painter friend, walked off to join them, and started an animated conversation.

Stanley Wiltshire glanced down at Elizabeth's almost empty glass. 'May I get you a drink? Red wine, isn't it?' Elizabeth managed a reply and they walked together over to the bar. As they did so two young men and a girl burst through the bar door.

'Well, say what you like, I won't be asked if I'm carrying shit by some—' 'Shut up, for goodness sake.' The girl looked round the bar. 'Just be thankful you weren't carrying.'

Her companion calmed down a little. 'OK, OK, let's have a drink here and split.'

Elizabeth noticed Stanley Wiltshire never

37

took his eyes from the trio. When they were served with three pints of cider, he turned back to Elizabeth. 'I'm so sorry, it was those . . .' He summoned the barmaid and ordered a half-pint of bitter and a red wine.

The three young people downed their drinks and moved off. As they left an elderly man entered and hesitated. 'Come on, Grandad, don't hold us up, we've got some living to do.'

'Charming,' the man said and crossed to the bar close to Elizabeth and Stanley. 'Dear young things. One feels hanging is too good for them, but let's hope they may have an accident in their broken-down, battered-looking car outside, if it's theirs.'

The remarks were made lightly, almost in fun, but they had an effect on Stanley. 'Don't say that. They have got parents who would probably be devastated if anything happened to them.'

The elderly man looked surprised at the effect his words had had. 'Pity their parents didn't teach them better manners then,' he said and walked off, carrying his whisky.

'Let's sit down.' Stanley Wiltshire seemed shaken by the man. Elizabeth followed him round the side of the bar to an empty table and they sat down opposite each other.

Elizabeth's shyness disappeared. 'It was a horrid thing to say, but I really don't think he meant it. He was just furious at what they had said to him.'

Stanley nodded. 'I know, Elizabeth, I know. I over-reacted.'

Elizabeth thought back to Mary's long hand clasp and her broken-off remark, 'So sorry to hear . . .' So sorry to hear what? She looked at the man opposite her, comparing him with her husband. Stanley was thin and tall. Henry was shorter, stocky. His eyes were brown like Nina's—that's where she had got those pebble-hard eyes. Henry's were not as hard, more apologetic. Henry was balding, his hair mousy, what was left of it. Stanley's was still thick, wavy, though white. She guessed Stanley was about Henry's age, perhaps a little older. His hand, his left hand resting on the table, boasted no wedding ring, but had one or two small brown marks on it, larger than freckles. Elizabeth longed to put out a finger and touch one of the marks. In spite of his greeting smile, Elizabeth could sense a sadness there, not just because of Mary's remark, or his reaction to the young people, but it seemed there, like an aura. She wished she dare ask, or say something to encourage him to talk to her about whatever was making him sad.

Another glass of red wine, another half-pint of beer, and Elizabeth found out a little more. Stanley lived alone in a house about two streets away from the Black Horse. He was a surveyor. 'Have to break bad news sometimes to house buyers.' He shrugged his shoulders.

'Not a very dramatic job, I'm afraid.'

'What would you rather have been?' Elizabeth asked.

'Well, it would have been nice to tell you I was a retired astronaut, or a captain of international industry, or even flew Concorde.' He smiled, almost laughed. 'Rather than a chartered surveyor.'

Elizabeth laughed. Their laughter seemed to loosen the atmosphere.

'Will you have dinner with me on Friday?' He put out a hand and covered hers.

The difficulties of a dinner date, what excuse to make, flew through Elizabeth's mind, but she replied almost as quickly: 'I'd really like that, Stanley.' It was the first time during their conversation that she had used his name. Her shyness had kept her from saying it before.

'Shall I call for you?'

'No, no.' Elizabeth shook her head. 'I'll meet you here. I'd rather, if you don't mind.' She felt Stanley's blue eyes questioning, fixed on her. Elizabeth looked directly at him. 'You don't know anything about me.'

'Or you about me.' He did not let go of her hand. 'Let's leave it like that for the moment.'

They both got up and went round to the crowded bar. Elizabeth felt she had been sitting with Stanley for hours, in another world.

Mary Hughes was still there chatting away.

She came over as she saw Elizabeth. She seemed unaware that she had not been in the crowd all the time. 'Ready for off?' she said. Elizabeth nodded. With a handclasp and 'See you here at seven?' Stanley had gone.

Mary led the way out to the car-park. 'Sick of orange juice,' she said, laughing, as she got into the car. Elizabeth knew her friend was very strict about drinking and driving. One glass of white wine, then orange juice. They drove home, Mary still talking about the model, the class. 'Andy's looked like a stick insect,' she said. 'And Bill's like a Barbie doll.' Neither mentioned Stanley Wiltshire and Elizabeth was glad. Mary knew about Elizabeth's problems at home after that disastrous outburst at her house over coffee, but she never mentioned it. Neither did she mention again her son, just as she did not speak of tonight's meeting with Stanley. Maybe, like Elizabeth, she felt that it was better to stick to the lessons they were both enjoying and not spoil it by indulging in personal gossip.

At Elizabeth's house she made just one overt remark: 'Bang the door hard, it doesn't catch very well. Things any better indoors?'

'No, not really.' That was all that was said.

Indoors, things were as usual. Henry was reading the local paper. He looked up as she came into the room. 'Your class is mentioned in the *News*. Says what a success it is and that

41

your teacher won some watercolour award.'

'Yes, he told us about it, and we're having a little party on Friday evening to celebrate.' Elizabeth was almost breathless at her own rapid inventiveness.

'Oh, another casserole,' Henry said, but without rancour.

'No, I'll get two TV dinners and Nina can put them in the microwave.'

'She won't like that.' Henry shook the paper and turned to the next page.

'Then I'm afraid she will have to lump it, Henry.' Elizbeth's voice was firm.

'Lump what?' Nina's voice came from the door of the sitting-room.

Elizabeth explained. 'I'm going to a party.' She flushed, avoiding her daughter's eyes.

'Oh, found a boyfriend, Mum, have you? And I've got to do the meals?'

Then Elizabeth did look directly at her daughter. Her grey eyes met her daughter's brown ones. 'Dream on,' she said and felt great satisfaction in saying it. She went through to the kitchen. 'Anyone want a coffee?' she called. It was, she felt, the least she could do.

She felt slightly but quite deliciously guilty. Perhaps it was the coffee. Elizabeth lay looking at the square of light in the bedroom for a long time. The coffee apparently did not affect Henry. He was asleep about ten minutes after he had switched off the light. He snored—not a loud aggressive snore but a soft breathy one, rather more irritating, his wife sometimes thought, than a real snorting one. She speculated on her date (childish way of putting it) for Friday night. Where would they go? What should she wear? She thought of his hand on hers. Could almost feel again the warmth. Should he have done that? Should she have drawn her hand away? She would order a taxi to the Black Horse but he would expect to drive her home. How could she get out of that? Where did he live? She began to panic, to wish she had refused his invitation. It was all too complicated, too risky. What was she hoping for?

She sat up, her heart pounding. He would wonder why she had arranged to meet him at the pub. She clasped her bare shoulders and rocked a little to and fro, still staring at the space of light.

Then the panic subsided. If he asked her why, she would say, tell the truth. I didn't want you to know where I lived. If he didn't understand, well, he didn't. She wondered how married women began affairs. Several of her friends had, it was so frightening, so difficult. Perhaps it was just the beginning that was so difficult, perhaps things worked out. Probably one date was all he or she would want, perhaps, perhaps, perhaps . . .

She lay down, cold. She must just take things as they came, see how it all worked out.

Perhaps his eyes were not as blue, his hand not as warm, perhaps she was so sick of Henry and Nina that he had looked more attractive than he really was. That thought calmed her down. Her heart slowed down to its normal rate. She cuddled down under the duvet and grew warmer. Look forward to it, for God's sake. At least you've been asked! On that more optimistic thought she eventually fell asleep.

CHAPTER THREE

Friday morning did not begin well. Nina started her usual chant, 'Don't need to go in till late this morning, free period.' This, Elizabeth had learned, was nine times out of ten a lie. She forced her daughter to go and in revolt Nina tucked her skirt well up into her belt, making it at least six inches shorter than the school decreed.

Henry had a sore throat and would not join in the argument until Nina had departed. 'Perhaps it was a free morning,' he said in a rather hoarse voice.

'Rubbish. It's Miss Meadows this morning—history.'

Elizabeth was well aware that a battle raged between Nina and Miss Meadows. Henry and she had met the history teacher at a parents' evening a few weeks ago—or rather, had been accosted by her. She was a tall, big-boned woman, rather masculine, with short black hair, sharp pointed features and large red hands, with which she gesticulated as she talked, holding them out palm upwards at the end of each sentence. 'I can do little with your daughter.' She had addressed Henry and Elizabeth while standing out of earshot of the other teachers and parents. 'While in my class she is inattentive, rude. She has no wish to learn, she is also disruptive during class.'

Henry had tried as usual to stick up for Nina, but for once he had met his match, at least in the Miss Meadows area.

'What is she like at home, Mrs Mason?'

As the question was asked of her directly, Elizabeth decided on a straight answer. 'Very difficult. I suppose like many teenagers she calls school boring—everything is boring, school, television, books, even games.'

Miss Meadows nodded in agreement. Elizabeth had noticed that the teacher's eyes were very like Nina's, hard, brown, pebble-like. Miss Meadows pursed her lips until they were a thin and implacable line. 'The fact that Nina appears to dislike me intensely does not help.'

'Oh, she dislikes me too, Miss Meadows, she always has.' The observation had slipped out, perhaps before she had given it thought, but she did not regret it, indeed it had been a relief to say it, to someone with more understanding than Mary Hughes.

Henry had been shocked. 'Oh, come, Elizabeth, of course she doesn't dislike you, she's your child.'

Miss Meadows, however, was not at all shocked. 'Daughters can dislike their mothers and their teachers, Mr Mason, believe me.' Another father and mother approached her. She excused herself and walked away with them, smiling this time. Their child was obviously a good pupil.

'What a dreadful thing to say.' Henry was still shaken by her remark.

'Well, it's true, Henry. You just won't believe me. I've said it God knows how many times.'

He had shaken his head in disbelief and taken a cup of coffee proffered to him by a pupil. Nina, of course, had not been there, not even mentioned that some pupils went back to the school to help at the parents' evening. But that meeting had revealed to Elizabeth the hatred Nina felt for Miss Meadows. Whenever she mentioned her to Nina, the reply was always much the same: 'That old cow, I hate her. She shows me up whenever she can,' or 'Butchy Meadows. More like a man than a woman. I wouldn't like her near me.'

Elizabeth looked at her husband. 'Is your throat very sore, Henry? Should you perhaps take the day off?'

He shook his head. 'No, can't possibly, we are too pressed at the moment.'

46

He got up from the breakfast table. Elizabeth went to the front door with him. She knew that, as usual, Nina was on his mind. Just outside the door, he turned. 'You don't think Nina was telling the truth, do you, it really was a free—'

'No, no. It's Miss Meadows. You've heard what she calls her. She hates her and would skive from any lesson she takes.'

Henry nodded. 'Perhaps so.' He walked round to the garage, coughing and rubbing his neck.

Elizabeth watched the car drive out into the road. The morning sun was blazing, low in the spring sky. She saw her husband put up a hand to adjust the visor. The car drew away between the cherry trees, the fruitless cherry trees, just beginning to swell into bud. They would soon be flowering. They were so regimented, planted in line and at equal distances one from another. Henry had said he would be late. April drawing nearer and the end of the tax year always made the firm busy, he said.

Nina would be home about five or before. She would tell her how to cope with the TV dinner that she would get from the supermarket this morning. Polly to walk, her morning walk. Not through the leafless cherry trees but further up in a wide, hedged field that Elizabeth found more pleasant and was a change for Polly. A light brunch, a cup of coffee, then get ready. She looked at her watch. Nine o'clock. Ten hours before she would see Stanley. A long time. She sighed, closed the front door, called Polly and snapped on her lead. The dog gyrated round her, winding the nylon extending lead round her skirt. 'Morning walkies, Polly,' she said, unwinding herself and shortening the lead. As she closed the front door, she pushed it to see if it was latched. She looked at Polly 'Wonder if he likes dogs?' she said aloud. 'Or cats?' she amended, realising for the hundredth time she knew so little about him.

The day passed slowly: a visit to the supermarket for the TV dinners, ironing. She took special care with Nina's school blouse—guilt again? Another walk for Polly, a light lunch, very light. Her apprehension grew as the time to get ready approached. Nina came in, not in a good mood, her eyes red.

'That woman, Meadows. You knew it was her day and you made me go.' She threw down her bag of books; some spilled out on the hall floor. She made no effort to pick them up, threw her coat over a chair, said 'Shut up' to an excited Polly's greeting and followed her mother into the kitchen.

'The TV dinners are in the freezer.' Elizabeth opened the appropriate freezer drawer. 'Just take them out of their boxes and pop them in the microwave—you know how to do it.'

'I may go out, I don't know yet.'

'What happened then with Miss Meadows?' Elizabeth felt the least she could do was ask.

'Oh, what do you think she did? Picked on me as usual, asked me why my skirt was pulled up to my crotch and did I think it looked attractive!'

'Well, Nina, you do hitch it up. You know the regulation length.'

The girl's rage overcame her, She was holding a carton of orange juice in her hand. She suddenly threw it across the room towards her mother. The cap flew off and the juice gushed out all over the table and began to drip on to the floor. Elizabeth picked up the carton, avoiding treading in the spilt orangey mess on the floor, stood it upright on the kitchen table and went across and closed the refrigerator door. When she reached the kitchen door she turned. 'You must choose what you want to do first, Nina, clean up that mess, then walk your dog, or walk Polly, then clean up. Perhaps the latter would be a better idea, the walk may calm your temper down a little.'

She felt quite detached from her daughter at that moment. Perhaps Nina felt the detachment for she stood for a moment gazing at her mother. 'I'll take Polly first,' she said.

They went out of the front door and Nina slammed it, but perhaps not quite as hard as usual. Elizabeth glanced at the orange liquid still spreading over the black and white tiled kitchen floor, still dripping from the table on to the kitchen chair and from there again to the floor beneath. By the time Nina had got back the juice would have congealed a little, be even more difficult to clean up. She shrugged her shoulders, made herself a cup of tea, treading carefully. Having drunk it, she left the kitchen, ran a bath and locked the bathroom door. She put in some bath oil, another little 'pamper' for herself, and put on her bath cap to protect her hair. She relaxed. Make-up, dress, shoes, all ready in the bedroom. She hoped Henry would be late at the office and not arrive home in time to see her new dress, smell her new perfume. Still, if he did, he probably wouldn't notice anything different about her.

He wasn't home when the taxi arrived. Nina had been home, left Polly in the sitting-room and gone out again, no clearing up in the kitchen. Elizabeth fed Polly in the sitting-room, shut her in there, so that she wouldn't create more havoc by putting her paws in the sticky juice and spreading it about. Henry, poor Henry, with his sore throat if he still had it, would be greeted with maybe no supper and a mess. Well, it would perhaps teach him a little more about his daughter.

'The Black Horse, Wellington Street. Do you know where it is?'

The taxi driver grinned. 'Oh, yes, miss. Trust me, I know where all the pubs are.'

Elizabeth stiffened a little and wondered again if she had been right in suggesting this meeting place, but it was done now. The journey seemed much shorter than usual and as the taxi drew up into the Black Horse car-park, she could visualise the door of the hall where she painted each week, not very far up the street. She paid the cabman, and probably overtipped him in her anxiety for he gave her a wide smile as he drew away. She walked very slowly across the gravel between one or two parked cars. The Black Horse usually started to fill up when they arrived at about nine o'clock. Even so its amber lights shone welcomingly.

She pushed open the door into the small reception area, crossed it and stood hesitatingly at the entrance to the bar. She felt a great urge to give it all up, the whole idea, call another taxi and go home. Then she thought of the spilled juice, probably still all over the kitchen floor. The TV dinners, all the unpleasant things to face if she did go home. Then another unpleasant thought rushed at her. Just supposing he hadn't come? Well, that would be that. She boldly pushed open the bar door and went in.

She saw him at once. He had been sitting in his normal place but as she entered and he saw her he got up, came across with hand outstretched and took hers. 'I'm so glad you came,' he said. Elizabeth noticed that he was more lined than she had realised; creases in the corners of his eyes deepened as he smiled, and round his mouth, a full generous mouth, were more lines, laughter lines perhaps, because they also deepened and increased as he smiled, revealing white even teeth.

She looked around the bar. 'It seems bigger,' she said, at last managing to smile back at him.

He nodded in agreement. 'That's because all your painter friends are not here, filling it up, but I expect it gets full later.' He steered her towards the door, turning to wave a good-night to the barman.

'Night, Mr Wiltshire,' he called, putting a cigarette to his lips and preparing to light it.

'Nice chap that, he never smokes when I'm in the bar, he knows I hate the smell of it.'

They walked out into the cool, dark starry night.

'Here's my car.' It was standing almost beside the front door of the pub, a Rover, like Henry's, Elizabeth thought, but it looked bigger, perhaps a bigger model. It was difficult to tell the colour, in the orangey glow from the window it could have been black, dark blue or dark green. Elizabeth settled in the seat and searched around for the seat belt. In helping her, Stanley's hand touched hers: she felt a little shock at his touch. His eyes met hers, lingered for seconds, then he did up his own belt and they drove smoothly out of the car-park and turned right. Further away from home? A little thrill went through her, like fear.

They joined the traffic. Elizabeth glanced at Stanley; he spoke. 'I've booked a table at the Silver Knight. Do you know it, have you been there?' She shook her head. Stanley cornered smoothly. 'I hope you will like it, the food's good, usually. Now I've said that, it probably won't be!'

Elizabeth hated herself for asking the question. 'Do you go often?' Indeed, she had to clear her throat the first time she started.

Stanley looked serious. 'I used to,' he said. There was a sadness in his answer and a reserve that made Elizabeth wish she had never asked him. She vowed to herself that she would not ask a question, say a word—just enjoy the evening.

The car slid to a halt and the Silver Knight loomed in front of them. There were several cars parked around. A silver Metro like the one Elizabeth owned stood alongside an imposing red E-type Jaguar. A blue BMW was their nearest neighbour. As they drew nearer the door, Elizabeth looked up into Stanley's face. He put out a hand and touched her face gently with the back of his fingers. Something happened between them—what it was, Elizabeth could not even begin to understand, didn't even try. The moment passed and they moved forward through the wood and glass doors into the entrance hall. A little breath, a sweet-smelling warmth greeted Elizabeth. Since that magic glance her heart rate, which anxiety and perhaps guilt had been making her conscious of, had calmed down. Relaxation, trust, a true and wonderful sense of companionship flooded through her.

The rest of the evening was trance-like, the meal perfect, the wine, the service, the talk over coffee and liqueurs went on and on and could not be stopped. Afterwards they drove out into the country and he stopped the car at the end of a road that ran uphill. There they looked out into the valley where the town lights twinkled and beamed, and cars as small as beetles flashed along the outer roads or crawled beetle-like in the city streets. They talked, hands clasped. Stanley, not looking at her as he spoke, told and told and told—as she had told—and what they told was strange, like clearing a field of weeds and nettles and stones and rubbish, ready to plant. Elizabeth had never talked so intimately to anyone before. There had always been, even with very close friends or relatives, a need for reserve, for hoping they would guess. Here with him, there was no holding back. She could, once started, tell him everything. He was second in the telling, she was first.

It was quite late when at last they drew up at her door. 'This is it, where it all happens?' He got out of the car and came round to open the door for her. Just for a second he clasped her to him.

'Not here,' she said gently. They parted.

'Wednesday then,' he said, and released her hand slowly and with reluctance. He watched her put her key in the lock.

The house was in darkness except for the rather dim light in the hall. Elizabeth let herself in quietly, glancing at the little grandmother clock in the hall—twenty to two. She switched off the hall light. In the bedroom Henry was snoring, his usual quiet snore. She sat on the side of the bed and took off her shoes, one slipped from her hand and made a small sound as it hit the rug. Henry turned. 'Oh, had a good party?' he said. His nose got blocked at night, hence the snoring and the rather guttural way he asked the question.

'Fine, lovely party. Tiring, though,' she said.

'Yes.' He turned back to his original position, his back towards her. 'Can't do these knees-ups now we are older, eh?'

'No, you are so right, Henry,' she said.

He started to snore again. As she had passed she had noted the door of Nina's room was shut. Was she in or out? Elizabeth felt she could not care one jot. She slipped on her nightdress, creamed off her make-up, crept to the bathroom and cleaned her teeth. She looked in the mirror over the washbasin. Her face, devoid of make-up, looked younger, nothing mattered now that Stanley liked that

55

face, had touched her cheek gently with the back of his fingers. She could almost feel his touch again. Elizabeth wanted him so much, with such longing, such desire, she trembled. She looked down at her hands, which were clutching the edge of the porcelain basin so hard that her knuckles gleamed white.

In bed at last she lay, sleepless but without the least wish to sleep, gazing at the rectangle of lighted window and started at the beginning. She remembered almost word for word the story of his journey to the here and now, the things in his life that had brought him to sitting, watching the twinkling lights, the starry sky, beside her, no one else. Could it be true that this was a lasting thing, or was it just a brief encounter? He had nothing to escape from. She had so much. A home, husband, child. Would it lead to her heading away from everything she had and hated?

She turned on her side and the first words of Stanley's story came back to her. 'What can I say to justify my actions, what can I say . . . ?'

*   *   *

Stanley had married, he told her, when he was twenty-five to the one, the only love of his life. Annette, beautiful, blonde, wilful. He really had never looked at anyone else. He had met Annette at a dance when he was twenty and she nineteen. She had flirted with him, they had gone out together for a while, then she had left him for someone else, perhaps more handsome, more wild, adventurous. He had watched and waited, watched and waited for five years. 'Find someone else, for goodness' sake,' his friends had said so often, pairing him off with other girls, pretty girls, lively girls, quiet girls. It had been useless, always she was in his dreams, in his mind, Annette. She had married and left her husband and baby after a year. People were shocked. 'Leave your baby, dreadful!' But to him it didn't matter. After her divorce he had married Annette. He had been in heaven. Everything she had done, been guilty of, was nothing to him. He loved her, no matter what, but someone else came along, younger, richer, and off she went after him, leaving Stanley after six years.

Stanley had been devastated, hurt beyond hurt, but as several years passed, his work became almost an obsession. Anything to forget her. Annette never got in touch with him, did not ask for a divorce. He heard she lived now in Florida, that was all, until one day she had turned up on his doorstep.

It had been a Sunday morning, early, sunny and warm. April. He had just been preparing to go out, every minute detail seemed to be etched on his mind. Elizabeth could understand why. He had opened his front door, just as a heavy April shower had started, and there Annette had stood. She had looked

57

up at him for a few seconds, then collapsed at his feet. She had leukaemia.

'What could I do?' he said to Elizabeth. sitting in the car gazing over the lighted sky to the hills beyond. 'What could I do? She was still my wife.' He had looked after her for three long years, no longer loving her, that feeling had long gone, but pity and kindness and, Elizabeth thought, a natural honour had made him see it through to the end. Annette had had remissions, gone to parties now and again and behaved much in her normal fashion. Then the disease had finally been the cause of her death. She had gone to hospital one week before. Stanley had been with her when she died. 'The sad thing was, Elizabeth, that even though I hated to see her suffering, I could not love her any more. I did not even like her. What could have happened to all the love I had always felt for her, where had it gone?' The long story had ended and Elizabeth could find no fault in him.

He seemed to have scaled mountains compared to her molehills, yet Elizabeth could see another side to it. Her troubles were all around her. His had gone away—leaving scars perhaps, but they had gone away.

* * *

Elizabeth turned and looked at the electric bedside clock, the figures gleaming red. 4.20

a.m., still dark outside. There was a sound, a faint roar, a motor bike? She got out of bed, gently opened the bedroom door and slipped into the upstairs hall. Henry's and her bedroom window gave a view of the road, but not of the front door. She looked down, not moving the net curtains. She was right. There by the front gate was a motor bike and just getting off the pillion, taking off her helmet and shaking out her hair, was Nina. Elizabeth watched. The boy took off his helmet and they kissed, a long kiss, then with a key Elizabeth didn't even know her daughter possessed— and which she was certain Henry didn't know about—Nina unlocked the front door. The boy had followed her. Elizabeth couldn't see them but she guessed they were kissing again. She was about to turn and creep back to the bedroom when she noticed that to the left, the sky was curiously red, not the pink of dawn, but red. 'A fire somewhere,' she whispered to herself.

She climbed back into bed having gently shut the bedroom door. She did not, at the moment, want to confront her daughter or get in any way involved with her actions. She heard the front door close, the quiet grind of the wheels of the bike on the road, obviously being wheeled away by its owner. He would start the engine presumably when he was further away. She heard the gentle closing of her daughter's bedroom door, glanced at the

59

bedside clock again. Twenty five to five. She switched on her electric blanket. The warmth and the mixture of thoughts turned to muddled half sleep and a little later deeper sleep. Nothing had disturbed her husband; he had gently snored through it all. He certainly would not have slept, or indeed gone to sleep at all, if he had known Nina was out. She must have fooled him by going to bed, maybe early, then slipped out again. Out all night—what had she been doing? Elizabeth had not been able to see the boy's face, only his brown wavy hair as he kissed Nina. Her dreams were full of Stanley, motor bikes, Henry driving Stanley's car, Nina climbing out of windows, and the red glow in the sky like sunset.

She woke later than her usual time, it was nearly nine o'clock. Downstairs she could hear Henry either making tea or clattering the cups and saucers. She got up, slipped on her dressing-gown and went down to the kitchen.

'Morning, I tried not to wake you.' Henry was pouring water on to the tea in the teapot. 'You were late in, but was it a good party?' Elizabeth nodded and sat down at the kitchen table. 'I was going to bring this up to you.' He put the steaming cup of tea in front of her.

'Nina's not up?' Elizabeth asked.

'No, I called her. She went to bed quite early.'

'Did you have your TV dinner, Henry?' she asked.

60

He looked slightly uncomfortable. 'No, at least, yes. I had mine. Nina went out.'

'What's the matter with that girl?'

'Oh, she had to go out.'

Elizabeth got up to pour herself a second cup of tea.

'For goodness' sake, Henry. Why do you not try to see how undisciplined she is?'

'Well . . .'

He was going to stick up for her again, Elizabeth felt, and her irritation got the better of her. 'Very soon she will do anything she feels like doing and God knows what trouble she'll end up in.' Elizabeth said nothing about the time she had seen Nina come in, or the motor bike, or the boy, but she did ask him, 'What time did Nina come in then, last night?'

Henry answered at once and with complete conviction. 'Oh, not late, about twenty past ten. She told me she had been round to Margaret's. It was a little later than we had agreed upon, but she went straight up to her room. I went to bed early too.'

Elizabeth nodded. 'I see.'

'You see what, Elizabeth?' Henry's voice was sharp.

'Well, I feel she can so easily fool you Henry. She could have gone out again. You were sitting here, looking at the television, you might not have heard her go out again.'

Henry shook his head firmly. 'No, I saw her light on. I mean I looked, I could see it on

61

about ten to eleven, under the door, her door, then when I went up to bed about ten minutes later, her light was out, so there you are.'

'Good. Well, at least you knew she was safely in bed, Henry.' Elizabeth felt curiously detached and said nothing further.

Henry nodded. 'You enjoyed the party?'

Elizabeth smiled at him. 'Yes, you were just awake enough to ask me when I came in last night.'

The telephone rang and Henry went into the hall to answer it. They used a cordless telephone and he came back into the kitchen, talking into it. 'How was it started, do you know, maliciously or accidentally?'

Elizabeth looked at him and mouthed the words, 'What is it?'

He shook his head and went on talking. 'Yes, of course. We will be here this morning, my daughter too, if you wish. Right.' He put the phone down on the kitchen table. 'The school was set on fire last night, or rather this morning sometime. They want to ask all the pupils, they think it was malicious, a pupil or someone employed there, I don't know.'

'Well, thank goodness Nina was safely in her little bed.'

'Yes, indeed, but she wouldn't do anything like that, it was probably some lager louts or . . .'

Elizabeth went upstairs, paused and looked out of the window, remembering her daughter and the boy on the motor bike, remembering the red sky. She opened Nina's bedroom door. Only the top of the dark hair was showing. Her daughter was curled up in the foetal position she always slept in.

'Nina,' she said, not too loudly. Nina stirred, turned over, but her brown eyes did not open, and she gave a little snort rather like her father. Elizabeth closed the door and went back into the bedroom to dress. The problems of her husband and daughter seemed utterly secondary. The thought of Stanley and the possibility of escape obliterated any other feelings. As she sat in front of the dressing-table mirror, she felt a slight smile which would not leave her lips.

Elizabeth felt reluctant to go down and listen to Henry's worries about the school fire. She supposed someone would come—the police presumably—to question Nina. Was that the way it was done, she wondered? Had Nina set fire to her school? Elizabeth was almost sure her daughter was capable of doing so and she had seen her arriving back. She carefully made her face up. Wednesday, Wednesday, Wednesday drifted through her mind.

A peal of the front door bell brought her back to today. Quarter past ten. She went downstairs and arrived in the hall just as Henry was admitting a young constable and a pretty, neat, fair-haired policewoman.

They all walked through to the sitting-room.

Henry had dressed in his weekend clothes. He turned to Elizabeth. 'They have come to ask about the fire. My wife . . .' He introduced the three and they sat down at his invitation, the young constable with notebook and pencil. At that moment, Nina walked into the room. She looked at the policeman, then at Henry. 'What's happening?' she said. She looked pale and her brown eyes were half shut. 'I was asleep!' she said accusingly.

Henry introduced everyone again. The young constable spoke. 'There has been a fire at the school you attend and we understand . . .'

Nina slumped in a chair. She had put on an old pair of jeans and a woolly jumper at least four sizes too big for her. 'Well, so?' she said, running her fingers through her hair.

'We are asking pupils and teachers if they were aware of any disturbance in or near the school.'

'What time did the fire start?' Henry asked.

'About two in the morning, or perhaps later—we can't be sure, but it was started by someone who knew their way about the school.'

Nina scratched at the polish on her nail. 'How do they know that?' she asked, lowering her eyelids and giving the young man an almost flirtatious glance.

He hesitated. 'Well, the garden shed had been broken into and a can of petrol kept for the mower had been stolen and we presume used to start the fire.'

Nina shrugged and resumed picking at her nail.

'How much damage has been done, constable?' Henry asked.

'Quite a considerable amount, sir, the whole of the bicycle shed and the end classroom have been gutted.'

'We only want to know your daugher's movements last night, sir,' the young woman spoke.

'Oh . . . my daughter came in at twenty past ten and went straight to bed, didn't you, Nina? I was in all evening.'

Nina nodded. 'That's right. Dad always notes when I come in, or go out for that matter.' There was an edge of sarcasm in her voice, Elizabeth felt, not lost on the policewoman.

Questions were asked of Nina. Did she know anyone who had a particular grudge . . .? To all their questions she shrugged, drew the corners of her mouth down in a little grimace. She reacted a little more positively in describing how she had spent the preceding evening with her friend Margaret and corroborating her father's statement that she had got in at twenty past ten and, having called out 'Good-night' to her father, had gone immediately to bed.

The two police officers left, apologising for the time they had taken up, explaining that all pupils were being questioned, and their parents, and, of course, school employees and personnel.

'As if Nina would do such a dreadful thing!' Henry protested after they had left.

'As if, indeed.' Elizabeth replied.

In the kitchen she felt totally incapable of making lunch. She went back into the sitting-room and accosted her husband. 'Let's go out to lunch, Henry. I just don't feel like coping with cooking.'

'Right. We'll go out, I'm sure it's upset you as it has me, this school thing. Arson is a terrible crime. I'll ring up Harvey's, see if we can get a table for three.'

Nina had just come downstairs again and heard the conversation. 'Not for me, Dad. I've got a date.' She was dressed to go out. Another woolly on top of the large one and high-heeled black boots her mother had not seen before.

'Is that . . . ?' Henry asked as the sound of a motor bike stopped outside the front door.

'No, it isn't. You didn't approve of my last boyfriend. This is someone else, so don't start whingeing.'

There was a knock at the door. Nina made a move to go and answer it but Elizabeth, nearer the kitchen door, beat her to it. The boy she let in could well have been the one she had seen with Nina. His hair colour and the way it waved were similar. As he entered the hall Elizabeth was sure she noticed a smell of burning, of smoke.

Nina came into the hall. 'This is Jacko, Mum. We're going out.' She almost pushed the boy through the door and out and pulled the door shut firmly behind them.

Henry came out into the hall. 'Who was that?'

'One Jacko.' Elizabeth did not mention the smell of smoke which had accompanied the boy.

'Where has she gone?'

Elizabeth shrugged, rather like her daughter. 'Out.'

Henry went back into the sitting-room. Elizabeth went into the kitchen to make mid-morning coffee. She was well aware that her husband hated weekends and would much rather be safely tucked away in his office. Here, in his own home, 'Neeny's behaviour' was closer to him, her shortcomings more obvious. As Elizabeth took in the coffee he looked up from the newspaper.

'What was he like, this Jacko, did you say his name was?'

'Oh, usual. Jeans, scruffy-looking, rather nice hair. Wavy hair though, not one of those awful brush cuts that seem to be the thing just now.'

As she drank her coffee Elizabeth felt she could still smell the smoke. Maybe he . . . ? She cut off the thought. She didn't want anything to worry her, to come between the wonderful

67

thought of next Wednesday. She focused her mind firmly on Stanley's face. His lovely smile, his eyes crinkling as he smiled. The thought of Nina watching the flames in her waste-paper basket, the enjoyment in her eyes as she had been watching the flames before she had doused them with water, rather pushed his face from her mind. Would she set fire to the school? Damn the girl. She was pushing her dream away.

All the way to Harvey's Henry went on and on about the fire. 'Well, let's try and forget it for the moment, Henry and have a nice lunch. We don't often treat ourselves, do we?'

Henry had difficulty in parking the car in the rather small carpark. He left enough room on the driver's side for him to get out without hitting the next car with the door, but not enough on Elizabeth's side. 'Never mind, I'll move across.' Elizabeth squeezed herself past the gear handle and steering wheel. Henry, preoccupied with the small space he had got, did not even hold open the door for her.

The roast beef was overdone, according to Henry, and the glasses of wine which he ordered were expensive. Other than that, he went on talking about the fire—Nina—hoping no one had seen the police calling at the house. He looked slightly nonplussed when Elizabeth suggested a second glass of wine. 'Have one yourself, Henry,' she suggested. 'We both need it, don't you think?' On the whole it was not a particularly enjoyable meal, with Nina and the school fire looming over it all like a black cloud. Elizabeth wondered— should she tell him about Nina's habit of burning clothes? Or her suspicions about the boy Jacko?

She decided she could not—the trauma it would cause! She guessed, too, that Henry would be completely against telling the police any of this. She knew he would concoct anything, even lie, to protect Nina. Apathy overcame her. What would be the use? They finished the meal. Henry, in Elizabeth's opinion, undertipped the waiter. But then, on the very few occasions they came out together, he always did undertip.

'Let's have coffee at home,' he said. 'It's very expensive here. 75p a cup.' Elizabeth did not answer, couldn't answer. She merely got up and made her way out of the restaurant.

The local paper featured the school fire on its front page. The picture showed the completely gutted bike shed. Two fire-mangled bicycles still leaned drunkenly against each other. The end classroom abutting the shed was also badly burned, the smoke-blackened windows glassless, the window frames completely destroyed. The piece written round the pictures was fairly non-committal. 'The police were investigating,' which usually meant they had no clues at the moment. 'Arson was suspected' was a little more positive and there was a comment that arson was a serious crime and usually the motive that could be suspected was revenge for some real or imagined injustice, frustration because of some failure or, less frequently, pyromania, a love of fire itself—the thrill of seeing the flames and smoke. As she read it Elizabeth thought of her daughter, sitting watching the clothes burn in her waste-paper bin, of the boy's jumper smelling of smoke or burning. The feelings and suspicions were so deep, yet Elizabeth could think only of Stanley. What did it matter if the whole damned school was flamed to the ground, what if Nina and the boy *had* done it? Nina, she was sure, was quite capable of doing such a thing.

Henry had taken the paper and was rereading the whole article again, his face wrinkled with concern. Never, thought Elizabeth, would he suspect his beloved daughter of doing such a thing. Even if he had seen her with matches in her hand at the bicycle shed door. Nina had been rather quiet on their return from the restaurant. Jacko had not been mentioned and she had cleverly avoided Henry's attempts to talk about the fire at the school. Elizabeth felt nothing but contempt for them both. It was a lovely feeling and seemed to absolve her from any pangs of guilt.

She had already prepared her excuse for next Wednesday, why she had been delayed so

70

long after the class. She had thought it out carefully, lying beside Henry, both their bedside lights off, only the window for her to gaze at. Henry asleep, she wide awake, plotting next Wednesday. She was going to blame Mary for her late return from the painting class. Mary's car had refused to start and someone else had brought her home. That was the plan at the moment.

Elizabeth was not entirely happy with this. Should Henry look out, he would see Stanley. *That* would matter, because if Stanley brought her home again . . . She argued with herself, staring at the window. Not that Henry was very likely to open the front door to see who had driven her home, or indeed worry because she was late. She wondered just how soon Henry would begin to worry, no matter how late she was. How long ago had he ever bought her flowers or any kind of present? Mother's Day? Yes, he might have done that, to thank her for Nina, she supposed.

CHAPTER FOUR

Next Wednesday Elizabeth did not enjoy the painting class. The model was there and posed in the same position as the last time. Elizabeth tried hard to concentrate on the canvas, but she couldn't. Mary, painting beside her, looked at her once or twice. 'Having trouble, Liz?' she asked.

Elizabeth nodded. 'Just a bit,' she said and felt her cheeks reddening.

Mary did a little more to her picture, then turned to Elizabeth again. 'He's a very nice bloke, Stanley—be careful, Liz.' Her painting companion could only nod. 'I suppose you won't want a lift this evening?'

Elizabeth shook her head. 'Not if he's there,' and both women started to laugh.

'Oh, I think he'll be there,' Mary said.

The teacher looked in their direction with a shade of disapproval. 'Something funny about the pose, or the model, or the work in hand?' he said, looking at them over his glasses. One or two people around Mary and her companion murmured 'No, nothing,' and the class resumed its serious demeanour.

Elizabeth had never found the class so long. She tried very hard to push the meeting with Stanley out of her mind. He had said he would be there, but would he? Suppose since he had seen where she lived, had perhaps been made more conscious of her background—her husband, her daughter . . . What would they do tonight? They had so little time together.

Mary gave her a nudge. The teacher was addressing them all: 'I thought a painting weekend for those who can get away would be enjoyable.'

Enjoyable! The possibility of escape was

intoxicating. Elizabeth felt almost sick with apprehension and excitement. Could she leave Henry and Nina, then go to the painting weekend, but spend it with Stanley? Would he agree? She was committing adultery. He, of course, was not. The programme for the weekend was being handed round and the green piece of paper, covered with instructions and costs, was thrust into her hand. She couldn't read it. The letters seemed blurred and running into each other.

Several people during the coffee break mentioned the fire at the school. All sorts of guesses and theories were put forward. 'You can't tell young people off about anything these days,' one woman remarked with some bitterness. 'I objected when a couple of young boys about twelve skateboarded up my drive. They put up two fingers at me. I said they were very rude.' She dropped two lumps of sugar in her coffee. 'The next day all my polyanthus were pulled up and thrown in the driveway. I didn't see them do it, but I know it was them!'

An older man nodded in agreement. 'They are completely out of control, some of these youngsters. Even their parents can't punish them for anything because of reprisals!'

Amid this outburst of animosity Elizabeth thought of her own daughter and the new boyfriend. No, Nina wouldn't go quite so far as to start a fire at the school and 'Smoky Jacko' could simply have been near a harmless

73

bonfire. Anyway, it didn't matter. Nothing mattered, except the imminent meeting in the pub. Please, please, she prayed, let him be there.

*   *   *

He was there, seated at the bar in his usual place. As they walked into the bright lights, Mary gave Elizabeth another little nudge. Elizabeth turned towards her friend. 'Mary, this is—'

'Don't try to explain, just get on with it—I would.'

'Would you?' Elizabeth felt she was almost begging for reassurance. After all, this was wrong. Henry, she felt, would never be unfaithful to her, but then . . . he had Nina, Neeny, to watch over, worry about. Love. Perhaps that was enough? But it was not enough for her, did not even include her.

She crossed the bar, her heart quickening, her cheeks growing pink, like a young girl. Stanley met her half-way from his seat. He drew her away from the chattering crowd and they sat down at a table in a quiet part of the room.

'It seems such a long time between Wednesdays, darling Elizabeth,' he said.

'I know.' She put out her hand and clasped his. He raised it to his lips and kissed her fingers.

74

Everything seemed so natural, so perfect, as if, instead of a couple of weeks, Stanley had been part of her life for years. He looked at her and smiled his lovely warm smile. The place was filling up now and as she looked across towards the crowd, she couldn't see any of her painter colleagues. Even Mary was hidden from her view, though Elizabeth heard, as she looked, Mary's loud laugh.

'Let's get out of here. Need you go home just yet?'

Elizabeth shook her head. She knew Mary would understand if she disappeared and did not need the lift home.

'There's a little café just up the road, we can get a coffee and maybe even a sandwich, if you can stand gingham tablecloths and plastic flowers?'

Elizabeth laughed. 'If you can, I can.'

'Oh, I've never been in there, just seen it in passing, but it's often nearly empty.' They both got up. 'We will leave the car here, then walk back and I can drive you home.'

The evening was slightly chilly, the stars clear and twinkling. 'Frosty night,' Stanley said and slipped his arm through hers. During the short walk to the café, they were silent, Elizabeth comparing Stanley with Henry, the boredom, the harassment and at times the sheer hurt that her husband seemed totally unaware of. He had not even been slightly interested in her painting, except to make a derogatory remark when she had done any work at home. Nina, too, brought her no joy as a daughter, indeed mostly heartache and worry. But now, she realised her feelings were changing and not just because of Stanley; the caring she had once felt for Henry, for the house, for the garden and had tried to feel for Nina had long since disappeared, melted into an unbearable nothingness. She still did the housework, tended the garden, washed Nina's clothes and ironed them as she did Henry's, but she didn't care any more.

'I'm sorry about this, but it's the only place I could think of where we could talk and it wouldn't make you too late home.' Stanley interrupted her thoughts and she looked round the bright warm little café he had brought her to. He was right about the gingham tablecloths he had spied through the window. They were pink and white and gleamed with starch and cleanliness. A fat, short young waitress came up to them. Stanley looked at Elizabeth. 'Coffee?' he asked. She nodded.

The little waitress said, 'Right. Nothing to eat then?'

Stanley shook his head. 'Are we in a hurry?' he asked.

'No, I'm going to say Mary's car broke down if I'm late.'

He smiled at her. 'All for my sake?' he said.

'No, for my sake too.'

'I want to kiss you, but somehow these tablecloths look as if they would be shocked,' he said.

They both laughed and the tension in Elizabeth, which had built up a little with her thoughts of Henry, released. 'Stanley, look.' She took the green sheet of paper out of her handbag and handed it to him to read. 'Could we . . .?' She dared not say more but watched his face as he read it carefully, then placed it on the tablecloth when the coffee arrived. It smelled delicious.

'It's good coffee,' the fat little waitress said, stressing the 'good'. She smiled and two dimples appeared in her cheeks. 'Are you sure you won't eat? We've got egg and chips, sausage and chips, bacon and egg and tomatoes and sausages and baked beans and chips.' She paused, 'No, you don't look like truckers.' She took herself off again. They sipped their coffee which was delicious.

'Egg and bacon, sausages and tomato sounds good to me.' Stanley leaned forward, his arms on the table, his eyes full of mischief.

'I'd love it, but not the beans,' Elizabeth said.

'I believe I've brought you to what is known as a good pull-up for truckers.'

'I believe you have!' Elizabeth felt so good, so happy. Henry and Nina seemed a million miles behind her, but Stanley had not picked up the green slip of paper again. Elizabeth

77

longed for him to say something. He called the waitress and she seemed delighted they had decided on a meal. At last Elizabeth had to ask him. 'What do you think, Stanley?'

His face and expression became guarded. For a moment, a truly awful moment, she felt she had got it all wrong. Desperate for affection, she had assumed his feelings for her were as strong as hers for him. She'd been a fool. He looked towards the counter, then back at her. 'Are you saying you would like to spend the weekend with me, Elizabeth?'

She felt like getting up and running out of the café along the road to anywhere, anywhere except home. Suddenly she felt once again the firm, warm pressure of his hand on hers. 'Elizabeth, I wanted you to say you want this, explain to me, what do you want me to say?'

She knew he was right. She was not being open or honest in just handing the little brochure to him. 'I want to spend the weekend with you, Stanley.'

The grip on her hand grew a little tighter. 'Elizabeth, our meeting has been brief, we are attracted to each other.'

She nodded. 'Well, do you want to be with me?'

He smiled at her, his eyes gazing into hers. 'Of course I do, to be able to hold you in my arms.' He picked up the green paper.

'Can you manage to get away, from work I mean?'

Stanley laughed. 'Try and stop me, my darling.' Relief flooded over Elizabeth as he handed her back the green slip. 'Fill it in, it's a lovely place. I'll even paint if you want me to.'

The food arrived, they ate their meal. A couple of truckers came in and the little waitress smiled and twinkled. They finished with more coffee.

'I'll always love this place,' Elizabeth said as they walked out into the chilly night and back to the Black Horse and Stanley's car.

Once outside her own house, Elizabeth clung to Stanley. His kiss was more passionate, deeper, and went on till she felt almost overwhelmed by the desire to stay with him, not go into the lighted house, where husband and daughter would be waiting for her, but with little anxiety at her lateness.

'Good-night, darling. We'll talk about plans for the painters' weekend next Wednesday.'

'No, no, telephone me before then, it's all right during the day—well, not at weekends but . . .'

'I will. We'll try and arrange something.' He kissed her again and she got out of the car. As he opened the door for her he looked at the house. 'No twitching curtains or welcoming open front door,' he said.

She shook her head and watched him shut the passenger door, go round and get in and slam the other door. The car drew away. Elizabeth felt her heart go with it. Would he telephone, would she see him again before next Wednesday? She felt she couldn't wait that long. The red lights of his car drew further and further away, turned a corner and were gone.

Elizabeth shut the front door behind her. She could hear the television in the sitting-room. Nina's room light had been on, she had noticed while she was outside with Stanley. She went into the sitting-room. 'Mary's car broke down,' she said in answer to no question from Henry, who looked at his watch, then switched his eyes back to the television.

'I thought it was something like that, I had the casserole with Nina.'

'Oh, right. I'll put the bolt on the front door if she's in.'

Elizabeth went back into the hall, shot the bolt that in Henry's eyes would keep them all safe, then went upstairs. Henry's complete lack of concern about her late arrival home had done a lot to wash away her feelings of guilt. Some husbands would have rung the hall where the painting classes were held and, as it grew later, would have worried more, rung the police perhaps. Now, if Nina had been out . . . As she passed Nina's door she heard no sound, opened it, having knocked and got no reply. The room was empty. Elizabeth went in. As usual, the room was in a mess. She straightened the bed, shook up the pillow, picked up some discarded clothing.

She turned to the dressing-table. It looked dusty, as though Nina had spilled face powder, but she didn't use face powder. Various lipsticks, two open. Elizabeth tried one. Almost black, she thought, it looks awful. She looked around for a tissue, opened a drawer, some screwed-up brassieres, a pair of tights. She tried another drawer, the small one on the right side of the dressing-table. A few folded envelopes, letters perhaps, but what surprised her was what lay on top of the white paper. Five or six condoms, still in their flat blue transparent packets. She almost laughed. Her motherly wish to take Nina to the planning clinic, Henry's horror at the idea that his pure little girl needed such a visit . . .

Then as she was about to leave the room she saw the face of Miss Meadows, cleverly drawn, twisted and distorted with hate and rage. Jacko's work? Nina could not draw like that. Even more sinister was the circle of flames, drawn with orange and red crayons, almost all round the head of the teacher. Elizabeth thought of the fire at the school. No, Nina wouldn't put a human being at risk. Her clothes, a doll, the school sheds but surely not . . . ? No. Elizabeth closed the door behind her.

She'd better draw back the front door bolt again. Henry wouldn't check it now. Silently she ran downstairs before returning to her own bedroom and wiping the rest of the dark lipstick from her lips. She was shaken and

81

suddenly thirsty.

'You coming down again?' Henry called from the bottom of the stairs.

'No, I don't think so, I feel rather tired with all that waiting about.'

She heard Henry go back into the sitting-room, heard him switch off the television wall plug, the standard lamp, the hall light and braced herself for the moment when he would come upstairs.

She sat in front of the mirror of her dressing-table for some time, taking off her make-up, rubbing moisturising cream into her neck. Henry appeared at last, undressed and went into the bathroom. She could hear the splashing of the water into the basin as he cleaned his teeth. In the bedroom he climbed into bed but did not lie down and switch off his light as he usually did. Elizabeth thought he might ask about her evening, about Mary's car breaking down, but no.

'You know, Nina's idea might be a good one, to ask young Harper to dinner one night. What do you think?'

'Who? Oh, the new one in your office. Yes, if you want to.'

He switched off his light and lay down. 'We'll see, shall we?'

Elizabeth nodded, folded back her bedclothes and got into bed.

'Nina was quite good tonight, helped with the meal and came in early.'

Elizabeth nodded again. 'Perhaps, Henry, she behaves better when I'm not there. She's so fond of you.'

He turned and looked at her, his face pleased. 'Oh, no. I don't think it's that, Elizabeth. Maybe she's getting to the age when she likes looking after someone, even if it is her old father.' He lay down again.

'Yes, perhaps that's it, Henry.' She hoped that Nina's 'old father' would not wake up and hear her come in. Why didn't she care that Nina was out? A normal mother would worry, she was sure. She wondered whether she was out with Smoky Joe and an unwelcome image of Miss Meadows in flames flashed before her eyes. She switched off her light and thoughts of Stanley calmed her. Was she in love? She thought so. In all her life she had never before had this longing to be with another person and it astonished her how all-consuming this desire could be.

She did not find it easy to go to sleep. She dozed, and in between dozes she heard the stealthy opening of the front door, the careful closing, the slight click as the bolt was shot into place. Clever of her daughter to think of doing that. She would imagine that her father had forgotten to push it into place and that he would then think he had remembered to do his nightly task. Elizabeth heard the one stair that creaked—really, Nina should have learned about that stair creaking. She heard the bedroom door shut, put to gently. She looked at the luminous dial of her bedside clock. Two thirty. What did the girl do until this time in the morning? Elizabeth listened for the crunch of wheels on the gravel but heard nothing. Well, all the family were in now, the happy united family! She went off into a deeper sleep.

CHAPTER FIVE

The next morning Henry sat down to his toast and cereal breakfast. Usually he took it on the run, but this morning he seemed unusually relaxed. 'Young Harper put his foot in it yesterday,' he said with some satisfaction.

'Really?' Elizabeth felt a profound lack of interest.

'Yes, he was laying down the law about how much better the filing system was in the firm he had worked in before coming to us.'

'Not a very wise thing to say,' Elizabeth said dutifully.

'No.' Henry accepted a second cup of coffee. 'Nina's idea to ask him to a meal was rather good, I thought.'

'Oh, have I done something right?' Nina came in. She looked white and tired. Elizabeth felt little sympathy for her daughter, knowing what time she had come in the night before.

She was still in her dressing-gown.

'Free period?' Elizabeth asked, then, 'Oh, it's Miss Meadows' morning, isn't it?'

Nina put on her whining expression and turned to her father. 'Must I go, Daddy? I don't feel very well.'

Henry drained his coffee cup and stood up. 'Is it Miss Meadows this morning?' he asked.

'Yes, it is, but Daddy, it's awful. She picks on me.'

Henry looked sideways at his wife, no doubt remembering their visit to the parents' evening and Miss Meadows' description of Nina's behaviour in class. 'Well, you'd better go and try and be a good girl.'

Nina stamped her foot. 'Daddy, for God's sake, stop talking to me like that, I'm nearly sixteen.'

Henry murmured something in reply.

'Go and get dressed and then have some breakfast and you'll feel better, Nina.' Elizabeth spoke firmly, but she needed both of them out of the house in case Stanley telephoned.

Nina flounced out of the room but soon came down, dressed. She refused the toast her mother had made. As she came into the kitchen the usual two hoots came from the road. Henry decided suddenly he must rush and disappeared. She heard his car draw out with relief.

It was Margaret's mother's turn to take the

two girls to school this morning. 'I'll kill myself if that bitch is nasty to me, you don't try to understand. She humiliates me and you don't care, neither does Daddy.' Nina didn't wait for a reply but went out, banging the front door behind her. Elizabeth gave a long sigh of relief, sat down at the table and buttered the rejected toast. It was still warm and tasted pleasant. She poured herself more coffee, turned off the radio and gave herself up to thoughts about the painters' weekend. Would Stanley be able to come? Should they go to the painters' weekend or would he suggest going somewhere else, to a hotel perhaps? The painters' conference centre would be easier in case Henry needed to get in touch with her. She longed for a telephone call, but Stanley did not ring that day. Elizabeth made Polly's two walks shorter than usual in case she missed his call.

Nina came home in a fairly good mood. Elizabeth had got some of her favourite Country Slice Mr Kipling cakes for her tea. She devoured these.

'How did you get on with Miss Meadows, Nina?'

'She is a diabolical bitch, showed me up as usual about the date of some European war or other, as if it mattered.' She reached out for a fourth cake, then thought better of it. She was trying to slim without any noticable success. 'One thing I found out though. She's retiring

86

soon, bought herself some crummy thatched cottage near Ryston.' Ryston was a small village, almost joined on to the town by estates in the last few years.

'Oh, when's that to be?'

Nina drained her teacup and put the cup back with a clatter. She was a clumsy girl, her mother thought, watching her brush the many crumbs off her school tunic on to the floor.

Polly came in from the garden. 'I'll take her out.' Nina picked the dog up. She immediately started licking Nina's face. Elizabeth watched with her usual wonder at the change in her daughter's expression and demeanour. When she held or caressed the dog, her face softened, became loving. She looked almost pretty. Polly jumped down. Nina snapped her lead on to her collar and without a word to her mother or a thank you for the favourite cakes, went out of the back door, slamming it as usual. How many times? Elizabeth thought as she carried the tea things to the sink to wash. How many times had she, sometimes sharply, sometimes gently, according to her irritation level, said, 'No need to slam the doors, Nina.' Sometimes she had got a reply, 'Oh, sorry, OK,' sometimes not, but the doors continued to be slammed. Perhaps all teenagers did that, she was not sure.

Miss Meadows retiring, she thought as she put the plates and cups and saucers on the draining board. I bet she will be glad. She remembered the rather sharp features, no doubt honed into sharpness by girls like Nina. Surely there must be some who wanted to learn, wanted to go on to university, make something of themselves. Nina, when asked, just wanted to leave school as quickly as possible. Elizabeth believed she and her friend Margaret shared an ambition to be a singing duo, or be models. But Nina, even when asked by Henry what she wanted to do, was evasive. 'Look after animals' had been—at least to her mother—the most hopeful answer. She seemed to have a genuine love of animals and, on Elizabeth's suggestion, had approached the local vet to see if she could do anything on a Saturday to help the vet nurses. The vet had not been particularly helpful and Nina, easily put off, had not tried again.

Henry came home about seven with moans about the traffic, but did repeat his remark of the morning that he'd like to ask young Harper to a meal. Elizabeth agreed and said, 'Fix a day, Henry, but not a Wednesday,' then had a panicky thought it might be a weekend, the very weekend she wanted most of all to be free, so amended it to 'Monday or Tuesday?'

Henry nodded. 'Yes, Tuesday's a good day. Shall I ask him?'

Elizabeth agreed and Henry said he would try out next Tuesday for the invitation. 'He's not a bad chap—too young for the job in my estimation. Don't know how he got it, influence somewhere I expect.' Elizabeth knew he was bitter about the young man's appointment.

Henry took his drink through to the sitting-room and turned on the television. 'Chops for supper,' Elizabeth called to him. 'Needn't put them on for a moment. I'll have a drink with you.' She poured herself a small whisky, added a good dollop of soda and took it through to the sitting-room.

'Neeny in?' Henry asked.

'Yes, she's upstairs with Polly.'

'Humph.' Henry did not take his eyes off the screen and did not address a remark of any kind to his wife. Elizabeth was strangely comforted by his habitual indifference to her presence.

Stanley, Stanley, she thought. I am due for something better. No phone call today though. As the thought went through her head, the telephone rang. Her heart leapt, she went out to the hall. It was Stanley. 'Sorry to be so late, hectic day, but I felt I must speak to you. The weekend sounds wonderful, or rather reads wonderfully.'

'Can you get off?' she asked, keeping her voice down.

'Sure, no problem, but see you Wednesday?'

'Yes, yes. It's lovely about the weekend.'

'You are speaking quietly, so it may be difficult for you. I'll ring off and wait for Wednesday, which seems a long way away.'

'Oh, not too long, darling.'

She put the telephone down, thrills of sheer joy running through her. A slight noise made her look up. Nina was at the top of the stairs looking down at her, Polly beside her. 'A friend,' Elizabeth said, then felt a fool for saying anything.

Nina began to descend the stairs. 'Oh, right,' she said. Was her voice full of disbelief, or was Elizabeth just imagining it? She couldn't be sure. She felt her daughter's eyes on her as she went into the kitchen to turn the grill on over the chops. How long had Nina been listening? Those brown eyes of hers gave nothing away.

Oh, well, Elizabeth thought. Let her think what she likes.

She heard Henry greet Nina with 'Good day at school?' and Nina's answer, 'Bloody diabolical,' and his reply, 'Don't use language like that, Neeny.' As she carefully turned the chops she waited for Nina to come into the kitchen and make some comment about the phone call, but she did not appear. Elizabeth served the meal.

'These chops are very good.' Henry cut into his cutlet.

'They are too tough, I don't like chops. Polly!' Nina called the dog who bounded in from the kitchen where she had been finishing her bowl of Pal. 'Here you are, you have it!' Nina picked up the chop from her plate and

90

handed it down to the dog who grabbed it, turned round tail in the air, her fat little bottom waggling, the chop in her mouth.

'Neeny, you know you shouldn't feed Polly at the table! This meal was cooked by your mother for us, not for Polly.'

Elizabeth went on eating, numb to the scene around her.

'I hate chops.'

She came back to earth. 'That bone is not good for Polly. If she splinters it, it may choke her and stick in her throat.'

Nina immediately jumped up. 'Oh God, I didn't think of that! I'll go and take it from her, just give her the meat bit.' She left the room and called anxiously for Polly

Elizabeth and Henry went on eating. 'When will she learn anything?' she said.

'Oh, come on—she's bright enough. It's just at that age you are a bit rebellious.'

Henry finished his meal. Elizabeth finished hers, collected the two plates and went out to the kitchen. She left Nina's unfinished meal on the table.

In the kitchen she opened the freezer to get out ice cream. In doing so, she glimpsed her daughter tapping the telephone. In a flash, she knew Nina suspected her of something and was dialling 1471 to find out the number of the last caller.

'Ice cream, Nina?'

Nina put the telephone back in its rest with

a bang. 'Oh, right. Yes. Is it peach?'

'Yes, it's peach. Who were you phoning?'

'Just a friend.' Nina looked slightly sheepish.

'Oh, I see, just a friend. Did you get the bone away from Polly?'

Nina nodded. 'It's on the kitchen table.' She walked into the dining-room. Elizabeth followed, carrying the ice cream.

Her heart was beating uncomfortably fast. Had Nina managed to get the number Stanley had rung from? She thought not. She hoped not. She looked across the table where her brown-eyed daughter sat scooping her ice cream. Those brown eyes were suddenly raised. She looked directly at her mother, a long steady look. Elizabeth was the first to drop her eyes. Then she looked up again. Now Nina was concentrating on her ice cream. Elizabeth could not make up her mind. Was there a slight mocking smile on her daughter's full lips? What could she have done to make the girl think . . . Had she noticed the perfume, the make-up, the hair-do before the painters' class?

The meal finished, Elizabeth cleared the table and Nina went upstairs to watch her own television. The telephone rang again, this time Mary. She had heard Mrs Albright was not well and not coming to the painting class next week. Did Elizabeth want a lift? 'That is kind, Mary, but I have decided to be a devil and drive myself. This being afraid of driving in the dark is silly.' Mary had agreed. As Elizabeth put the phone down she smiled. That call would obliterate Stanley's, not that she thought Nina would try again, prying little toad.

CHAPTER SIX

Monday turned out to be a very bad and stormy day in Elizabeth's household. When Henry came home it was one long and boring tirade. Words like 'ineffective', 'inadequate', 'poor thinkers', 'no initiative', then 'arrogant young pup' which usually, and did in this case, referred to young Harper. This was rather unfortunate as he was invited the next evening to dinner. However, the invitation caused Henry more irritation and frustration as the young man rang up during the evening to say he could not manage the next day but could he postpone it to the following Tuesday evening? Elizabeth took the call and found his excuse and request quite reasonable. She agreed and put the phone down. When she told Henry he blew his top.

'Young whippersnapper—who does he think he is? You should have said no, we are booked that day.'

Elizabeth shrugged. 'What does it matter, Henry, we are not booked and one day is just as good as the other.'

'That's not the point. I don't want him to think we go nowhere, have no—'

Elizabeth felt weary and broke in: 'Henry, we don't go out, or get invited out much, do we? So what does it matter?'

'It does matter, we don't want him to know whether we get out much or not, do we?'

'Yes, we do!' Elizabeth felt guilty for comparing how she thought Stanley would behave in such a situation—although she didn't know, and was only guessing, she felt sure he would be pleasant.

Then earlier on that black Monday Nina had lost Polly while she was out on her after-school walk. She came home distraught. Polly had disappeared in the field up the road and she had searched and searched and called and called. 'She was just playing. I was throwing her ball for her, she brought it back, then suddenly she didn't and there was the ball and no Polly. Oh, Mum, she may go on the road and get killed.'

Elizabeth comforted her, even put her arms round her shoulders. Nina blew her nose and tears poured from her eyes. Why does she feel so much for Polly, yet apparently nothing for me? Elizabeth always thought this, every time Nina was distressed, usually about an animal. Why did she love them so, such an unloving girl?

'Come on, we'll take the car out and go and

look for her.'

They toured the streets, scoured the field, Nina becoming more and more hysterical. 'It was my fault, my fault. I let her go too far after the ball.' Nina wiped her eyes with the innumerable tissues Elizabeth supplied her with from the glove compartment. Suddenly there was Polly walking along the pathway towards home. 'There she is, there she is!' Nina screamed. Elizabeth was as pleased as Nina without the hysteria, she was genuinely fond of Polly. She stopped the car. Nina jumped out and called the little dog, who ran up to her, barking, tail wagging furiously. 'Oh, darling, where have you been?' Nina clasped the little body to hers, carried her back to the car. Elizabeth watched her, wondered if her daughter would thank her for helping with the search. No, all she could do was talk to the dog. Elizabeth wondered too at the word 'darling'. Whenever did Nina use that word? 'Daddy darling', perhaps, yes, if she were wheedling him to let her do some forbidden action, but 'Mummy darling'? Certainly never in living memory.

As they drove home, Elizabeth thought about what she had told Mary on the phone. Yes, she would banish this ridiculous fear about driving in the dark. After all, the evenings were drawing out now. She could drive to the painting class in daylight, and manage the dark drive home. Even that, in high summer, would be in daylight. It would give her more freedom to stay with Stanley, and it would be better if he didn't drive her home each time, with this nagging suspicion that Nina was suspecting something, watching her. Yes, she was determined. All or most of her friends drove at night, why not her? The thought made her feel free, more independent of these two people who seemed to take her completely for granted. As long as meals were prepared, the house cleaned, washing done, sex occasionally, very occasionally, available, that was as it should be.

Henry, when told about Polly's disappearance on his return home, said, 'Nina would be terribly upset. That dog means everything to her.'

The day was rounded off by another unpleasant event. Miss Meadows telephoned, asking them to excuse her for the rather late call, but she would be grateful if they could call and see her on the following day at about eleven o'clock in the morning. When Elizabeth suggested that it would be difficult as her husband would be at work, she said, 'Then perhaps you could come and convey what I have to say to him afterwards.'

'What is it?' she had asked.

'I would rather not say over the telephone.'

Elizabeth had had to agree to go and see her.

Back in the sitting-room she told Henry

what Miss Meadows had said. Henry dismissed it as unimportant. 'Some naughtiness she has been up to. They are all the same.'

Elizabeth tried to convince him Miss Meadows had sounded serious.

'Well, why did she want to see you as well?' Henry seemed barely to be listening to her. 'No, you will be able to handle it'.

'Damn it, I don't want to handle it, Henry. She's your bloody daughter too, you know!'

He looked up then, surprised at her vehemence. Elizabeth hardly ever swore. 'Well, you know I can't take the day off, just like that.'

'Why not? Just the morning, family problems,' she suggested.

'Family problems!' Henry's voice was mocking.

'Well, isn't it?' she had insisted.

'No, of course it isn't, just a storm in a teacup.'

He dismissed the matter and the next morning departed to work, grabbing a cup of coffee before he took off. Perhaps, Elizabeth thought, because he didn't want to talk about her visit to Miss Meadows, or because he had forgotten all about it. Nina too departed for school. Nothing about her mood made Elizabeth think she knew anything about Miss Meadows' request to see her parents. She did the usual chores, washing up, beds, dusting, then went and dressed in her one tailored suit, with discreet make-up. She did not want to go, especially alone. She drove to the school at quarter to eleven, feeling nervous and apprehensive.

As Elizabeth approached the school she wondered where to park her car. The well-kept lawns and tidy paths seemed car-free. She turned to the left and, a little further towards the corner of the building, she saw a neat row of clean, shining vehicles parked, their noses close against a blank wall. There were one or two spaces, equally divided by equally neat white lines, each car having a 'home' of its own. Elizabeth took a chance and slotted into one of the spaces.

She walked round to the front door of the school and entered a large, silent, well-polished hall. A young woman approached her from a side door. 'Did you want something?' she asked, her voice echoing a little in the space.

Elizabeth smiled. 'Thank you, yes. I've come to see Miss Meadows, she's expecting me at eleven.'

The girl pointed up the stairs at the side of the big hall. 'Headmistress's office. Says so on the door. She's deputy head, see. Knock before you go in.'

'Of course,' Elizabeth answered her. 'Are you a pupil?'

The girl was not in uniform and seemed curiously self-possessed. She laughed. 'Pupil, no. I'm a cook. I work in the kitchen. Pupil! I've got a kid too.'

She looked all of fifteen, Elizabeth thought, and some sympathy for Nina went through her mind, remembering her saying, 'I'm not a child.' She wasn't, Elizabeth supposed. She was a young woman.

Elizabeth found the brown door with the white letters: HEADMISTRESS. She knocked as instructed and a voice answered almost sharply, 'Come.'

Miss Meadows sat behind a large desk covered with books and papers, half-glasses perched on the end of her nose. The eyes that looked over them at Elizabeth were slightly red and tired. 'Ah, Mrs Mason.' She looked at her watch. 'Right on time, but alone?'

Elizabeth nodded, advanced into the room and closed the door behind her. 'Yes, as I said on the telephone, my husband could not get time off. He is an accountant and very busy at this time of the year, tax and everything you know.'

Miss Meadows nodded, taking off her glasses and placing them on the desk in front of her. 'I understand, but I would have liked him to be here.' She sat down and motioned Elizabeth to a seat on the other side of the desk. 'Do sit down.'

There was a tap on the door. A fair-haired girl opened it and peered round. 'Coffee, Miss Meadows?'

'Please, two cups.' Elizabeth would have refused but it was impossible because the girl nodded and disappeared.

Miss Meadows looked down at her clasped hands on the desk before her. They were rather red hands, shiny, the nails clean and short.

'You wanted to see us, Miss Meadows?' The woman was so hesitant, so obviously reluctant to start what she had to say. Elizabeth began again. 'My husband is . . .'

Miss Meadows raised a hand. 'Oh, I do understand, I'm just waiting for the . . .' At that moment the girl came in with two cups of coffee on a tray. She looked rather shyly from one woman to the other as if she was intruding on something very private, as indeed she was. This became only too clear as Miss Meadows began to speak:

'Mrs Mason, I am very distressed at what I have to tell you. As you will remember, when we met before I did acquaint you with the difficulties I was having with your daughter Nina.' Elizabeth nodded and was about to speak, when Miss Meadows raised a hand, indicating her wish to continue. 'Since that meeting, owing to the unfortunate illness of Miss Leaman, our headmistress, I have left that particular class and someone else has taken over my duties and, alas, has fared no better at your daughter's hands. She has been just as disruptive. However, that is only by the way, I am afraid.' She pursed her lips until they almost disappeared. 'Something that cannot possibly be overlooked.' Elizabeth's heart missed a beat. Was it the fire? Had they discovered some other clue as to who had actually started the blaze? 'No, Mrs Mason, cannot be overlooked as your daughter was actually, as it were, caught in the act.'

At that moment Elizabeth felt toward the stiff-laced, sharp-featured woman as impatient and frustrated as she might well make Nina feel and she burst out, 'Well, for God's sake, Miss Meadows, what has she done? You seem to be keeping me in suspense for no reason.'

The deputy head clasped her hands together, looked down at the paper in front of her as if what she was about to say was written there. 'Nina was caught in break smoking cannabis, Mrs Mason. Not only that, she was found to have another, I believe the term is 'roach' in her desk.'

Miss Meadows could not know that Elizabeth had breathed a sigh of relief. Not the fire then. She hastily drew her mind to the new problem. 'Cannabis!' It was quite a shock, but really a lot of kids experimented with it, probably many more in the school. 'Miss Meadows, many young people do want to try these things and soon get over the silly craze.'

Miss Meadows reared in her seat, glared at her companion with eyes wide. 'Silly craze, is that what you call it? We call it a serious offence that must be punished.'

'Yes, yes, of course, but it would worry me more if you thought she was giving any away, selling it.'

Miss Meadows sniffed, straightened the papers on her desk and looked as if she were preparing herself for the final blow. 'She will be suspended of course and the police will have to be informed.'

Elizabeth was horrified. Henry would be so upset, his little girl! 'When did all this happen?' Elizabeth marvelled at her daughter's silence about the whole affair.

'Friday.'

'Friday? But today is Tuesday,' she said. 'Why leave it so long to tell us?'

Miss Meadows herself looked upset. 'On Friday, Miss Leaman, our headmistress, had a stroke.' She looked as if she might easily burst into tears. 'On Friday we discovered Nina's ...' She paused, took off her glasses and placed them carefully on the desk. 'It may be, Mrs Mason, that that discovery caused Miss Leaman's illness. She was very proud of her school, you know. We had better see Nina now.'

She pressed a bell on her desk and the young woman, who had brought the coffee poked her head round the door. 'Yes, Miss Meadows?'

'Will you tell Nina Mason she may come in now.'

The girl nodded and withdrew.

'Does Nina know I'm here?' Elizabeth asked.

Before any answer was given the door opened and Nina came in. She looked over at her mother. 'Where's Daddy?' she said.

'Nina, please sit down.' There was another chair on the same side of the desk as Elizabeth's. Nina sat down stiffly, leaned back in the chair and clutched the wooden arms. Her knuckles showed white, which made Elizabeth suspect that her daughter was not as relaxed as her facial expression would have one believe. Miss Meadows looked directly at the girl. Nina looked back at her.

'I have told your mother about you being in possession of an illegal drug Nina. She is, of course, shocked.'

Nina gave a dry, husky short laugh. 'She doesn't look shocked to me.'

Both women ignored this. 'Your mother will take you home now for a suspension whose duration will be decided by the school governors.' She put her glasses on again and looked down at the papers on her desk.

'Off school! Good! Look, it's not long till I'm sixteen, then I can leave the poxy school anyway, can't I?'

Her eyes went from her mother to Miss Meadows and back again. Elizabeth was quite shocked now, really shocked. 'Nina, you know how your father wants you to go to university.'

Nina's lower lip stuck out in the way so familiar to her mother. 'I want a job,' she said. 'I'm sick of school.'

'Well, I may have retired and left before you come back. Holidays are only a few weeks off and I retire then.' Miss Meadows spoke sharply.

'Well, I shan't be sorry.' Nina muttered the words under her breath almost, but they were loud enough for Miss Meadows to hear.

'That I can quite believe, but in spite of what your feelings are towards me, I feel I have done my best to help you.'

Elizabeth felt she must reprove her daughter. 'Nina, please don't be so rude.'

Miss Meadows put up her hand. 'Go and collect your books and all your things and bring them back here.' Her voice was cold. Elizabeth felt she had never been in the presence of two people who hated each other as much as these two, their animosity made her almost shiver. Nina got up and left the room.

Miss Meadows gave a long sigh. 'I quite realise I have been a complete failure with your child, Mrs Mason.'

Elizabeth shook her head but did not speak for a moment; quite suddenly she felt tears pricking her eyelids, then running down her cheeks. 'So have I. Nina detests me, maybe she lacks love from me. Her father adores her.' She found herself pouring out all her dislikes, her boredoms, the banalities of her home life to this stiff-backed woman opposite her. Everything of course except her new relationship with Stanley. Miss Meadows listened with apparent sympathy. Elizabeth wiped her eyes and apologised.

Nina did not appear and Miss Meadows seemed to feel that after Elizabeth's outburst, the silence should be filled. She talked about her retirement, the cottage she had bought. 'It is thatched, Mrs Mason, a large, rather wild garden. I can have a dog or a cat. I have no relatives so I shall live alone. I do now, but in a flat, which is not the same, is it?'

'I've never lived alone.' Elizabeth tried to appear interested. 'I should think it would be rather nice.'

Miss Meadows shrugged. 'We shall see,' she said and shut off the conversation as Nina came into the room carrying a holdall of books and some shoes and a raincoat, draped over her arm.

'I'm ready, Mum,' she said without even a glance at the deputy head.

Elizabeth got up. 'Miss Meadows . . .' she said.

'You will be hearing from us, Mrs Mason. Goodbye for the present, Nina.'

Nina laughed. 'Goodbye for ever, Miss Meadows.' She turned and went out of the door, the stuffed holdall banging against the lintel.

Elizabeth followed. She felt deeply ashamed that Nina was anything to do with her. They drove home in complete silence. Elizabeth felt her daughter's glance sliding towards her several times on the journey. She was imagining this evening. Henry's reaction, the rows. How he would manage somehow to make out it was her fault. The old accusation would be voiced again: 'You don't supervise her enough, she's still a child. You shouldn't let her wear clothes like that, goodness knows what people will think of her.' Well, cannabis would be a change, that would really make him blow his top, really upset him too. Wednesday, Wednesday, should she tell Stanley about this? Yes, she felt she had to tell someone, but would it make him feel she was just using him as someone on whom she could unload her troubles?

Arriving home, Nina collected her things, but left her raincoat in the car. 'Well, Polly will be pleased to see me if no one else is,' was her only comment as she entered the house. This was true. Polly barked in welcome. 'I'll take her for a walk.' Nina put on the dog's lead and went out of the back door. Elizabeth went through to the kitchen and poured herself a large glass of sherry. She felt she needed it, and lunch could go hang. If Nina was hungry she could go and get herself some fish and chips when she came back. But three o'clock came and Nina was not back. So lunch was passed and forgotten with no meal being served. It was not until five that she eventually reappeared.

'Did you have cannabis in your desk as well?' Elizabeth asked. Nina had fed Polly and given her a clean bowl of water before slumping down on a kitchen chair by the table and accepting a cup of tea and some ham sandwiches Elizabeth had made. There was no answer to her mother. 'Where have you been, Nina, have you had any lunch?'

She ate all the ham sandwiches offered and gave one to a hopeful Polly sitting beside her. 'I had a roach in my desk apparently,' she said, pushing her cup across the kitchen table for a refill.

'A roach?'

'A cannabis cigarette.'

Elizabeth poured the tea and pushed the cup back to her. 'So, why was it there?'

'Someone put it there. Any cake?'

Elizabeth shook her head. 'You were very rude to Miss Meadows, Nina.'

'That cow! At least she'll be in that bloody cottage of hers when the school condescends to have me back, which I hope is never.' She pushed her chair back. 'Come on, Polly.' She went up to her room, Polly pattering behind her, more door slamming.

Elizabeth stood at the kitchen sink washing up the cups and saucers. She dreaded Henry's return, dreaded it. Having to tell him about

107

what he had termed 'a storm in a teacup'. He would be shattered, his darling little girl into drugs! She really felt sorry for him. How would Stanley handle this kind of thing, she wondered? With more understanding for his wife, she felt sure. Look how good he had been—again she felt herself spilling over with tears. Stanley, his love. Henry's indifference. Nina's behaviour. Miss Meadows, the whole sorry mess.

She felt sorry for Miss Meadows. As for the school itself, it was probably full of problems— the fire, children playing truant, all that was quite enough to cope with at retirement age without drugs and rudeness and the obvious hatred she must realise Nina felt for her. Elizabeth wiped her eyes on the tea-towel. Well, let's hope she would be happy in her thatched cottage, she deserved it.

Henry was more than upset at the first telling of the morning's visit to the school and its reason. He would not believe it. Nina might be headstrong, naughty sometimes, yes, rude even—but drugs! Someone had left the stuff in her desk, someone who wanted to get her into trouble. Elizabeth's 'Henry, she was smoking cannabis!' seemed to fall on deaf ears. 'She wouldn't do that, my little girl, not drugs, it's all a mistake!'

Nina of course had to face her father eventually, though she stayed in her room the rest of the day. About eight o'clock she came down with Polly, put her on the lead and snapped at her father, 'Polly needs to go out and she comes first before everybody. If you want to talk to me, you'll have to wait till I come back.' The front door slammed as usual.

Elizabeth felt genuinely sorry for her husband. He looked as she knew he would be—shattered. When she suggested dishing up the meal he refused, saying he could eat nothing. They sat, waiting until Nina returned. Even then she fed the dog again before she would sit down and talk to her father. Elizabeth opted out. 'I've had all I can stand today, Henry,' she said firmly, and as the sitting-room door closed on the two of them she drew a great sigh of relief. She went up to the bedroom and stretched out on the bed.

She rang Stanley on the bedside phone.

'Hello, this is an unexpected delight,' he said.

'Slight family crisis and I have a minute to myself. I'll tell you about it tomorrow or I may decide not to. We will see. It may be too boring to repeat.'

'You couldn't be boring and I can't wait for tomorrow,' he said.

'That helps so much, I cannot tell you.' There were tears in her voice. 'I'm turning into a bit of a cry baby,' she said.

'I'm so sorry that you're hurting, I hurt too for you,' he answered.

She could not stop crying now and had to

say 'Goodbye' and put the telephone down. She felt wretched and yet rapturous. Stanley's words and voice had perhaps made her cry, but he was there to tell if she wanted to, there to support her as she did want him to. What a funny woman she was, she thought. Even now she could not feel for her daughter as she was sure Henry was feeling. She lay there for about an hour before she heard the sitting-room door open and Henry call out, 'Elizabeth, where are you?' The dreaded hated yoke was on her shoulders again.

Supper was hardly touched. Nina was silent and directly Elizabeth brought in cups of coffee after clearing away the almost untouched sweet, she jumped to her feet. 'I'm going out,' she said.

'It's late and I think you should stay in.' Henry's voice was unusually firm.

'Why, think I might go on the drugs again?'

'Don't speak to your father like that, Nina, and sit down.'

Nina looked at her mother. 'Oh, leave me alone!' she said and left the room.

Elizabeth looked across at her husband.

'What have we done wrong?' he asked.

'What have *you* done wrong, Henry! Spoiled her to death, made her think her smallest whim must be indulged.'

Henry got up, pushed the table in doing so. The coffee cup turned over, sending a cascade of coffee over the table top. Elizabeth went to the kitchen and came back with a handful of kitchen roll paper—sopped up the mess. She felt so angry, so furious that she could easily, at that moment, have walked out of the house and out of these two hateful people's lives. She heard the front door bang.

Nina's going out, to boys, drugs, sex, the slamming door always seemed to indicate a broken rule, a broken promise. She stood in the dining-room doorway looking at her husband. 'I've had enough,' she said.

He looked at her. 'What do you mean?'

'I don't know, but I've had enough.'

She went upstairs and longed for Wednesday.

CHAPTER SEVEN

Nina seemed to enjoy not having to go to school. She was defiant, particularly towards her father. To Elizabeth she hardly spoke at all. Henry took the next morning off and went to the school to see Miss Meadows. He came back in a very chastened mood. He sat down heavily in his armchair. He looked older. 'What did she say?' Elizabeth had to ask at last, handing him a cup of coffee, pretty heavily laced with whisky.

He sipped the drink before he replied. 'Nice!' he said, then, 'Miss Meadows . . .' He

111

paused and took another sip. 'She said the police would not be informed. No more cannabis has been found, all the pupils have been questioned.'

'Well, that's good news so far—no police at least.'

He nodded. 'But Elizabeth, she said that Nina was very rude to her, almost all the time. She was disruptive. Then things about when she was frustrated and held up other people's learning.' He drank the rest of his coffee, put the cup down on the little table beside him with, Elizabeth noticed, a shaking hand. 'Why does she act like that at school? She doesn't at home.'

Elizabeth laughed, the laugh mocking. 'Henry, she behaves disgracefully at home. The only thing Nina really loves is animals. We should try to make her go to university and suggest she becomes a vet.'

'She'll never get to university now, I feel. She is determined to leave school and, as she puts it, "get a job".'

He got up. 'I must get back to work.'

'What about lunch, Henry?'

He shrugged. 'Don't feel like eating, anyway, I must get back.'

After he had left, Elizabeth felt so sick of the whole thing, she left the house, went and walked in the fields.

To humiliate Henry even further the arrogant young pup telephoned to say he could not manage their kind invitation on the following Tuesday. Could he put off the visit and let Henry know when it was more convenient—a sick mother was his excuse. Henry chose not to believe him.

The painting class was slightly bigger. Three more people had joined—maybe they had heard about the model. Elizabeth would have much preferred to give up the time to being with Stanley, but the weekend had to be thought of. If she did not attend the painting class, she would not know more about it. She was torn two ways. Should she suggest that Stanley came to the Western Concourse, as the place was known? Several people brought their husbands, according to some painters who had been before to other weekend courses. Or . . . should they go to a hotel and be alone together for the whole glorious weekend? The class painted and drew the same model. Elizabeth was bored and restless. 'You are not in the mood, Mrs Mason,' the painting teacher suggested, frowning.

'No, I'm afraid not,' she had to admit, but made various small alterations, to while away the lesson.

Just before the end of the two hours the teacher dismissed the model and said he had an annoucement to make about the weekend at the Western Concourse. It was to be in four weeks' time. Friday, starting about four, and ending on Sunday after four, so it would be two nights. Maybe they, Stanley and she, could steal the Sunday night in a hotel. Her heart fluttered at the thought of it, to sleep with him, hold him in her arms, be in his arms. No Nina, no Henry, no rows, no problems. She would love to stay in a hotel for the three nights. But Henry would want to telephone her, want the address, in case of a crisis with Nina. Now she would be forced to leave Nina at home, no school, free to do as she liked with her boyfriends, girlfriends. Well, go she would. Forms were handed round to be filled in. She folded hers and put it in her handbag to show Henry, before she filled it in with—she hoped, and prayed—his blessing.

The lesson finished at long last. The jangler jangled his keys, everyone packed up, the three new painters decided they would like to come to the Black Horse as well. Elizabeth put her painting gear into her car, looked around her at the dark night. She had to brave driving home through it, but she did not regret her decision.

Mary asked her as she came out, 'How did the driving go?' then realised it had been daylight when she drove there. 'Oh, of course, it was light then, hope you get on all right on the way home.'

'Thanks, Mary. Black Horse first though.'

Elizabeth drove the short way to the pub and parked neatly, noticing a motor bike parked beside her. She made a mental note not to get too near it when she backed out to go home. She locked her car and looked around for Stanley's car. There it was. Her heart quickened and she followed the others through the door into the brilliantly lit room. Cheery bar! Only orange juice for her tonight, she thought as she blinked in the light after the darkness outside. She had hardly got accustomed to it when a voice beside her, almost in her ear, said, 'Hello, Mum.'

It was Nina, and beside her stood the boy she had named as Jacko, the boy who Elizabeth had thought smelled of smoke. He was still wearing the jumper and pulled at Nina's arm, 'Come on, we have to go.'

Stanley suddenly emerged from around the curved bar, a wide welcoming smile on his face. He advanced towards them.

'What are you doing in here, Nina? You're not old enough, you're only fifteen,' Elizabeth asked hurriedly. She looked accusingly at the boy, who pulled harder at Nina's arm.

'All right, Mum, keep your knickers on, we're just going.' The girl smelled of beer. Jacko, if that was the boy's name, pulled her towards the bar door and they disappeared through it, just as Stanley reached her. She was shaking.

'Who were they?' he asked, taking her hand.

'My fifteen-year-old daughter who has just been suspended from her school for smoking dope,' she said, 'and the awful part is, Stanley,

115

I believe she may have started a fire in the school too!' She put her hand up to her mouth. 'Supposing she had seen us together?'

Stanley put his arm round her shoulders and led her to the door. 'Come on, darling, you've had enough of her for the moment.'

Elizabeth shrank back. 'We can't go to that little café, she might be there, Stanley, she might be anywhere.'

'OK, we'll go to my place. Give you time to get over seeing her here. We'll have a drink there, then I'll bring you back to your car and, if you feel able, you can drive home. Come on.'

They got into his car. The night was still and warm; the motor cycle had gone. Elizabeth tried to relax. Stanley looked at her. He took her in his arms and gave her a long lingering kiss. Her body seemed to melt away under his lips, she wanted him so badly at that moment. He released her and started the engine. As they drove out of the car-park, Elizabeth felt as if her whole body was still on fire. Never, never, even on their wedding night, had she felt anything like this for Henry. It had been a ritual act and, as the years went by, something carefully planned to take place at the right time, the whole sad effort to make a baby. A baby that took so long to happen and then brought Nina into being. Was that loveless act, at least on her part, responsible for how the girl was? They drew into a driveway. Stanley's house, the place she had so longed to see.

It was not at all like Elizabeth had visualised. It was not particularly large, but a pretty house, covered with young golden Virginia creeper at this time of year. The leaves gleamed bright and yellow in the car lights. The front door was under a porchway. 'Come in—take care not to tread on the bun.'

Elizabeth looked down and in the porch light could see two white circles of a bun, cut through the middle and lying on the tile floor. 'What?' she was going to ask, but Stanley, unlocking the door, interrupted her.

'We have nesting swallows by the porch.' He pointed up to the right of the porch roof. 'Mrs Evans, my cleaner, puts the food out every evening and by morning it's gone.'

The door opened into a small hall. In the middle stood a well-polished round table, on which was a bowl of roses. 'How lovely!' Elizabeth touched them gently with her fingertips. They went into a room on the right, and as he switched on two lamps, the room was revealed. More flowers, a chintzy room, rather a woman's room than a man's. 'How pretty,' Elizabeth said as she looked around. There were no photographs, none, and very few ornaments. The big sofa and chairs had loose covers of flowery chintz, their skirts well pleated and creaseless. The furniture was well polished. Stanley, she felt, noticed her surprise. 'After my wife died I seemed to leave everything to someone else. My sister Marion refurbished the house, made it totally different to how it was when Annette was living here, and eventually—dying.'

He moved over to the drinks cabinet. 'What can I get you?'

'Anything, I don't mind.'

'That was a shock, wasn't it, seeing Nina there?'

Elizabeth nodded.

'But she didn't see me, so, for the moment, it's all right.'

'For the moment.' Elizabeth took the brandy he gave her. She felt utterly miserable. She turned suddenly and looked at the man sitting beside her. 'I've never been in love before, Stanley,' she said.

He looked back at her. 'I don't believe I have either, Elizabeth. I thought I was with Annette. I was certain I was but now, with you, feeling as I do, I know I wasn't.'

He took the brandy from her and placed the glass on the coffee table in front of them. They drew together. To feel him holding her was the most wonderful moment of Elizabeth's life. She felt herself melting at the closeness of him, his hand caressing her breast sent a thrill through her that made everything other than this moment unimportant, almost non-existent. No Henry, no Nina, no drugs, no slamming doors, no lies, only she and the man who was about to become her lover.

Upstairs in his bedroom, she let him

undress her, amazed at her own feelings. She has always been shy of being seen naked, even with Henry. Here with Stanley, as more of her nakedness was revealed, she suddenly felt proud of her body, her flat stomach, the well-shaped breasts with prominent nipples, made so by her lover's caresses. In bed at last, their bodies entwined flesh to flesh. She gave herself up completely. This was love, lust. She didn't care which.

Elizabeth arrived home two hours later. Henry was up and in a state. Nina had not come home. She had gone out at about eight fifteen and said she would not be late. He stormed on. 'And now it's nearly half-past eleven.' Then, as an afterthought, 'And where have you been?'

'The Metro wouldn't start, so I called the nearest garage. They were reluctant to come. I had to wait.'

'What was the matter with the car?'

'I don't know, spark plugs, I think he said. It didn't take long, it was waiting for him.'

'You could have rung.' Elizabeth snapped back at him: 'You could have rung me. You know we go to the Black Horse. I've told you that, Henry!' She prayed he hadn't.

'I was so worried about Nina,' he said, not apologetically.

'I'm sure that put everything else out of your mind,' Elizabeth said but, as she knew it would be, the sarcasm was totally lost on her husband.

'Where is she?' he said distractedly.

'Out with Jacko or whoever the current heart-throb is, Henry. I'm going to have a shower and go to bed.'

'What, with Nina still out?'

She shrugged. 'Staying up won't make her come home any earlier, or any later.'

She did not say a word about seeing her daughter in the Black Horse with Jacko. The fact that his daughter had been in a public house, under age, would only upset him more, much more. All Elizabeth wanted to do was get into bed, in the dark, and relive the last two hours, relive and re-feel.

She took a shower, though she was reluctant to wash away the smell of her lover's body. Once in bed, she lay gazing at the window, living again each wonderful moment of that short, too short time. They had been in a double bed, and as they lay afterwards side by side, he had answered a question she had only thought. It seemed he could tell what she was thinking. 'No, this isn't the bed shared with Annette. My sister changed it for hers when she got divorced.' She had laughed. 'How did you know what I was thinking?' she had asked him. He had taken her face in his hands and kissed her. She felt the tingle as she remembered. 'I know, I just know,' he had said.

Henry interrupted her thoughts. 'Nina's

come home,' he said.

She looked at the gleaming red figures of her bedside clock. 'One thirty, that's not very late. Wait until she's sixteen.'

Henry sounded scandalised. Elizabeth retreated back into her world of love. Various noises, domestic noises that she was used to, seem to reach her through a veil. Henry undressing, the sound of the shower, his muttered remarks about Nina's attitude. 'She was quite hysterical.' Sounds of teeth cleaning, then 'I heard that motor cycle driving off, skidding all the gravel up.'

She curled up and closed her eyes. At last Henry stopped talking, got into bed and snapped off his light, remarking before he fell asleep, 'You should go and have a word with her, you're her mother.' Elizabeth waited until his soft little snore began, then she dismissed Nina and Henry from her mind and returned to Stanley; where could they meet again, when would he suggest?

*   *   *

During the next week Henry and Elizabeth were asked to attend the school, this time without Nina. Miss Meadows was still in charge. Elizabeth asked after the headmistress and was answered very gravely by the deputy head: 'I am afraid she will not, according to the doctors, be able to return to her duties here, or indeed even to teach again.' Miss Meadows blew her nose, straightened her shoulders and resumed: 'This unfortunate happening will not alter the fact that I am retiring at the end of term. The board of governors has decided, I think with great leniency, to make Nina's suspension for that time only.'

Henry suddenly broke in: 'Does that mean she will be able to start school again at the beginning of the new term?'

Miss Meadows nodded. 'We hope with amended ways and attitude, Mr Mason.'

Henry looked at Elizabeth, ever hopeful, she thought. 'That is good. The whole sorry business will be forgotten?' He looked hopefully across the desk.

Miss Meadows regarded him with a rather solemn expression. 'Not forgotten, Mr Mason. Of necessity, it must go in her records and of course greater supervision will be used on your daughter.'

Elizabeth sighed. 'Henry, I don't think she will come back. She'll be sixteen in four weeks' time—she hates school, studying and all that goes with it.'

Miss Meadows shrugged as if it were of little importance to her one way or the other.

'Oh yes, she will see how necessary it is to get to university, to continue her education, Miss Meadows, I am sure I can persuade her,' Henry said.

Again that almost indifferent shrug.

Elizabeth felt Henry did not understand, could not even imagine the hostility that had built up between Nina and her teacher, but she said no more, it was no use.

They both got up, both shook hands with Miss Meadows. Henry had such a preoccupied air that Elizabeth thought he must already be planning his persuasive speech to his beloved Neeny. As she shook hands she said, 'Have a happy retirement, Miss Meadows, and please try to forget Nina's rudeness and naughtiness to you.'

Miss Meadows smiled, a real smile. 'Thank you, Mrs Mason. I cannot tell you how I am looking forward to it.'

They left the office. The school. Elizabeth was conscious of the smell, what was it? A mixture of young girls' bodies, chalk, shoes, waxed floors. Even with all the computers, all the new technology, the smell of school remained the same. She mentioned it to Henry as they passed through the big hall to the main entrance but, as she knew it would be, his mind was on Nina.

'I'll make her see sense,' he said positively. 'I'm sure I can, it would be foolish to give up now. I'll manage it.'

'I hope you will be able to, Henry,' Elizabeth said without much conviction.

In the car they did not speak again. Elizabeth's mind was totally occupied with the thought of the painters' weekend and telling

Henry about it, how to break it to him.

During that same week, however, something happened for the better, or to Elizabeth's mind for the better. Nina took herself off most mornings, either walking Polly, or meeting someone. She gave no indication of what she was doing, or where she was going. But, at the weekend, she came into the kitchen. Henry was just getting a beer from the fridge. Elizabeth was preparing the evening meal.

Nina was smiling, an unusual event to say the least. She dried Polly with a clean tea-towel. Elizabeth made no comment. Nina, having put Polly's bowl down and watched the little dog start her meal, looked up at both her parents. 'I've got a job,' she said.

Henry started. 'No, Nina! You must go back to school. Is the job just for—?'

Nina shook her head. Henry was about to say more, but Elizabeth broke in, putting up her hand. 'Let Nina tell us—about the job, I mean. Is it a permanent job, Nina?'

The girl nodded vigorously, her dark hair swinging to and fro. Her hair was thick, and her mother always thought it moved beautifully and fell back into place when she shook her head or the wind blew it about. 'Yes, it's for keeps. At the vet's. He said he could take me on now—when I'm sixteen, that is. It's what I want, so don't go on, Dad!'

Henry left the kitchen. Elizabeth knew his disappointment was acute. 'Well, Mum?' Nina

124

looked at her mother, wanting a fight perhaps, Elizabeth couldn't be sure.

'I think it's a very good idea, Nina, I think you are very good with animals. When do you start?'

Nina looked at her mother, her brown eyes not as hard as usual. 'Well, straight away. Till my birthday, I won't get paid or anything. Till then I'll just go in, you know, to see what goes on.' She patted Polly's head. 'Are you going to blow your top about uni, Mum?'

Elizabeth shook her head. 'No, I'm not, Nina, but your dad will be disappointed.'

'He'll get over it.' Nina turned. 'What's for supper?'

'Sausage and mash, or sausage and chips.'

Nina said, without turning back, 'Make it chips, I prefer chips.'

No need to put them in the oven yet, Elizabeth thought. She poured two whiskies, added water and, with a glass in each hand, went through to the sitting-room to listen to what she knew Henry's arguments would be, remarks about the failure of his little Neeny to realise her own brightness, cleverness, what she could do if she chose, all to be, in his opinion, thrown away. After all he, they, had done for her. Elizabeth steeled herself, went into the room and handed him the whisky. 'A chaser for you, Henry,' she said pleasantly.

It began. 'Doesn't she know what a bright mind she has, Elizabeth?'

125

She sat down and sipped her own drink and listened, or really didn't listen. In her mind, she was in Stanley's arms.

'Are you listening to a word I say, Elizabeth?' Henry's words got through to her. 'You're just sitting there looking vacant,' he complained.

'Of course I'm listening, Henry, and I know what a big disappointment this must be for you.'

He drank the rest of his whisky and got up. 'I'm going to talk to her. Is she in her room?'

Elizabeth nodded. 'I should leave it for the moment,' she advised.

He shook his head. 'You would leave it, I won't!' he almost shouted and stamped out of the room. Elizabeth finished her whisky and went into the kitchen to put the sausages under the grill and the chips in the oven.

Nina came down to supper and ate with appetite. Henry played around with his food. He was clearly more upset by the conversation he had had with his daughter than he had been before he went up to talk to her.

'Sorry it's only sausages, dear,' Elizabeth offered the apology, 'but I knew you were lunching out with your client Mr Simms, so I thought you wouldn't want a big meal.'

Henry grunted a reply, pushed aside his plate and left the dining-room. Mother and daughter looked at each other, a long look, brown eyes met grey.

'Going out tonight, Nina?'

The girl nodded. 'Yep.' There was a little silence, then Nina pushed aside her empty plate and put her elbows on the table, her chin cupped in her hands. 'You don't give a toss about all this really, do you, Mum?'

Elizabeth started to protest, saying 'Of course I do!', but Nina didn't give her time. 'I mean, if I go back to that poxy school and go on to university, you couldn't really care less, could you?'

Elizabeth managed to interrupt her long enough to say, 'It will upset your father, Nina, you know it will.'

'Yes, yes, but not you and I know why.'

Elizabeth felt a sudden shock. There was malice in the little twist of Nina's mouth, yet amusement in her eyes. She knows, she knows, but how? Elizabeth thought.

'I saw him kiss you in the car outside. I was with Jacko. We left the bike up the road because Dad didn't know I was out.'

'You shouldn't deceive your father like that.'

Nina really laughed then. 'That's good coming from you, Mum.'

'It was just . . .'

'Just?' Nina laughed again.

Elizabeth sat down abruptly. 'Well, are you going to tell your father?'

Nina shook her head. 'No, Mum, not just now. Maybe sometime but not now.'

Elizabeth felt a sharp stab of fear. What did

her child mean? 'Maybe sometime.'

Henry came back into the dining-room. 'I'm going out,' he said.

This was unusual. Elizabeth thought of the beer and the whisky he had had. 'Not driving are you, Henry?'

He shook his head. 'No, I'm going for a walk.' He did not look at Nina. The front door shut softly.

Polly strolled in, looked expectantly at Nina. 'Yes, Polly, time for your walk.' She left the room, Polly following her, the dog's fat little bottom wagging from side to side. Elizabeth usually found Polly's walk amusing but this time she couldn't raise a smile.

Elizabeth cleared the table. She was disconcerted because Henry had gone out. She had wanted to talk to him about the painters' weekend. Now he might stay out late, and when he returned he'd want to talk about Nina, Nina, Nina. Well, she would look at the news and go to bed. Pretend to be asleep when he came in. As she washed up she wondered how long Nina would keep silent about her meeting with Stanley.

CHAPTER EIGHT

The fact that Nina knew had far less effect on Elizabeth than she expected. Maybe she felt that one day Henry would have to find out that she had fallen in love with someone else, deeply in love, and could no longer stay with him. Did it matter if it were she or Nina who told him? Her indifference almost frightened her.

The next two Wednesdays were sad and disappointing. Elizabeth felt she could no longer tell trivial lies about the car or her friend Mary so she had to bear only spending a short time with Stanley. He was not so patient and was delighted when the painters' weekend was settled. They agreed that it might be better to go to the Concourse instead of a hotel after quite a lot of persuasion from Elizabeth. 'Let's be honest, darling,' he said many times. 'Tell Henry how we feel. There is nothing to hold you there, Nina is grown up.' Something held her back. Nina—for some reason she wanted Nina to be sixteen before she left.

At the moment Nina seemed happier than she had ever been through her difficult and rebellious childhood and teenage years. She was glued to any television programme about animals, animal hospitals, animal treatment. One night she would not come for her meal but told Elizabeth to keep it hot for her because she must see a programme. Henry had been furious. He was not quite such a doting father now that his Neeny had become a job seeker. No university. Perhaps nothing to boast about at work now. He used to be constantly telling his colleagues about his clever daughter, Elizabeth knew. She had put the meal to keep hot. 'Let her see the programme, Henry. It's about the work she wants to do, can't you understand that?' Nina had tossed off a 'Thanks, Mum' when she had eventually come into the dining-room. Elizabeth could not be sure of Nina. She thought she was perhaps sucking up to her for some reason. The girl was so difficult to read.

The week before the longed-for weekend an incident occurred which brought the 'sins of Nina' back with a vengeance. Miss Meadows telephoned. It was Friday evening and she asked if she could call on them the next morning, Saturday. She had something she would like to tell them face to face. Nina could or need not be present, it was entirely up to her parents. She would not say any more. Elizabeth suggested eleven o'clock and Miss Meadows agreed and rang off. Elizabeth told Henry who immediately bristled up and wanted to know why the woman was coming and why Elizabeth hadn't asked him if he would see her. 'She's just coming for a cup of coffee and to tell us something she feels we should know, Henry, just let's welcome her and listen to what she has to say.' Henry was reduced to a mumbling, grumbling silence and returned to the television programme he had been watching.

Nina was out, and she decided not to say anything about Miss Meadows' visit. If she was in, well, that would be that. If she was out, well, no matter. Nothing really mattered to her at the moment, whatever Miss Meadows had to say, whatever Henry's reaction would be, or Nina's. Perhaps the woman was coming to say the suspension was over and Nina could go back for the last few days of term. In that case she hoped Nina would be out. Certainly she would refuse to go back, maybe hurl abuse at the deputy head and the whole thing would be noisy, vituperative and horrid. But it didn't matter. The only thing that did matter was the weekend with Stanley. Three nights. Elizabeth had lied to Henry about the length of the course. Stanley and she were to spend the Sunday night in a local hotel which Stanley had already booked.

The next morning Elizabeth got up early. She was slightly worried about Miss Meadows' visit. She hoped it was not going to stir up the whole affair of the wretched cannabis again. She was pleased the way Nina was going. She seemed pleasanter, more approachable, even to her mother. Henry seemed to be rather left out at the moment, but that, she was sure, would alter the moment Nina wanted something, extra pocket money, a new pair of shoes.

Elizabeth got out some little cakes from the freezer, put coffee cups and brown sugar on her best tray. She was determined to make Miss Meadows welcome and hoped that she had some good news about Nina—though she could not imagine why she was coming, especially on a Saturday morning. Nina, having got up late—her day off from the vet's was Saturday—had taken Polly for her comfort walk, come back and was now sitting at the kitchen table eating toast and leafing through the paper. Henry had finished his breakfast and was walking round the garden, pulling the occasional weed from the rose border. Elizabeth wondered if he remembered Miss Meadows was coming in less than an hour's time. Neither had told Nina she was coming, but Elizabeth now decided she should be told—after all the visit was about her.

'Nina, Miss Meadows is coming for coffee,' she said.

'Who?'

'Miss Meadows,' Elizabeth repeated.

Nina threw down the piece of toast on to the table, dropped the paper on to the floor. She looked enraged. 'What! You've asked that cow to coffee here?'

Elizabeth shook her head. 'No, she telephoned last night to ask to come, she has something to tell us.'

'About me? It can't be anything else, can it?'

Elizabeth nodded. 'I thought—your father and I thought,' she amended hastily, 'that you might want to hear what she has to say, why she's coming.'

Nina shook her head. 'I don't want to see the old bag. You know I've finished with her. I never want to see her again, the old freak!'

'All right, all right, you don't have to be there, she's coming at eleven o'clock!'

Nina made for the door. 'I'll go out.' She went to the telephone, presumably to phone Jacko, and sometime later, about twenty minutes, the front door banged and she was gone.

Henry came in. 'You haven't forgotten Miss Meadows, Henry?'

He shook his head. 'No. Nina's gone out?' Elizabeth nodded and went into the kitchen to prepare the coffee and to check that the little cakes were completely defrosted. It was almost eleven o'clock.

Miss Meadows arrived on the dot of eleven, just as Elizabeth had expected. She took her through to the sitting-room, sat her down. 'I'll just get some coffee.'

'No, no, thank you.'

'Oh, please! It's all ready.'

Miss Meadows, who had half risen, sat down again. 'Very well. But what I have to tell you is—'

Elizabeth interrupted her. 'Whatever it is, there is no reason to refuse my coffee.' She smiled, but her visitor did not smile back. She sat, straight-backed, in the sitting-room chair she had chosen to sit in.

133

Through in the kitchen, Elizabeth called out to Henry, still in the garden. 'She's here! Go in and talk to her, for goodness' sake.'

He stopped to wash his hands at the sink. Elizabeth followed him through to the sitting-room carrying the tray of coffee and cakes. Henry, as she would always expect, had not offered to carry it for her.

'Good morning, Miss Meadows.' Henry walked over and shook her hand and then sat down on the settee, leaving Elizabeth to pour and hand out the coffee.

Miss Meadows sipped the coffee, refused a cake, cleared her throat and spoke. 'Mr and Mrs Mason, I have rather bad news for you—'

Henry broke in: 'Not more drugs, Miss Meadows?'

She shook her head. 'No, no. The headmistress will not be able to resume her duties, and a new head has been appointed.' She paused then, as if to justify her own position. 'I, of course, would have been asked to fill the appointment had I not been retiring.'

Elizabeth, as Henry did not speak, felt it necessary to acknowledge this remark. 'Of course, I am sure you would have, Miss Meadows.'

'I have bought a small cottage and wish to move in at once. It's at the end of . . .' She paused. 'Not far from the school. It's thatched and rather pretty.'

Elizabeth suddenly realised she knew the

134

cottage. 'Oh, the charming thatched one, right at the end of Harding Road. I've seen it when I was walking Polly, our dog.'

For the first time Miss Meadows really smiled. 'Yes, yes, I'm pleased to have it, Mrs Mason, but I must go on and tell you the rather unpleasant news. The new deputy or acting head does not agree with my suspending Nina. At the school governors' meeting, while agreeing to act as head, she insisted that Nina be expelled.'

Henry jumped to his feet. 'They can't do this, Miss Meadows. I shall appeal or do whatever one does!'

'It's not my business now, Mr Mason. It is out of my hands. My opinion is entirely irrelevant.'

Elizabeth felt sorry for the woman. 'It's good of you to come here and break the news to us.'

Miss Meadows shook her head. 'You will get a letter, of course, but I just wanted you to know.'

At that moment Nina burst into the room. She immediately addressed Miss Meadows. 'That your dog outside in the car?'

'Yes, Nina.'

Elizabeth kept silent but Henry had to throw oil on the fire. 'Miss Meadows just called to tell us you are expelled, not suspended!' He got up and left the room.

Nina turned to the visitor. 'Do you think I

135

care? I wouldn't have gone back to the rotten place anyway. Trust you to make it as bad as possible for me. You don't deserve to have a lovely dog like that.' Miss Meadows and Elizabeth tried to speak but Nina carried on. 'You've always been rotten to me. I hate you.' She turned on Elizabeth. 'What are you feeding her cakes for when she's ruined my life?' Both women again tried to speak but Nina was still shouting. 'I hate you and I'll never forgive you. I know where your new house is. You'd better watch out!' She flung out of the room, through the hall and they heard the front door bang. Polly came into the room with tail wagging. She went up to Miss Meadows, who patted her. Quick as a flash Polly rose on her hind legs and took the uneaten cake from Elizabeth's plate and ran off.

It was one light moment in a storm-filled half-hour. 'Take no notice of my daughter, Miss Meadows. She is helping in the veterinary surgeon's clinic. Soon she will be sixteen and they have offered her a job there. She really loves animals, she perhaps could become a veterinary nurse.'

Miss Meadows nodded her head slowly, stroking Polly's head. The little dog had come back to her having devoured her illicit cake. 'I feel I failed Nina, Mrs Mason. I don't know why but I do.'

Elizabeth sighed. 'She's not an easy girl, Miss Meadows. As I told you, I've never managed to get on with Nina. Her father has, but then I think he did it by spoiling her.'

She accompanied her guest down the path to the front gate, shutting Polly in the kitchen. In the car was a young golden labrador, delighted to see his mistress.

'He's lovely,' Elizabeth said.

'He's my pride and joy.' Miss Meadows' face lit up. She looked quite different. She got into the car, wound down the window to say goodbye. 'Thank you for the coffee, Mrs Mason. I came because, well, I thought it would be nice if you knew it was not my decision. Tell Nina that, if she will listen.'

'I will,' Elizabeth answered as the car drew away into the sunny morning. She looked up and down the road. There was no sign of Nina or Henry.

What she wanted most in the world was to telephone Stanley, but one of them might come back. She went into the sitting-room to collect the coffee cups. Henry had not drunk his, her cup was half empty and Miss Meadows' was still almost full. Elizabeth had been quite startled by the ferocity of Nina's attack on Miss Meadows. The desire to flee to Stanley was overwhelming. The warmth of his body next to hers would banish all thoughts of this morning, Henry's rage and her daughter's rather frightening threats.

Henry came back, still storming about the injustice of the school, what he was going to do about it. Demand to see the acting head, see the board of governors or whatever they were called. Write to the council, his MP . . . He went on and on. Elizabeth did try and placate him once or twice, suggesting that Nina was happy in what she was doing and would make a good veterinary nurse if she decided to be one.

'Let her make the choice, Henry, let her do what makes her happy.'

'Veterinary nurse! If she had gone to university, she could have become a vet, or a doctor!'

Elizabeth gave up. It was no use. If Henry could not accept Nina as she was, she could not help him. 'Henry,' she wound up, 'if you make a fuss about this, stir up the whole miserable business, you will only do more harm. Leave it, I beg of you, leave it.'

He had stormed at her then, accused her of all sorts of things. Ignoring her daughter's behaviour, not caring. Not being a good mother, never blaming Nina. Elizabeth listened, hurt and miserable, but argued no more with him.

Nina did not come back for lunch. Henry had a particularly large whisky then grumbled his way through the meal. After lunch was cleared, Elizabeth took Polly for a long walk in the fields, much to the little dog's delight. Putting on the lead as they came out in the quiet road, Elizabeth took a short cut which took her into the end of Harding Road. There

138

was Miss Meadows' little retirement cottage. It was very pretty, the garden full of spring flowers. The thatched roof distinguished it from the rest of the houses. Indeed, it was slightly away from the road, an ideal spot for a retired teacher and her lovely dog, Elizabeth thought, and hoped she would be happy there.

She guessed, from the state of the garden and the freshly planted summer flowers, that maybe she was already living there. She wondered just what the teacher had done to build up such hostility between the girl and herself. Perhaps Nina's hatred would extend to others, who knows? But she hated the way her daughter had threatened her teacher and, after the fire at the school . . . Elizabeth blanked out the thought and continued on her way, smiling, her mind away from anything except the weekend to come. She decided to tell neither Henry nor Nina that she had seen Miss Meadows' cottage. They would wonder why she had even looked at it. Anyway, Nina had said in her outburst of hate to Miss Meadows, 'I know where your new house is. You'd better watch out!'

Good God, was the girl capable of . . . ? 'No. No, no!' Elizabeth said aloud. But, as she said it, she knew she was not altogether sure. 'Come on, Polly!' Elizabeth began to walk more quickly, trying to get away from her own thoughts and suspicions. If only she could talk to Henry, voice her fears to him. But she had never been able to do that. Never. Best keep everything to herself as she always had.

*   *   *

The letter from the school arrived on the Tuesday and Henry was as furious as he had been on hearing Miss Meadows' news. Elizabeth's interpretation was that the deputy head had wanted to soften the blow before the letter arrived. Henry, on the other hand, argued that Miss Meadows couldn't wait to tell them the news and had merely come to gloat. Nina agreed of course. Nothing would alter what they thought, or their dislike—or, in Nina's case, her sheer hatred—of Miss Meadows. In the end, Elizabeth gave up and decided that, no matter what she said, it would not change them.

So, she gave up talking about it and would not help Henry draw up a letter to the chairman of the school governors. Neither would she agree to talk to the newly appointed acting head. Anyway, she knew Henry would probably do no good by going there, writing or telephoning.

CHAPTER NINE

The Wednesday before the painters' weekend, Elizabeth did not even bother to go to the class, but spent the time in Stanley's house. They drank wine, made love. The two and a half hours flew by. They arranged for Elizabeth to drive to a garage very near to the Black Horse, and leave her car there for three days and nights. They would go to the Concourse in Stanley's car. Even to be driven by him was a delight.

Thursday went by . . . Friday morning. Before Elizabeth set off, Henry was fairly irritating, but in her state of euphoria every remark fell off her like water. Henry went on and on. 'I don't know how you can go away for a weekend with this hanging over our heads.'

She tried to be patient. 'Look, Henry, Nina is fine. She doesn't want to go back to school. What difference does it really make?'

Henry literally snorted. 'Expelled from school—that will look good on her CV, won't it?'

Elizabeth hadn't thought of that, but she tried to brush it off. 'Well, I expect lots of people who have been expelled from school have made good.'

Henry got up. 'Well, I must go, I can't say I understand your way of thinking, Elizabeth.'

He left. No kiss goodbye. No 'Have a nice weekend, enjoy yourself.' Perhaps he didn't care one way or the other.

Elizabeth went upstairs. She was meeting Stanley at eleven. She took a lot of trouble with her make-up and hair. She had bought a new frock and a new trouser suit, a very pretty nightdress and really splashed out on some even prettier bras, panties and other items of underwear. She had laughed at herself when she had packed these 'pretties', reminded herself she was fifty-six, 'nearer sixty than fifty' as her grandmother would have said. On her fiftieth birthday six years ago, she had bought rather a similar trousseau, hoping it would make Henry look, admire, assure her that she was just as attractive as she had been. Silly. She knew Henry had not even noticed. Nina had been ten then, as difficult a ten-year-old as she was now. If she had seen what Elizabeth was packing now, she would have repeated her words, 'Dream on, Mum.' But this was no dream—it was true. She snapped the case shut.

The front door banged. Nina going to the vet's. She got up earlier now, walked Polly, who was allowed to go to the vet's with her. Maybe it would work out for the girl. Anyway, this weekend she was free and she picked up her suitcase, her handbag and made her way downstairs. She felt jaunty, young. On her way, driving to the Black Horse and the garage, she felt her heart quickening, her cheeks growing

142

pinker. 'Now, steady, girl!' she said aloud. 'We have a lot to go through,' and she knew she was not thinking of Nina or Henry, just Stanley and herself. She at last pulled into the garage and saw Stanley outside, already waiting for her.

He was standing by his car and, as she drove in, at first he did not recognise her car. He was squinting into the sunlight. He looked a little different to her. Older, perhaps thinner? What he had been through, seeing his wife through her last and probably painful and lingering illness, seeing her through it all although she had been unfaithful to him, loved someone else. Elizabeth felt such a surge of love for him, such an overwhelming wish to be with him, love him, try to make up for those sad years. She felt at that moment, as she drove past him into the garage, that she could not leave him after this weekend. She would like to run away with him and hide for ever.

*　　*　　*

The receptionist at the Concourse, a middle-aged, well-groomed woman, greeted them and on hearing their names, 'Mrs Mason and Stanley Wiltshire', booked into a double room, gave no indication of surprise or interest. She handed them each a key with a large blue tag marked 23, and asked them to sign a form, handing each a separate one. Smiling vaguely

143

she said, 'Your room is on the first floor, there is a lift if you need it.' She pointed a red-varnished fingernail across the hall to where a sign said 'Bedrooms 21 to 35', and turned to the next person waiting behind them.

A large and tough-looking porter appeared. He picked up their two cases as if they were feather-light and carried them along the corridor to room 23. He held his hand out, Elizabeth thought for a tip, then realised he wanted the key. Inside the pleasant snug room he plonked the cases down, refused Stanley's tip and said, 'No tipping, sir, until you leave.' No smile, no other remark. He was off, down the corridor at a quick stride.

Stanley and Elizabeth turned to each other and burst out laughing. 'No questions asked here, darling,' he said and kissed her. 'I bet they won't be quite so casual at the hotel on Sunday. We'll have to be Mr and Mrs Smith there.' They read the meal rota on the door. 'Breakfast at 8 a.m. Coffee will be served at 11 in the large reception room. Lunch at 12.30. Tea at 4 p.m., 4.30 on day of arrival. Dinner at 7.' Then a list of lessons and lectures, all of these being optional. Paints must be supplied by pupils. Stanley was genuinely interested in another booklet on the dressing-table. 'Look at this,' he read out. 'Car maintenance weekends. Creative Writing. Advanced French weekend.' He looked at Elizabeth. 'That last one sounds good, darling, wouldn't mind an

Advanced French weekend!' So the weekend started on a light and lovely note.

They joined the tea-takers and Elizabeth met one or two of her own painting class but, with the exception of Mary, who was not there, they thought Stanley was her husband and she did nothing to alter the misconception. After a very good dinner with a bottle of wine Stanley insisted upon, Elizabeth said she must telephone Henry to say that she had arrived safely and all was well. It was then she got her first shock.

She had to wait a little while outside the telephone booth. Several wives had the same intention, ringing husbands to say they had arrived. Whilst waiting she rehearsed what she would say to Henry. Should she ask to speak to Nina too? She decided yes—after all, before she had left she felt she was improving the mother/daughter relationship a little, not much perhaps, but a little. The feeling that her daughter really loved animals, probably better than humans, had made a bond, if a tenuous one, between them, or so she imagined. She grew impatient as the person before her seemed to be going on and on talking into the phone. Elizabeth hated every moment she had to stay away from Stanley, who was in the bar waiting for her. There was one more lecture tonight at nine, on Monet, and Stanley had decided he would like to hear it. Elizabeth felt he was quite genuine about this. About ten more long minutes passed and at last the woman came out of the booth with a muttered apology to Elizabeth. 'Telephoning home,' she said. 'There's always a hundred things, aren't there?'

Elizabeth doubted that would be likely in her case. She went in, put in her card and dialled her number. The telephone rang for longer than she expected. Perhaps Henry had gone to a movie, just lately he had surprised Elizabeth by saying he wanted to see a movie that had been advertised on television. The ringing went on and she was about to replace the receiver when it was answered. 'Henry?'

It was not Henry and it was not Nina, it was someone else, a woman with a rather husky attractive voice. 'Is that . . .?' There was a pause, then 'Oh, excuse me. Henry, I think it's for you, I . . .'

'Hello, Elizabeth, you arrived safely, what's it like there?' Henry sounded flustered.

'Who was that?'

'Oh, Nina's friend, Helen.' He called out, 'Nina, do you want to speak to your mother?'

Then Nina's voice, always rather clipped on the telephone, sounded now as if she were suppressing a giggle. 'Hello, Mum, how's it going?'

'Nice place. Lecture tonight, no painting till tomorrow.'

'Oh, that's convenient, I bet you're pleased about that.'

146

'Yes, I am a bit tired, Nina. Who was that on the phone, who answered the telephone—before your father, I mean?'

'Oh, her. Helen, my friend Helen.'

'I didn't know you had a friend called Helen.'

'Oh Mum, you don't know all my friends, she . . . she works at the vet's.'

She put the telephone down with her usual heavy-handed bang. Elizabeth had intended to speak again to Henry, hesitated . . . Should she ring again? There were two people waiting to use the telephone, so she decided against it. After all, she had kept her promise and rung up to let him know she had arrived safely.

'Helen, Helen?' she said as she crossed the hallway to join Stanley, who was sitting in a large creton-covered chair chatting to a man in a similar chair. He looked up and stood as she approached.

'All right, darling?' he asked. She nodded. He looked at his watch. 'Half an hour before the lecture. Shall we stroll in the garden?'

'Yes, it's a lovely evening.'

The grass was soft and green under their feet, but Elizabeth was puzzled and preoccupied by the telephone call. It was unusual for Nina to bring friends home. Even Margaret, who Nina had for a long time referred to as her 'best friend', had never been to the house, though Nina frequently went to Margaret's. Elizabeth had often said to her daughter, 'You can always bring Margaret in after school for tea, Nina.' The response had been typical. 'What for?' Elizabeth had replied sharply, 'Well, you spend enough time in her room watching television or listening to tapes, I thought perhaps . . .' Nina's reply had caused offence to Henry as well as herself: 'Well, she's got a decent room, not like my little cell.' He was hurt as well. 'What more can she want up there, we've done all she asked, given her everything she asked for.' Her answer, 'Perhaps that's the trouble, Henry,' had not gone down well with her husband. 'Well, as I bought her the computer and the TV and the music centre, I suppose anything she does wrong is my fault.' Elizabeth remembered she had left the room. Nina, her beloved daughter, could stir up trouble, cause a row, in the blink of an eye.

All these thoughts were chasing through her mind as she and Stanley strolled across the lawn in the pleasant grounds of the Concourse.

'You're looking very thoughtful and rather sad, Elizabeth. I hope you're not regretting coming?'

'Oh no, no indeed, Stanley. It was just the telephone call. I wish I hadn't made it. Let's forget it, shall we?'

Stanley would not be satisfied with that. 'Why, what did Henry say, or was it Nina?'

'No, I hardly spoke to Henry. Nina's friend Helen answered the telephone.'

'Oh, I see,' Stanley answered, but it was obvious that he didn't.

Elizabeth tried to explain. 'It's unusual, that's all, Stanley, for Nina to bring a friend home. Her best friend, as she calls her, never comes to our house, though Nina goes to hers quite often.'

Stanley shrugged. 'Well, maybe she is changing her ways, your Nina. Surely that's a good thing?'

As the lecture ended and most of the others drifted to the bar or to what was called 'the Picture Room', where the better painters and more skilled of the crowd could exhibit their pictures, Elizabeth and Stanley went up to their room. Both were too tired to make love that night. They lay side by side with their bodies touching. Elizabeth almost hated feeling herself drifting off to sleep. Sleep seemed such a waste of time, the short time they had together. However, sleep she did and suddenly it was morning and Stanley was switching on the Teasmade. He saw she was awake and smiled that lovely smile.

'Tea or coffee? This thing makes both.'

'Tea please,' she answered and stretched. She felt like a purring cat and far younger than her years.

The day flew by. Elizabeth took no part in the painting. Stanley and she went to one lecture on Abstract Painting just, as Stanley put it, 'to show willing'. They motored out to a hotel on the river and had lunch on the lawn listening to the lapping of the water on the banks. A massive, important-looking water rat was on the opposite river bank; it sat up on its haunches and looked at them for a minute or two, then scurried off. They ate strawberries and cream after their light lunch. The sun shone softly on them, dappled by the young green leaves high above on the trees' branches.

Everything was magic. They toured round, drank tea in a little thatched cottage garden tea rooms. The cottage momentarily brought Miss Meadows to Elizabeth's mind. She hastily banished the thought. They arrived back at the Concourse, bathed, changed and joined the rest for dinner. That night Elizabeth was made love to and made love as she had never before. By morning she knew her lover had made it impossible for her to stay with Henry. Somehow she had got to summon up the courage to tell the truth, as Stanley said. Be honest and tell him she must leave.

At lunch time, or just before, she and Stanley were having a drink in the bar when one of the waitresses came in, looked round and made her way towards them.

'Mrs Mason, isn't it?' she said. Elizabeth nodded. 'You are wanted on the telephone. We don't usually answer the outgoing telephone but I thought it was my boyfriend, but it's for you.'

Elizabeth sprang to her feet. 'Something

must have happened,' she said and made for the door.

'Don't worry, it may be just a routine call. I'll come with you.'

It was Nina. 'Hello, Mum, don't panic. I just thought I'd tell you, I don't want to upset Dad.'

'What do you mean, upset Dad?' Elizabeth tried to control her voice and looked at Stanley as she said it.

'Well, tell him about your little goings on. I take it you're not spending this weekend alone. Don't worry, I won't if you do something for me.'

'What?'

'Get me a new music centre, mine's duff, packed up last night. I want a Panasonic and I won't tell Dad.'

Elizabeth could not answer for a moment, then she said, 'That's blackmail, Nina!'

'Oh, Mum, a present for your dear daughter after her being so tactful, don't give me that!' She hung up.

Elizabeth was shaking as she put down the receiver and told Stanley.

'Don't worry, darling. Remember we are determined, aren't we, to tell him ourselves? This makes the telling more urgent, doesn't it?'

'How could she do it, a daughter of mine? Blackmail, deceit. What must you think of me, Stanley?'

'Remember, I've had problems too, darling, and came out the other side and found you.'

'Shall I get her the music centre? We could go into town on Monday morning, before we go home?'

He shook his head. 'No. She's only young and we don't want to let her think such schemes work.'

'She'll tell him, Stanley.'

He led her back to the bar. 'Don't let her ruin our weekend, my sweet.' He took her hand. 'Don't forget, it's all different now. I'm here, we are together.'

Elizabeth looked at him, deep into his blue, blue eyes. He was right, she was no longer alone, fighting a battle with two difficult unloving and unlovable people. She was supported and loved.

'If she tells him, she will have lost her power to demand things. She won't tell him.'

Elizabeth felt Stanley was right.

The rest of their time flew by. The night spent in the hotel was wonderful but the packing of Elizabeth's suitcase and the journey back to the Black Horse were almost more than she could bear. When they arrived at the garage to collect her car the 'Goodbyes' were dreadful but Stanley was adamant that Henry should be told. He could see she was almost frightened of going home and offered to get in touch with Henry if she wanted him to. The tears flowed down her face as she drove away.

It was as late as Stanley and she had been able to make it, late evening. To add to her misery, it began to rain a thin drizzle. She arrived home knowing that Henry would be back and probably Nina in her room.

She was wrong. No one was in. She looked at the kitchen clock. Unusual for Henry to be out. No Polly to greet her either! She went upstairs and unpacked and as she was doing so, she heard the bang of the front door. Nina and Polly. She called out, 'That you, Nina?' She stood at the top of the stairs, Nina at the bottom.

'Oh, you're back. I thought you'd make it last as long as poss.' Nina laughed. 'Must feed Polly.' She went into the kitchen.

Elizabeth finished her unpacking, then went downstairs. Nina turned round from putting the dog's bowl of food down. 'I'm going out again, Mum, we'll have some fish and chips.'

Elizabeth nodded. 'I thought someone might have prepared a welcome home meal for me,' she said drily.

Nina shook her head and was about to leave the kitchen. 'Oh, by the way,' she said, 'you needn't worry about the music centre. Dad bought me one. I need something else though, I'll tell you what later.'

She disappeared, first upstairs, then out of the front door. Elizabeth opened the door and called to her, 'Where is your father? Working late?'

153

Nina turned round, a strange expression on her face. 'You could say that,' she said, slamming the front gate shut and disappearing up the road. Presumably, Elizabeth thought, toward the bus stop, but she really could not bring herself to care much, one way or the other. She made herself some sandwiches and coffee, took them through to the sitting-room and switched on the television. She began to feel Stanley was right. Henry should be told and she should pack up and leave. The resolve cheered her but she wondered if she had the courage to tell him when he came back that night. With the weekend so fresh in her mind, perhaps it was a bad time, or would the thought of her lover give her more courage? She got up and pottered round the room. She felt like a child picking petals from a daisy, only this time it wasn't 'He loves me, he loves me not' but 'Shall I tell him or shall I not?'

Nine o'clock and Henry still had not arrived home. Working late? But this was later than usual. He had been working late a good few nights during the last few months. Even having to bring work home sometimes. He blamed it on the new young accountant—what was his name, Harper?

Elizabeth suddenly felt unbearably tired. She couldn't cope with Henry tonight. It was too late and her mind felt unable to command the kind of sentences she wanted to. Tomorrow evening she would cook a nice evening meal. Tell him over their after-dinner coffee. Perhaps she would say to him, tomorrow morning . . . Yes she would! She was determined she would say, 'Try to be home early. I do have something nice for dinner. Maybe Nina will grace us with her presence. If not, it won't matter. I want to have a talk with you, Henry.' That was it! Elizabeth made herself a hot drink and went upstairs to bed.

Before she fell asleep she heard the front door open and close, heard Henry call, 'You back, Elizabeth?' She looked at her bedside clock. Twenty past ten. She pretended to be asleep. Henry came upstairs and looked into the bedroom. Elizabeth didn't stir or answer and he went downstairs again. She heard him go into the kitchen, the dull thud of the fridge door, then the sound of the television. Her resolve did not weaken. She would tell him about Stanley tomorrow evening. Nothing, nothing must put her off.

She would have all day to rehearse exactly what she would say to him. How she would break it to him. It was not going to be easy or pleasant. Maybe he would be pleased to see the back of her? Elizabeth cuddled down in the bed, her feelings more settled, more at ease with the situation. This was to be the end of one era of her life and the beginning of another. She did not know it, as sleep gradually overcame her, but a lot more would happen before the end of this era and the other one began, a lot more.

*   *   *

The next morning Henry did ask about her weekend, how the painting had gone, what the food had been like, how many painters had been there. He seemed strained, his attitude different. Elizabeth wondered if Nina had already said something about that kiss she had seen, or perhaps just hinted that there was something going on between her mother and another man.

Elizabeth asked, 'Was Nina all right, did she stay out very late or do anything horrific?'

Henry had been very adamant. 'No, she behaved very well, even hoovered on Sunday before you came back on Monday.'

Henry was not a good liar where his beloved daughter was concerned and Elizabeth thought, after he had left for the office, she would check the hoover bag. She had put a new one on before she had left, indeed after she had done the hoovering on the Thursday before the weekend away. How petty can you get, she thought, but she knew she would check.

As Henry was leaving Elizabeth plucked up her courage. 'Henry, could you manage to come home early this evening? You've been doing so much overtime lately and I do want to have a talk with you.'

156

Henry stiffened. He turned back from going into the hall to pick up his briefcase. 'A talk?'

'Yes, I need to talk to you. It's really quite important, can you manage to get away?'

He nodded. 'Yes. I'll make a point of it. You're right, Elizabeth, we do need to talk.' He picked up the briefcase, looked at her again as if he was going to say something, then turned away and opened the front door. Once there he hesitated, said, 'Goodbye then. See you this evening,' and the door closed behind him.

Elizabeth went back into the kitchen. He knows, he knows. Nina has told him, hinted to him, or perhaps he has suspected it because I have been different, more withdrawn, more preoccupied, less appalled than he about Nina's misdoings and her explanation. Well, it didn't matter one way or the other now. The shock had got to come to him. In a way, if he suspected, it wouldn't be such a shock.

Nina walked into the kitchen, still in her dressing-gown. 'I'm hungry.' She helped herself to a bowl of cornflakes, put on milk and a generous amount of sugar.

'Have you told your father—I mean, said anything about me?'

Nina shook her head, her mouth too full to speak.

'Are you sure?' Elizabeth persisted.

Nina laughed. 'Mum, I want you to buy me, or give me the money to buy, some cropped

157

trousers—you know, capris.'

'Blackmail, you're good at that.'

Nina laughed. 'Come on, Mum, let's go and buy some, have lunch at Shirley's, it's good there. Why do you think I've told Dad anything?'

'I suggested he got home early so that we could have a talk. He said we needed to talk, what else can that mean?'

Nina took more cornflakes.

'You will be late for the vet's.' Elizabeth cleared away the dirty crockery from the breakfast table and piled it on to the draining board.

'I'm not being paid yet, so I don't turn up at nine. Soon I will though, when they begin to pay me and I'm a working woman. Maybe he just wants to talk to you, you know, have a little Dad and Mum chat, why not?' She called Polly and gave her the remains of her cornflakes. Then she went upstairs to dress.

Elizabeth disapproved of Polly eating out of their dishes, but you might as well talk to the wall, she thought, as try and stop Nina. A stab of jealousy went through her. Nina, she felt, would always do just as she liked and go where she wanted, have sex when she wanted, stay out late, go to discos, always have a boyfriend. Elizabeth thought of her own teenage years. She had complied. Always in at night when they told her to be, a virgin when she married Henry. Put make-up on when she got outside

158

the house, because her father hadn't liked it. No red nails, no miniskirts. She had been a drip. What did this make Nina? Did she wish she had been more like her? Was that why she disliked her daughter, because she had the power to do what she liked when she liked? Maybe.

Now, since making love with Stanley, she knew what love-making should be like. Perhaps it all hadn't been Henry's fault. He was as much a novice as she, strict parents, little freedom had made him so, but love didn't come into it. Why had she married him? To get away from home, to get away from her office job which she loathed. Henry seemed suitable, a chartered accountant. Her parents had been pleased—no, delighted. A clean-living young professional man, a secure future, no apparent vices. She had done well for herself. Now it was all to break up. This evening, she was going to tell the truth about what had happened to her and that she had to say goodbye to him.

The day dragged by. No Polly to walk, she had gone to the vet's with Nina. Nina had told her parents, in a rare flash of humour, that Polly sat in the reception area in a basket, behind the counter, acting as if she were a recovered patient, who recommended the vet's surgery as the best in town. Nina also said Polly was not allowed to meet any of the incoming or outgoing animals in case she might catch anything from them. This had made Elizabeth smile, but not Henry, who was still regretting that his brilliant daughter had given up university. Elizabeth felt she would like to talk to someone, tell them about what she was going to do that evening, but there was nobody, not even any of her painting friends, that she would dare tell.

In the afternoon she rang Stanley, but he was not in his office, nor would he be for the rest of the day. She longed for Henry to come home, in one way, so that she could get the announcement over with, and dreaded it in another. Would he be hurt, wounded by his wife's admission of adultery, or receive the news with his rather deadpan attitude? Only things that happened to hurt or discomfort his daughter seemed to move him.

Nina came in at six, full of the story of a snake that had been brought in. She had actually held it. It would get better, the vet had said. She ate a couple of sandwiches and drank two cups of tea, then went upstairs with Polly. 'I won't feed her yet, it's a bit early and she had one or two titbits at the vet's,' she said as she raced up the stairs.

Soon music, Nina's music, was filling the house. Elizabeth called up and asked her, as she normally had to, to turn it down a bit. To Elizabeth's surprise, she did so. 'Wonders will never cease,' she said to herself as she started to prepare the evening meal. She opened a bottle of red wine 'to let it breathe', as Henry always said, took it through to the sitting-room with two glasses, a room where the evening sun made the room warm enough to make the wine drinkable. Oh God, she thought, let's get this over. Would they be able to eat the meal, roast lamb, roast potatoes, peas, cauliflower? Would all the effort be wasted after she had broken her news? She heard Henry's car drive in, the familiar crunch of the gravel, the slam of the car door. Her heart began to race. Nina came downstairs and fed Polly. She was dressed in slacks and her usual sloppy jumper which meant the motor bike and Jacko, that is if Jacko was still on the cards.

'You're not in for dinner? It's roast lamb,' Elizabeth said.

Nina shook her head. 'No, going over to Headly, we'll eat there, then we're going to the disco. All right?'

'I suppose so.' Elizabeth was relieved, but did not want to show it.

Father and daughter met in the hall. 'Going out, Nina?' Henry said.

'Yes, Dad.'

'Well, don't be late and tell that boy to be careful on that bike.'

'OK, will do.' The front door slammed and Henry came into the kitchen.

'I've opened a bottle of red wine, it's in the sitting-room.' Elizabeth felt slightly sick. They both went through and sat down, Elizabeth on

161

the sofa and Henry in his usual chair. He looked strained and not at ease. He poured two glasses of wine. She took one, sipped it and started to speak. 'Henry, I—'

He put up a hand. Elizabeth noticed the hand was trembling a little. 'No, Elizabeth, let me speak first, if you will.' She nodded. Her immediate reaction was: He knows what I am going to tell him. That little bitch Nina has told him. Not that she knows much, but she has told him something. When he began to speak, however, she realised how very wrong she was. 'Elizabeth, I really don't know how to tell you this, maybe you have suspected. I don't know. You may say, as I have said to myself, that at my age, this is quite—what word can I use—ridiculous, stupid, but I cannot help it. When you said this morning that we must have a talk, I did feel you have suspected that there was someone else in my life. Did you guess?'

Elizabeth felt that the breath was completely knocked out of her. Indeed, she had difficulty breathing. She put her hand to her chest. 'No, Henry, no, no. I certainly did not.'

Henry looked hard at her, his eyes disbelieving. 'Are you sure? Why did you want to talk then?'

Elizabeth drew a deep breath. 'Tell me all about it, Henry. Who is it and what did you want to do about it?' She wondered, as she said this, how many women had prepared themselves to admit a love affair outside their marriage only to be forestalled by their husbands at the very moment they had decided to confess all!

Henry began, obviously speaking with some difficulty, clearing his throat in a way which irritated Elizabeth. The sentence he began with was unfortunate, at least as far as she was concerned: 'Nina really started it.'

His wife could not resist. 'I'm sure she did and how did my darling daughter start this little affair?'

'Elizabeth, don't call it "this little affair". Please. She's much more than that and, anyway, I only meant Nina introduced me to Helen. She could hardly guess that—'

She interrupted him with some sharpness. 'Helen? Was that who answered the phone when I rang? Who is she?'

'Helen is the senior veterinary surgeon where Nina hopes to work. She is a charming woman and Nina thinks the world of her.'

'That's a plus, for Nina to think the world of anyone.' Elizabeth knew she was being a bitch, but she was already suspecting her daughter of helping her dear Daddy's opinion to grow and prosper to get back at her.

'No. You are misunderstanding Nina, as you usually do!' Henry's voice had become stronger, more positive. 'When the vet first turned her down as a young helper, not Helen by the way, Nina was extremely upset, very upset.'

'I didn't know she was particularly upset, she didn't say anything to me!'

'Well, did she ever?' Henry said sharply. 'However, she decided to try again. I was not pleased at her deciding against university, but she begged me to go with her to the vet's to try again and I did.'

'She wheedled you into going. Had she already met Helen?'

Henry looked slightly embarrassed. 'Well, she had. She told me she was nice and understanding.'

Elizabeth felt she couldn't stand any more. 'So you met her. Took her out to dinner once or twice, went to bed with her and now you're in love!'

Henry's face became slightly pinker. 'We have met frequently, of course. You are wrong about the sleeping together. Helen is not that kind of woman.'

'Oh, I see.' Elizabeth didn't see. She could not imagine not having slept with Stanley.

'I want a divorce,' said Henry. 'I feel our marriage has not been a particularly happy one and we are old enough to make up our own minds.'

Elizabeth nodded. She felt she could not, at that moment, tell him about Stanley. She wanted to, but she did not know how to describe her own love in the face of his for Helen. She got up. 'Thank you for telling me,

164

Henry, I need to think a bit, if you don't mind.'

Elizabeth got out of the room as quickly as she could. She smelled something burning in the kitchen but could not care. Let it burn, she thought, and went out into the garden. Polly was there and rushed up to her with a ball in her mouth ready for a game. Automatically Elizabeth took the ball and threw it across the lawn; the little dog came back carrying the ball. This time it was ignored. Elizabeth went to the bottom of the garden and sat down on the teak seat. She sat there a long time, her thoughts in a kind of chaos. This woman Helen, she visualised her as slightly butch. How old? She had asked no questions and Henry had volunteered no information. Had she stayed longer in the room he might have done so but, try as she would, she could not tell him about Stanley.

She shivered. It suddenly grew colder, but she did not for the moment want to go indoors and try and assume normality.

'You cold, Mum?' It was Nina walking down the garden with an old cardigan of Elizabeth's in her hand.

'Thanks.' Elizabeth put the cardigan on. She turned and looked at Nina who seated herself next to her. 'Did you know all about this, with your father, I mean?'

Nina nodded, took a packet of cigarettes with difficulty from her jeans pocket, pulled out a lighter. The jeans were cut off mid-thigh.

165

Nina's legs, smooth and shiny, ended in sandal-type shoes with very high heels. She lit the cigarette. Elizabeth felt she must say something. 'How long have you been smoking, Nina?' There was no disapproval in her voice, she really felt past coping with what people should or should not do.

Her daughter threw back her head, opened her mouth, blew out smoke and laughed. 'About as long as I've been fucking, Mum,' she said.

But Elizabeth refused to be shocked as she felt Nina wanted her to be. 'Oh, yes, and what do you think of your father wanting a divorce, presumably to marry your young friend Helen?'

Nina laughed again. 'Young friend, Mum? Helen's about forty-five!'

'You like her?' Elizabeth asked. She was watching her daughter with a new interest. The short top, just covering her breasts, the bare belly button, the ivory skin. The full lips, the long lashes, heavily mascara'd, brown eye shadow. The stone eyes now slid inwards and looked at her mother.

'Come on, Mum, she's right for Dad. He's not happy, you're not happy. Helen's great. She got me my first condoms, gave me a lecture, what to do, how to do it. You wouldn't have done that if I'd asked you. You would have put on a horrified act and said don't do it at all.'

Elizabeth did not answer. There was a ruthlessness about this child she had given birth to. A ruthlessness that appalled her, but there was something about it she admired. Everything she was saying was right. Henry was not happy and now maybe she felt he might have a chance of a better marriage, a better life.

'Your father hasn't . . .' There was no need to finish.

'Been to bed with Helen? No, silly old wrinkly. They don't agree with that, not before marriage. Can you imagine? Still, if that's how they want it.' She looked at her mother. Was it a sneer or a half-smile? Elizabeth couldn't be sure. 'You have though, haven't you? I could tell. You look blooming, younger all of a sudden. Oh, not only the new clothes, the perfume, the make-up. I could tell.'

'Was it to pay me out you pushed Helen and Henry together?'

Nina laughed and lit another cigarette. 'Partly. I thought it was a bit of a liberty and Dad's always done what I wanted, he's a pushover really.' She got up. 'I'll take Polly out. Two divorces—well, one really, but two intended.' She laughed. It was rather a rich vulgar laugh.

'Don't smoke in the street, Nina.'

The laugh was longer this time. 'That's how the fire started at the school. We were smoking, then I set fire to—never mind, the

167

classroom's rebuilt now.' She called to Polly: 'Walkies.' Polly came bouncing up to her and they walked back to the house to fetch the nylon lead.

It was too cold to stay in the garden any longer.

'Your soup's burnt. I turned the gas off,' Nina called as she went in the back door. It slammed behind her as usual. All that Elizabeth wanted at that moment was to talk to Stanley, yet in a way she was fearful. What a situation she was putting him into, wife-swapping almost. One thing she was certain of, she could never let him meet Nina—though how could that be avoided? Now, as she walked back into the house, she knew what was in front of her. She had to tell her husband all about her lover and try and be as frank with him as he had been with her. The break-up of a marriage—all, she felt, arranged by Nina. Nina had suggested the painting class, or at least encouraged her to go. Nina had found Helen for Henry, condoned the relationship, had known about and probably laughed at her relationship with Stanley. Nina was in charge. She could, if she felt like it, manipulate all four of them. What would she demand in return for letting two relationships develop smoothly? There would be something, Elizabeth was sure. In the kitchen, the smell of burning was still strong, although Nina had turned off the gas under the ruined saucepan. Elizabeth took the lid off and looked inside. The chicken carcass and vegetables, which she had intended for soup before tonight's dinner, were a black mass at the bottom of the pan, even the lid was brown. She took the saucepan out to the back garden, round to the bin and, taking the lid off, threw the lot in. It was one of her favourite saucepans but she thought, as she disposed of it, one less for Helen! She realised she was smiling as she came back to inspect the rest of the dinner. She opened the oven. She had left it on low, anticipating her talk with Henry. The lamb was slightly overcooked and the roast potatoes just singed round the edges, passable though. She put on a saucepan half full of water and when it boiled she added the peas and cauliflower from the freezer. A sweet? Well, there was ice cream. She felt rather proud of herself for being able to summon up a meal in spite of being told her husband wanted a divorce.

This done, she went back into the sitting-room. Henry looked up as she came in. He had nearly finished the bottle of wine, not like Henry. He was a one-whisky man usually, or a beer. She had never, even at their wedding, seen him even slightly drunk. When he looked at her now, his eyes were slightly glazed and he looked what her mother had always called 'slightly piflocated'. She had never liked using the word drunk. Elizabeth poured the remaining wine into her own glass and drank it rapidly. She felt that when she told him about Stanley, which she intended to do after dinner, it would be better if they were both 'slightly piflocated'. 'Dinner in ten minutes, in the kitchen, if you don't mind, Henry,' she said. He shook his head. She left the room, but before she did so, she went to the cupboard where they kept their very small store of wine. Thank goodness, there was one bottle left. This should surely get them through the next crisis that she meant to throw at him, but after they had eaten.

Henry did not see her take the wine out to the kitchen. She managed to open the bottle, usually Henry's job the very few times they had wine. She dished up the meal, called Henry, who came in from the sitting-room. On the way he managed to knock over a little bunch of walkings-sticks and umbrellas in a tall blue container in the hall. Elizabeth heard him mutter, 'Sorry, sorry,' and gather them up. Strangely enough at that moment she felt fonder of him, more sympathetic towards him, than she had done for years. 'What's this?' he asked when he saw the new bottle of wine and glasses on the kitchen table.

'Why not?' Elizabeth answered.

He sat down with a bump on the hard kitchen chair. Elizabeth carved the meat. They both ate their meal. 'Good lamb,' he said.

'Yes, there was going to be soup to start with, but after your news it got burnt up. The saucepan's in the bin.'

'Oh, couldn't it be cleaned?' he asked.

'Yes, but I wasn't going to clean it. If Helen feels like fishing it out, she can.' Elizabeth knew it was a catty remark, and Henry shrank from it. He poured them both another glass of wine and pushed his plate away. 'Very good meal. And I must say, you are taking this very well, I mean in a very sportsmanslike manner.'

'Yes, I think I am too.' Elizabeth stacked the plates on the draining board and cleared the table. 'Now, you go back into the sitting-room, Henry and I'll make coffee and bring it through. I too have something to talk about.'

'Yes, about the divorce and everything, of course.'

Elizabeth put on the kettle. 'Only instant tonight, Henry, but I have some cream. I know you prefer that to milk. Go on now, off you go.'

Henry got up. At the door he paused for a moment, held the lintel. 'I'm sure you will like Helen,' he said.

Elizabeth replied, already putting instant coffee in two cups, 'Yes, Henry, I am sure I shall love her.'

Her husband looked chastened. 'Sorry, old girl,' he said. Henry had not called her 'old girl' for what seemed like centuries. The wine no doubt, she thought as she waited for the kettle to boil. She put the cups and saucers on a tray. No coffee pot for tonight. As she walked through with the tray, she wondered what Nina was doing at that moment. Having sex with Jacko, or someone else, perhaps?

What would Helen make of it all? Perhaps she would manage to stop her slamming doors. One thing she was quite certain of, Nina would want to live with Helen and her father and not with her. That was a comfort.

All the carefully rehearsed sentences she had thought up to tell Henry about Stanley had completely gone out of her head. As she put the coffee tray down on the little coffee table, Henry began again about Nina's relationship with Helen, how she was looking forward to training as a veterinary nurse, what a good influence Helen was on Nina... Elizabeth handed him his coffee, took her own and sat down. 'And I think Helen will be able to do something to influence her way of dressing, and perhaps curb that dreadful habit of swearing she has recently developed.'

Elizabeth listened to as much as she could stand, then suddenly she cut him off in mid-sentence. 'Now for goodness sake, shut up a moment, Henry! I said I wanted to talk to you too.'

'Yes, I suspected, or thought, Nina had hinted at something.'

'Well, she didn't. I knew nothing about Helen, nothing at all, and now I want to tell you about Stanley.' She drank the coffee and wished she had brought a glass of what was left of the second bottle of wine through from the kitchen with her. 'I am sure you are right. This Helen will completely remake our difficult, sometimes insolent and unattractive daughter into a paragon, but she is my daughter too, you know, so don't talk as if Helen will turn into her mother overnight.'

Henry, she could see, felt perhaps he had overstepped the mark. 'I'm sorry. That was perhaps too much.'

Elizabeth repeated what she had already said: 'I want to tell you about Stanley, who is not and I hope never will be in any way responsible for Nina or her sometimes outrageous behaviour.'

'Who is Stanley?' Henry said, looking totally bewildered.

So Elizabeth proceeded to tell him. Helen and her presence had freed her from all sense of guilt. She could tell Henry everything, and tell him she did! Elizabeth held nothing back, that Stanley was her lover, that he had stayed with her at the painters' weekend. How much she loved him. Henry listened. During the pause for breath that she had to take after several of his questions, Henry went out and fetched the rest of the wine from the kitchen. He seemed horrified, or made out to be, that she had slept with her lover. Elizabeth told him nothing about Stanley's tragic marriage, only that his wife had died of cancer. They drank the rest of the wine and then the second

173

confession ground to a halt. There was really no more to say

Elizabeth collected the cups and saucers and glasses on a tray. Henry stood up. 'Let me take that for you,' he said, unusually to say the least. 'What do we tell Nina?' Henry sounded almost fearful.

'Not to slam doors, learn to act like a human being and be nice to Helen.' Elizabeth smiled as she said it.

Henry looked dismal. 'Aren't we taking all this too lightly, Elizabeth?' he said, sitting down at the kitchen table. 'After all, we did take a vow, for better or for worse.'

Elizabeth's spirits could not be lowered. She nodded.

'Nina will be shocked.'

This made his wife's smile break into a laugh. 'Nina shocked! That girl knows more than both of us. I have always said she disliked me almost from birth and she loves you, Henry.'

'Only because I have given way to her.' He traced a line in the kitchen table, a crack, with his thumbnail.

'Don't do that, you'll make it worse.'

Elizabeth was putting away the dinner plates when the front door banged. Nina. Her hair looked slightly wet. 'Is it raining?' Elizabeth asked. She felt curiously detached from both of them.

'Yep. You had your talk then, got it all

sorted?'

Her father looked at her. 'We've got a lot to tell you, Nina,' he said.

'No, you haven't, Daddy. I know it all, and before you get all steamed up because you've got to tell your poor innocent daughter you are going to do a reshuffle, it says in the *Sun* today that one in three couples divorce.'

They were both silent as she turned to go through the kitchen door. 'I'm drenched,' she said. 'I'm going upstairs to have a hot bath and a rest. Come on, Poll.'

She left the kitchen, a pause, and her bedroom door slammed.

'The *Sun*, since when has she been reading the *Sun*?' Henry asked. So like him to fasten on the least important. 'I'll sleep in the spare room,' he said suddenly.

'OK.' Elizabeth had been about to say it wouldn't make much difference, but thought better of it.

The rest of the evening was so full of tension that Elizabeth decided to go to bed at about ten thirty. She knew Henry was longing, now the full effect of the wine was wearing off and leaving headaches behind it, to talk about money. Elizabeth felt she couldn't care less. She went upstairs and telephoned Stanley, told him a little of what had been discussed: Henry's intended divorce and her relief and joy at the way things were working out for them. She put the phone down, feeling more

175

exhausted than ever. If only, she thought, Stanley and she could go off together, quietly, no fuss. But the divorce would be important to Henry and perhaps Helen. Maybe they would all have to meet, discuss. It was all, made it all, so cheap, sordid. All she wanted was Stanley, his love and a new late middle-aged life. A new beginning, with no thought of beastly material things.

At first she could not sleep. She heard Henry come to bed and the spare room door shut. Perhaps he was as glad as she was that everything was now out in the open. She lent up on one elbow. Nina was in. She could hear the music playing, fairly softly for Nina! What would become of her? She wished her well, but could not summon up any feeling of affection. She buried her face in the pillow and longed for Stanley. Was Henry longing for Helen? Probably. What fools people were to try to hide their feelings, even from themselves. Things change, people change, feelings change. 'Till death us do part.'

No wonder teenagers shied away from saying that. Making a vow that they might well not be able to keep. Were they wise? Her feelings would never change for Stanley, never, never. At last, with this lovely thought, she fell asleep.

CHAPTER TEN

Henry now appeared to Elizabeth to become completely self-centred. What was happening in her life, or even Nina's, became secondary to what was happening to him. Elizabeth tried, in the light of her own happiness, to excuse his almost obsessional behaviour. Before he went to the office in the morning, he talked about Helen, their plans, the pending separation with Elizabeth and the divorce. Helen was like a goddess in his eyes, understanding, loving, highly moral. She had never been married before and according to Henry never found the right man. She was forty-five, a little taller than Henry, according to his description, wore no make-up and had fair hair which she wore short.

When he returned from the office in the evening, the topic was the same. Helen, Helen, Helen. Nina, of course, agreed enthusiastically with her father's opinion and took obvious pleasure in letting her mother know this. 'She's great, Mum. Wonderful with animals. Polly loves her. She can do anything with them. They trust her, you see, they know she's trying to make them better.' On and on and on . . . It was, she supposed, inevitable when Henry eventually said he would like Elizabeth to meet her and could they ask her to dinner.

Nina was thrilled. 'Let's have her to my birthday dinner on Wednesday, Daddy!' She put on her most winsome expression.

'Elizabeth, would you mind meeting her? It would be the nicest, most civilised thing to do, wouldn't it? For Nina's sake.'

Elizabeth almost laughed out loud. Why should she do anything for Nina's sake? The girl had what she wanted. However absurd Henry's request seemed, she knew she would have to agree. She would have to stay here, cook and meet the wonderful, the perfect Helen. Qualified Veterinary Surgeon. Oh, God, why couldn't she just move out of here into Stanley's house? Should she do that?

Her long silence was broken by Nina's 'Come on, Mum, it is my birthday.' She bowed to fate. She could see Stanley any time she wished now, although Wednesday still seemed sacred.

Tonight she would tell Stanley all her troubles, doubts and fears. Tell him she had to meet Helen. Perhaps he should come to the party too, she thought. Be introduced to her husband and daughter, but the thought revolted her. Stanley and her relationship was a thing apart, not to be sullied by all this. She tried hard to realise, when Henry was not talking about his new love, that perhaps it was his first love. He had, like her, never realised what love was about. That thought made her a little more tolerant.

The dinner party was agreed to. Nina seemed as delighted as Henry. Helen, Elizabeth thought, must have something about her to make Nina like her so much, so much more than she herself had ever succeeded in doing. Alone with Nina, she asked her.

'Why do you like Helen so much, Nina?'

'Oh, she's ace, Mum,' was all she could get out of her, whatever that meant.

Henry phoned Helen, who said she would be delighted to come. Elizabeth felt the whole thing was in incredibly bad taste and couldn't wait for that evening to tell Stanley about it.

That evening she did not go to the class. She drove straight to Stanley's house. When she arrived it was truly wonderful to have him draw her into the house, his arms around her. In a moment he could tell she was tense, upset. 'What is it, my dearest?' he asked. She told him everything. There in his arms it all felt safe, nothing to worry about. 'Well, my darling, it's how he is. He has to do it this way. After all, once you have met her, you can move in with me—if you want to, that is.' He put his fingers under her chin and raised her face to his and kissed her very gently on the lips.

'To be with you is all I want in the world,' she said and burst into tears.

'Don't cry. Nothing to cry about now, sweetheart,' he said, wiping her eyes. 'This Helen means we can be together. Nina is, by the sound of it, happy with her. The dinner party will be awful for you but . . .'

She drove home late. No need to bother with any excuses or lies now. She felt reassured and almost happy. The upheaval in front of her, Stanley had agreed, would be daunting but he was there beside her all the way and eventually they would be able to marry.

Henry was both apprehensive and delighted that Helen was coming to meet Elizabeth. If he thought there might be a lot of stress for his wife, he didn't voice it. He constantly reiterated the words, 'It will be so nice for both of you to get together, get to know each other. I really do want a friendly party. I know you will like her, Elizabeth.'

She had only once been tempted into making a sharp sarcastic reply. 'I'm sure I will like her, Henry, just as anyone would like another woman who has stolen her husband!' She knew this was an unjust remark, but at the time she had just had to make it and was only too glad that Nina was not there to say the inevitable, 'Oh, come on, Mum. She certainly didn't steal Dad, you'd already got someone else.' Meanwhile she and Henry had to have a less dramatic talk as to what to give as a joint birthday present for Nina on her very important sixteenth year. They decided on a brand new computer with a laser printer.

The following week Henry took off work. He was very determined to do everything he could to forward the divorce. Helen was the 'other woman'. He visited the solicitor and then rather humbly asked Elizabeth to accompany him on a second visit. Elizabeth reluctantly agreed. Her suggestion, made while Nina was in the room, was that Helen and Henry should move in together, either in this house or Helen's, whichever they wished. She would go her way and he his.

Nina said, 'Cool, Mum, didn't think you had it in you.'

Henry was shocked, horrified. 'I am not like that, Elizabeth. I would not ask any woman to live with me without making her legally my wife.' He very definitely was not 'cool' as Nina put it. The argument went on, but in the end Elizabeth did accompany him to the solicitor and had to take part in what she felt was a horrible discussion about money, house, furniture, car, etc. Henry kept asking her if she was in agreement. She kept saying, 'Yes, yes, certainly. That's fine.'

She learned that Helen had a rather bigger house than theirs with a larger garden. Polly would love that! she found herself thinking. Nina and Polly would have plenty of room. How Nina behaved was now the responsibility of her father and Helen. With a little mental wince she thought of Nina as a 'stepdaughter'. Stepdaughter! How weird! But she was certain, indeed had been told, that Nina wished to stay with her father and Helen. Elizabeth was not in the least affected by this, she was relieved. After all, if Nina decided to go on in the vet's, Helen would certainly be the best person to advise and lead her.

After another and, to Elizabeth, very boring discussion, Henry decided it was unfair to have the dinner at home and he booked a table for them at the town's most expensive restaurant. 'Why should we ask you to produce the meal, it's simply not fair, Elizabeth.' She wondered if this change of heart had been due to Helen rather than Henry, but she was glad. She had absolutely no wish to cook for her husband's new woman and the decision was a relief.

When she told Stanley on the telephone he said, 'Certainly, you should not cook for them. The least Henry can do is pay for a meal out.' Elizabeth herself had not even thought of that, but dear Stanley had, and again she felt protected by him. How soon, she wondered, could she escape from all this and be enfolded entirely by Stanley's love and protection? The thought that it would soon be possible kept her going through the week.

Elizabeth debated whether to go out and buy herself a totally new outfit for the dinner, but decided against it. Later she regretted this decision but she chose from her wardrobe a dress she had not worn for ages. After all, dinner dates at expensive restaurants had not figured often in her married life. She tried on the dress. It still fitted perfectly. She was pleased about that. She had kept her figure, that was one comfort at least.

*   *   *

The evening of the dinner party felt like the beginning of a nightmare for Elizabeth. Was this, she wondered, how all men behaved when they had fallen in love with another woman? Henry, so anxious for her to meet Helen, kept apologising and eulogising: 'She is such a lovely person, I know you will like her. She's so forthright, so . . .' Once or twice Elizabeth had interrupted and said sarcastically, 'So different from me, Henry!' This had only made him apologise again. Apparently it did not occur to him that she was not mentioning Stanley at all, nor suggesting that he and Henry should meet. Nina too was very enthusiatic about her stepmother-to-be. 'She's OK, Mum, she's a real goer, know what I mean?'

Elizabeth didn't know what she meant and expected a large woman, homely and wonderful with animals. She almost expected her to stride into the restaurant in Wellingtons and a tweed hat. She said this to Stanley, and he laughed really heartily. 'I can just picture it, darling, but probably she's small, slightly weatherbeaten and with a firm handshake.' She was neither.

Elizabeth dressed with great care that evening. Helen was driving to their house for a pre-dinner drink. 'She likes gin and tonic, but

183

no lemon,' Henry said, fussing about in the kitchen. Elizabeth took no part in the drinks preparation but concentrated on her make-up until at last Henry called out: 'She'll be here in a moment, Elizabeth. Could you . . . sort of be here to welcome her? I wouldn't want her to think . . .'

Elizabeth at last came downstairs to, she felt, put her husband out of his misery.

'Neeny, are you ready?'

Then Nina appeared. A long skirt, black and shiny with a slit side, made her look taller, a tight scant top accentuated the swell of her young breasts, the neck was round, low and revealing. Her hair was swept up and knotted on top of her head in a spiky bundle, her heavy fringe caught back with a red clip. Elizabeth hid her feelings. Henry was about to say something but Nina forestalled him.

'Now, Daddy, you gave me the money to buy these clothes, have my hair done. You said buy anything I like and I have.'

At that moment the door bell rang. 'Saved by the bell,' Elizabeth said.

'What?' Nina said. The door opened and there stood Helen, taller than Henry, yes, but, otherwise in no way what Elizabeth had expected.

'Come in, Helen.' They shook hands. 'This is Elizabeth, Elizabeth, this is Helen. Helen Wentworth.' Henry stood back to let her enter and for once Elizabeth felt sorry for him. He

184

looked almost frightened and she could see a faint sheen of sweat on his forehead. They all stood stock still in the hall.

Helen looked at Nina and smiled. 'You look quite sensational, Neeny,' she said.

'Shall we go through?' Elizabeth had to say at last. She felt if she didn't take some kind of lead, they would be there for ever. Nina beamed at her guest and sat close beside her on the sofa. Elizabeth detected a definite hero-worshipping attitude.

Elizabeth now had time to take in the woman opposite her. Her fair hair was straight with a slight curl at the end. It looked natural but probably wasn't. Forty-five? Elizabeth could not remember if Henry had told her this or if she was guessing. Her face looked fresh, rather shiny, pink-cheeked. Weatherbeaten, no. A pale pink lipstick and a tiny bit of brown eye shadow gave her a rather fragile look. Attractive? Elizabeth tried to decide. Old maidish. Her dress was long-sleeved, high at the neck, with a collar. Floral. She wrote this off as too awful for words, but tried to remind herself that Henry would probably like that kind of dress. Helen's shoes, rather surprisingly, were stylish. Black patent, high-heeled and strapped across the foot. Should have been worn with no stockings and varnished toenails, but were not.

They talked, stilted conversation, about nothing. Henry said they were booked at the

185

Grange Hotel in Hanley.

'Pushing the boat out, Dad?' Nina was the only one of the four who seemed completely relaxed.

Henry coughed and then tried a smile. 'Of course I want you to have a nice birthday, Neeny.'

'They gave me a computer and the whole works. Pays to have a divorce in the family, eh, Helen? And Dad gave me enough money to get this gear.' She seemed genuinely pleased with the whole set-up.

Elizabeth, almost silent, tried to analyse the scene. Odd, she decided. Odd was the word. A marriage breaking up, two people at a crossroad, one going one way one the other, both with new partners, probably new lives. Polly sat between Helen and Nina. Elizabeth felt the little dog was the one she would miss most. As she felt this, tears pricked at her eyes, not because of Polly, she would have a devoted mistress in Nina as long as she lived and a doctor all her own. It was not that, it was goodbye to something that had gone on so long and ended without love or caring. How could life be like that? But it was and this tableau, in this sitting-room that she had taken care of, cleaned, bought things for, in a short time would be no more. From Henry's conversation during the days before the visit she had drawn the fact that Helen's house, nearer to her surgery, bigger, would be where

186

they would live. This house, her home and Henry's, would be sold and the contents sold too. Nothing in it evoked pleasant memories.

'Are you a gardener, Mrs Mason?'

She woke out of her thoughts with a sense of shock. 'Please call me Elizabeth,' she said automatically. 'A gardener? No, not really. I pull a weed out now and again but . . .' She wondered what had led the conversation to gardening.

'I love it, but alas have little time to spare. Sick animals are no respectors of time.' Helen smiled; her smile was wide, her teeth very white and straight.

Henry suddenly got up, looking at his watch. 'Time we set off,' he said. He helped Helen on with the light coat she had discarded when she sat down. Elizabeth picked up her coat in the hall and turned to Nina.

'Aren't you going to put something on? You'll freeze. It's not that warm in the evening yet.'

Nina shook her head. 'Nope. I'm warm enough as I am and I'm not going to, Mum, it's no use looking at me like that.'

Elizabeth shrugged and did not even look at Helen or Henry; both said nothing. Nina got into the back seat of the car and patted the seat beside her for Helen, a swift glance at Elizabeth as she did so. So husband and wife were in the driving and the passenger seat.

The drive to the hotel was full of prattle

from Nina as she told Helen and anyone who would listen the things she could do with her new computer. 'I can even study on it, Helen, play games, get in touch with people, it's going to be great.'

Helen broke in as they arrived at the Grange Hotel. 'Oh, what a lovely place, Henry. I've never been here before.' Her praises went on as they entered the spacious hallway. It was a beautifully appointed place, obviously had once been a stately home.

They were escorted straight away to their table as they refused the bar. The meal was superb. Everything went well until the coffee was served. They had moved from their table to the coffee lounge. All four were now more relaxed, the food and wine had helped. Henry ordered liqueurs with their coffee for everyone, except himself. When he was driving he would never drink more than one drink, a point in his favour, Elizabeth always thought. Because it was her birthday, Nina had been allowed two glasses of wine and now the liqueurs. Henry had chosen crème de menthe, not Elizabeth's favourite. She preferred kümmel but she felt Henry's choice had been for Nina's sake. 'Mm, nice peppermint,' Nina said after the first sip from the tiny glass. The waiter brought more coffee, then the storm erupted. Something Helen said to Nina, who maybe was feeling the drinks more than anyone realised.

'The computer, Daddy, I'm going to use it a lot for my education, you know.'

Good, I'm glad, Henry had answered. Then Helen said quite casually, 'You'll need to get your A levels for university if you want to become a veterinary nurse—a degree in zoology helps.'

Elizabeth knew in a second that Henry had not told her that Nina had been expelled. She knew he was deeply ashamed of the fact.

Nina looked across at Elizabeth. 'There you are, it's your fault. You made me go to her poxy lessons.' She burst into a torrent of tears and suddenly clung to Helen. 'She got me expelled, this lousy teacher. She got me expelled, so I can't go to university and be a veterinary nurse, which is what I want more than anything in the world.'

Helen tried to comfort the girl. 'Come now, we will see what can be done, Nina. Don't cry so, you'll get a headache.'

Henry summoned the waiter for the bill. 'It's the wine and the excitement, Helen.'

'I didn't know she had been expelled, Henry. Why didn't you tell me? I wouldn't have mentioned university.'

The waiter approached, the bill on a silver salver. 'Everything all right, sir?' he asked, looking at the sobbing Nina.

'Perfectly all right, thank you.' Henry placed his card on the salver. The waiter retreated.

'That old bitch Meadows, I'll kill her, I'll kill

189

her,' Nina screamed. She was really making a
scene, hysterical and out of control.

'Take Neeny to the car,' Henry almost
hissed at Elizabeth. There was nothing, as she
knew, that Henry hated more than a 'scene'.

'Helen will look after her, Henry. I must just
go to the powder room.' She got up and, like
the waiter, retreated. Once in the perfumed
pink-lit Ladies she gazed at herself in the
mirror. Yes, she did look older than Helen.
She had to admit it, but then she was older and
Stanley loved her, so what matter. She opened
her handbag, took out her lipstick and powder
compact, lightly touched her cheeks and nose
with the puff, repaired her lipstick and went
back into the dining-room, just in time to see
Helen, her arm around Nina's shoulder,
walking out. She followed them.

'Helen, everything all right?' she asked.

Helen turned, and smiled at her. 'Yes, better
now. Henry's gone to the car, to unlock it.'

Elizabeth smiled back. 'Nina's so fond of
you, Helen. Isn't it lucky, she admires you and
your work so much.'

Nina was still crying but quietly. Elizabeth
got into the front of the car again and Helen
and Nina in the back.

'You must tell me all about it, why you were
expelled, everything. Not now, but tomorrow
perhaps.'

'She was caught smoking cannabis,'
Elizabeth said clearly and concisely.

190

'It wasn't only that.' Nina, her voice thick with weeping, spoke up. 'It was the Meadows woman, she had it in for me all the time. Mum didn't understand, she was an old bag, I hate her.'

When they arrived home Helen decided to go straight back to her house. She did give Henry a chaste kiss on the cheek. 'A lovely meal, everything was perfect, Henry dear. I so enjoyed it. Wonderful restaurant.' She turned to Nina. 'Don't worry, darling, we'll sort something out. Happy birthday, dear.' She kissed Nina, who put her arms around Helen's neck and hugged her, then ran into the house, up to her room and the door as usual, slammed. Elizabeth went in, leaving Henry and Helen to say good-night. For some reason she felt unbearably depressed and longed for Stanley. But she did not feel at all inclined to tell him about tonight's drama, it was boring and nasty. Helen clearly seemed to have taken over what had been her family and she was glad of it. It meant freedom for her.

Henry was very upset. 'I made a mistake there, Elizabeth,' he said, following her into the kitchen when she was making a hot drink.

'Want one?' she asked, holding up the Horlicks jar.

'Please, I don't think I'll sleep a wink.'

'Mistake?' she asked.

'Yes, I should have told her that Nina had been expelled but to tell the truth, I was

191

ashamed.'

Elizabeth tried hard not to sound smug. 'Yes, secrets are not good, Henry. Stanley and I have vowed not to keep anything from each other.'

'Stanley. Oh, yes of course.' His answer made her smile a little. She could hardly believe that he could be so wrapped up in his own concerns that her affair was of so little importance to him. 'I must put it right with her,' he said accepting the hot drink she handed him.

'And Neeny?' Elizabeth used the nickname on purpose.

He hardly reacted. 'Yes, Neeny.' Suddenly he looked very tired and old. 'I'm going to bed,' he said, and went up to the spare room taking his drink with him.

Elizabeth felt sorry, she was so happy. What a pity Helen could not have stayed the night, slept with Henry, not necessarily for sex but just to comfort him and each other, but they had their own kind of morals. Elizabeth finished her drink, switched out the lights, bolted the front door and made her way to her own room. She looked at the bedroom clock. It was still quite early, ten thirty. Stanley would still be up. She sat on the side of the bed, switched on the bedside light, got up and shut the bedroom door, then lay down on the bed and picked up the telephone by the bed. She dialled Stanley's number.

'Hello, my darling,' he said.

'She didn't wear wellies and a tweed hat.'

'I didn't somehow think she would,' he said and love and laughter came down the line to her and almost obliterated the evening's ugliness.

*   *   *

In the morning Henry woke up first. 'Do you think it went all right?' he asked Elizabeth as she came through the kitchen door, still in her dressing-gown. He looked as if he hadn't slept a wink.

'You mean before Nina threw her wobbly?'

'Well, yes, I mean, Helen. The drinks here and the dinner. Did you like her, Elizabeth?' He poured a cup of coffee and handed it to her.

Elizabeth shook her head. 'No thanks, I'd rather have tea. Yes, I liked her.' She went across and switched on the kettle, then went out into the hall as she heard the 'plop' of the mail on the doormat. She came back into the kitchen leafing through a handful of plastic-covered catalogues and some advertisements. She found one letter, threw the plastic envelopes and contents on to the table and opened the letter. 'Oh, it's from Maisie.'

'Maisie?' Henry looked at her.

'Maisie, for goodness' sake, your first cousin. She says . . .' She looked again at the letter. 'Her dad's not too well and . . .' Henry was obviously not hearing or attending to a word. 'Yes. About Helen, I think she seems like a nice woman. It's difficult to form an opinion at that sort of occasion. I can only hope you will be very happy together.'

'Oh, we will, we will. I hope you will too.'

Elizabeth looked at him. 'That's the first time you have mentioned my relationship.'

'Yes, yes. It's all a bit unusual what we are doing, but I'm sure it's for the best.'

'Henry, you don't have to convince me.' She knew she had spoken sharply, but Henry did not seem to notice.

'And Nina, that was a bit unfortunate. I think she thought if she worked there at the vet's, she would automatically become a veterinary nurse.'

Elizabeth poured the boiling water into the teapot and brought it to the table.

'Well, remember her attitude to the career interviews. She was rude to the career adviser or whatever she's called, and didn't turn up the next time there was a careers meeting.'

Henry nodded. 'She's her own worst enemy. I hope Helen can help her.'

Elizabeth sipped her tea. 'I'm sure she will. After all, she's a professional woman.'

Henry nodded. 'Yes, you're probably right, but I didn't want to take a problem like that into the relationship.'

'Well, she'll probably leave home now she's

sixteen.'

'She won't—I won't have that, Elizabeth.'

'Whenever have you been able to stop her doing anything, Henry?' Elizabeth finished her tea and went upstairs to dress. On the way she passed Nina's bedroom door. It was slightly ajar. She knocked and went in. Nina was lying in her usual curled-up position, sound asleep. Elizabeth looked around the room. It was untidy, open drawers, a bottle of black nail varnish, the top lying beside it. The brush had made a tiny black pool. Stockings and tights hung out of one drawer. The new computer had the place of honour. It took up a large amount of room. Elizabeth found herself thinking that perhaps Nina should move into the spare room with all her bits and pieces and make this into the guest room. They had few enough people to stay. She pulled herself up with a mental jerk. It was nothing to do with her. She did not know anything about Helen's house, only that it was bigger.

Nina's joy at going to live with Helen, and, according to Henry, Helen's pleasure, as he put it, at having a 'ready-made daughter', had made the 'custody arrangements', if one could use that term regarding a sixteen-year-old, no problem at all. Elizabeth felt very slightly guilty as she stood looking down at the sleeping girl. Anywhere but with me, she thought and turned to leave the room.

Nina woke. 'I was sick in the night, I could

195

taste that horrible peppermint stuff.'

'Oh, do you feel better now?'

'I'm thirsty.' Nina buried her head deeper under the covers.

'I'll bring you up some tea.' She turned, the door had swung almost shut again. Elizabeth was shocked to see that the charcoal drawing of Miss Meadows was stuck up there. Looking more closely, she realised that it had been added to since she last saw it: just below the neck, a knife now protruded.

'Nina,' she said.

Her daughter put her head over the duvet and looked. 'What?' she said, still sleepy. When she saw what her mother was looking at, she laughed. 'Jacko did it. Good, isn't it? He wants to become a poster artist. I did the flames though and the knife.'

Elizabeth grasped the door handle and opened the door so that the picture became hidden again. 'I think it's disgusting.'

Nina laughed again. 'You didn't think I'd forget the old bag or how she treated me? She got me expelled, I know she did. Just to suck up to the new head. She always hated me. I told you that, she was a right sadist to me. She enjoyed making me look small in front of the others. I'll never forgive her.'

'Well, I think you should tear that picture up, Nina.'

Her daughter snorted. 'Not likely, not until she gets her come-uppance, then I will.' She burrowed down again. 'Can I have that tea, Mum? My mouth tastes awful.'

Elizabeth went downstairs. Henry was still in the kitchen. She wondered if she should mention the picture to him, and decided against it. She made more tea and took it up to her daughter's room, putting it on the cluttered bedside table. 'Tea, Nina,' she said. She got no answer. As she reached the door, she looked again at the drawing. It was Miss Meadows to the life. Elizabeth had never seen her look quite as menacing as that, but perhaps that was how Nina saw her. Well, Henry, if he saw the picture, must deal with it himself—or Helen, if she saw it. She wondered what Stanley would have done had he seen the picture. Her thoughts shied away from that. Stanley and she were separate, apart. Oh, Nina would still be her daughter, she might still see her, but the responsibility for Nina's behaviour would not be hers—indeed, with Henry's spoiling, it had never been.

The picture lingered in her mind, the painted flames, the knife. Nina must have quite an influence with Jacko to make him draw such a portrait. Was he an old pupil of Miss Meadows? In the glimpses she had caught of him, in the hall and getting off the bike, he had looked too old to be still at school, but he too might have been a victim of Miss Meadows' discipline.

Last night Helen had sounded very

197

pessimistic about Nina ever being accepted by the BVNA—that was what she had called it, Elizabeth believed—unless her school records and her academic records were good. There was more to being a veterinary nurse than just being good with animals. There were exams to pass, studying to do. Being expelled might make refusal absolute. She hoped not, but her mind was so full of Stanley. At their last meeting, he had suggested she move in with him. 'What's the reason for staying there, darling?' he had asked in his reasonable, quiet way. 'Maybe Helen won't move in with Henry, but that's up to them, isn't it?' Elizabeth agreed with him, but she felt she couldn't leave Henry to cope with Nina, the cooking, washing, the shopping.

More than anything she wanted to commit herself to Stanley. He had the house ready for her. He begged her to think about moving in with him. 'Just say you are coming to me because I want you so much, dearest. Goodness knows, that's true enough.'

Elizabeth wanted it too, as much as he did. She suddenly decided, helped by the fact that she was in Stanley's arms. 'I will talk to Henry tomorrow evening, Stanley.'

'Not talk to him, darling, tell him.' Stanley embraced her. 'Look, he's not alone. You're not walking out on a lonely man. He already has a woman he loves and who loves him. He cannot expect you to wait till the divorce goes

198

through and the house is sold or divided, it may take months.'

Elizabeth sighed. 'You are right. I'll tell him tomorrow and pack my things and come to you.'

She stayed the night with Stanley and went back to her own house, still her own house, mid-morning.

No one was in. She let herself in and went up to the bedroom. She let down the loft steps, got down two large suitcases and began to pack her clothes. When both suitcases were safely in her car, she opened a tin of tuna and made some tuna and lettuce sandwiches. As she did this she remembered buying the lettuce yesterday. The sandwiches would do for both herself and Nina should she come in. Then she remembered that Nina would get lunch from Helen at the surgery and Henry never came home for lunch. That's how it would be when she was no longer there. The thought reassured her. She decided to go out, shop for the last time for Henry and Nina, make a meal for them for this evening. The last supper. It would help pass the time too, when Henry came in. After he had eaten, she would leave.

* * *

The front door banged and Nina came in with Polly. She looked excited. 'We, I mean the

199

vets, gave a blood transfusion to a spaniel this afternoon.'

'Oh, yes? Where did they get the blood from?'

'A poodle, Mum, it was wonderful. Helen said she'd talk to Dad about my going back to school somewhere, a private school, if they'll have me. I will have to study like mad, all because of that bitchy old Meadows, but I'll do it, if Dad can afford it—it'll cost!'

Elizabeth listened. She felt she had nothing to contribute. Perhaps Nina would succeed— she had to say something.

'Good. I hope you make it, Nina.'

'Did you sleep with what's his name last night, Mum?' she asked, putting a meal down for Polly.

'Isn't that my business, Nina?' she said sharply.

'Yes, I suppose it is, but I wish Dad would get on with it too—Helen would, I know.'

Elizabeth looked up from the gravy she was making. 'How do you know such a thing?' She was a little shocked.

'Oh, I just know, that's all.' Nina looked at her mother with those hard brown eyes. 'I do.'

Elizabeth believed her. 'How's Jacko?' she asked.

Nina made a face. 'He's OK. We're really an item now, Mum. He's an OK guy really, a bit dim at times, but he does what I tell him. What's for dinner?'

'Lamb.' Elizabeth opened the oven door and basted the joint, a rather larger one than usual. Her heart started to race as she heard Henry's car drive in.

'It's always lamb,' Nina said, and went upstairs, followed by Polly. Her bedroom door banged. The telephone rang and the door opened again, Nina ran downstairs. 'I'll get it,' she called out then: 'Yes, I'd like to. Let's get Chinese. Mum's cooking lamb—for a change.' Heavy sarcasm in the last few words. She raced upstairs again, then back down with a large handbag slung over her shoulder, a mac over her arm.

Elizabeth watched her cross the hall. 'Won't be in for dinner, Mum—oh, hello, Dad.'

Henry came into the kitchen, the front door slammed.

'Will she ever learn to close a door quietly?' Elizabeth said.

'She was in a hurry, I expect.' Once more Henry excused, protected.

'I expect she was.' Elizabeth started to dish up the meal.

'Some wine?' Henry asked. She nodded. 'White or red?'

'White, it's lamb,' she answered and carried the meal through to the dining-room for the last time.

'I bought some crème de menthe, they call it Freezamint. I thought Nina seemed to like it and one now and again won't hurt, as a treat I mean.'

He put the bottle on the sideboard. Elizabeth made no comment. They ate their meal in silence. Henry leaned across to pour a second glass of wine into Elizabeth's glass. She put her hand over it. 'No, thank you, Henry. No more, I'm driving.'

He looked up, withdrew the bottle and put it down before he spoke. 'You're going back again tonight? I thought . . .' He waited; there was a pause. Elizabeth felt the tension. Did he guess?

'I'm driving back to Stanley tonight, Henry. My cases are packed and in my car, there are other things of mine I will need to fetch, but that can be later.'

'But the divorce, the money side of things, the—'

Elizabeth suddenly felt immensely tired. 'I'll wash up before I go,' she said and realised how banal the remark was.

'But Helen—'

She did not want to listen. 'Henry, you and Helen have things to settle, if you love each other, you will settle them. How you do so is not my business. I love Stanley and want to be with him.' Henry tried to say something, but Elizabeth stopped him. 'We are not young people, starting out in life with years and years in front of us, Henry, we are middle-aged. I want to spend the rest of my life with Stanley and I'm not going to waste any of it wrangling

202

about houses, furniture, possessions. Nina wants to live with you and Helen, she is old enough to make up her mind and she has done so.' She picked up the plates and took them into the kitchen, stacked them in the sink. 'Mrs Jones can do them in the morning,' she said. She had forgotten it was their cleaner's day the next day.

Henry stood there watching her as she slipped on her coat, picked up her handbag, went out of the front door, but did not slam it.

CHAPTER ELEVEN

Nina sat on her bed looking at herself in the dressing-table mirror. She held up her hands, pulled back her cheeks a little, making them look less full and round. Her skin was very white. She quite liked that. She remembered a book where the heroine had a skin like magnolia and she thought that was probably a description of her skin. Her eyes? The lashes were pretty good, with mascara even better. She wasn't good at eye liner—Margaret was ace at it.

Her neck wasn't swan-like at all. She did exercises every day, well—every day she remembered. Her boobs were too big, she worried about her breasts. The nipples were brown. Jacko thought they were great, but what did he know? She was naked except for a pair of black briefs. When she stood up the mirror wasn't big enough to take her whole body in—it cut her head off and reflected down to her pubic hair.

That had been a bit of a disaster. She had tried to shave it into a triangle like the models did but she had cut herself and hadn't managed to shape the black-haired triangle. 'Sucks,' she said and pulled the black briefs back on. Her middle bulged a bit too and her waist was not as slender as she would like it to be. Neither was she tall enough. She had bought some shoes with three-inch heels. She hadn't worn them to that poxy dinner. She tried them on now. They hurt a bit and her feet slid forward, making the strap over the toes cut in. Still, they made her taller!

She sat down again. Her hair was good. She could do anything with it. Now Mum was gone, she would let the fringe grow—she liked straight hair, hated curls. She leant forward and made a kissing mouth. Her lips were thick and, she felt, well shaped. She took a lip brush from the medley of stuff on her dressing-table, picked up a lipstick. Deep purple, almost black. She painted her lips carefully 'Great,' she said and leant back. She could, if she tucked her legs up under her, see all of herself in the glass. She posed provocatively, pouting her lips, half closing her eyes. 'Tasty,' she said and giggled. Then she turned sideways too, looking good, looking sexy.

'Wish Jacko was here,' she said, pouting her lips again. But then, he wasn't really what she wanted. Who she would really like as a boyfriend was Mr Jones. Jamie, the new PT teacher. He had a beard, long curling hair, a lovely smile and red lips, like he was wearing lipstick. His arms were brown. He had been in India, lived there for three months.

She sighed. She looked too young for him perhaps? Still, now she was sixteen—sixteen and two days. She put her arms around herself and hugged herself. 'I love me and I'm sixteen, on the threshold of life.' She had read that in a Mills & Boon.

Nina knew Mum had gone, the moment she came in, just by the feeling. Dad was in the sitting-room, the television on in front of him, an old film in black and white. Dad never looked at old films, never. He hadn't heard her come in, it was pretty late. She crept upstairs into the bedroom, or rather Mum's bedroom now. All Mum's clothes were gone, just a row of hangers left.

Poor old Dad, she thought. Still it serves him right.

Why doesn't he shack up with Helen?

Nina thought it would be lovely at Helen's. Cleaning lady all the time, two gorgeous golden retrievers, a horse, two cats—a ginger and a tabby. Polly had been there and got on with all the animals. How were they going to live here with no Mum? Who was going to do the cooking? 'Not me!' Nina said aloud. She must talk to Dad and Helen, get them to see sense. After all, Mum had moved herself in with her partner, or lover, or whatever. Did they still make love?

She tried to envisage them having sex. Mum! She had only just caught a glimpse of— what was his name? Stanley. Still, Mum was— what? She tried to work it out. Forty when she was born, now she was sixteen. Fifty-six, for goodness' sake! Did people still . . .? She grimaced. Awful, the thought of it. She dived into bed, rubbed the lipstick off with a tissue and cuddled down under the duvet. Dad would be gutted. She couldn't sleep.

After an hour or so, she got up. She opened a little box on the bedside table and took out a roach. She lit it and after a few deep breaths, holding it in, she went back to bed, lay on the coverlet, legs spread out. She felt great. Sixteen! She was grown up now, an adult. She looked across the room at the picture on the door. Jacko had done the face. Every night she added a flame. Orange and red crayon. She had not done one tonight. 'Well, never mind,' she said aloud. 'I'll give you one more night off, Miss Meadows.' She propped the pillow up a little higher. The face stared back at her. 'I hate you. You have messed up my life and I'll get you.' She drifted off to sleep, but even in her dreams Miss Meadows loomed like a

206

witch. What Helen had said about the impossibility of her being a qualified veterinary nurse, BVNA she believed it was, had rekindled her hatred of the woman pinned to her bedroom door. Mum had said where her cottage was. She'd go and have a look tomorrow.

*   *   *

Tomorrow came late. Nina didn't wake until ten past ten. Dad had gone. She woke, stretched, then thought of Helen. She telephoned the surgery, and got the receptionist. 'I've got a tummy upset, can you tell Helen?'

'Yes, I will. Is it bad?'

Nina decided to play it down in case she felt like going in later. 'No, not terrible, but I have to keep going to the bog.'

'Oh well, I'll tell her. Hope you'll be better soon.'

'Thanks. I'll come in if it stops.' She put the telephone down.

Polly got out of her basket, looking miserable. 'Poll, you've not been out. You must be bursting!' She got the collar and lead and took the dog into the garden, unlocked the back gate and walked up the road. Not Polly's usual walk but she was so delighted to have relieved herself she trotted along quite happily on her lead. When Mum was here she would have done that, let Polly into the garden. Dad didn't think.

Along the road quite a long way, then down a road of fairly new houses and bungalows, a cul de sac and, at the end, the thatched cottage. Miss Meadows' retirement home. Nina stood, partially hidden by a large bush. There was a garden adjoining a new-looking bungalow which stretched down the side of the thatched cottage. A man was mowing the lawn, an elderly man, who didn't look in her direction. There was a bottle of milk on the cottage doorstep. 'Perhaps the old bitch has died,' Nina said softly to Polly. The little dog pricked up her ears at Nina's remark, looked up at her, her brown eyes puzzled.

At that moment the front door of the cottage opened and Miss Meadows picked up the bottle of milk, looked at the man mowing the grass, disappeared inside again, closing the door quietly behind her. Nina remembered the times she had said to her, 'Go outside that door again. Come in and close the door quietly, don't slam it!' The sight of the woman made Nina feel physically sick. The humiliations she had suffered at her hands. 'Take off that lipstick at once, Nina!' 'Let your skirt down to the proper length, Nina!' 'Why do you wish to show us your crotch, Nina? Is it different from everybody else's?' It all came back to her as she stood there, hating the woman behind the now closed door. No one really knew how she had treated her. When she had made the taunt about Nina's crotch, the whole class had laughed, laughed at her, Nina. She had hated them too, but not as much, not nearly as much as she had hated the woman who had made them laugh and got her chucked out.

Nina stood there a little longer. The cottage was pretty, too good for a beastly woman like her. After being a sarcastic bully, she then retired to a dear little place like this. She didn't deserve it. She deserved to be in prison or in a tower block with really bad children messing in the lifts and covering the walls with filthy words. See how her sarcasm and hurtful words would work on children and teenagers like some of those who would tell her to 'Get lost', 'Bug off' or worse. That would make her know what teenagers could be like. She walked away, keeping carefully on one side of the road, just in case Beastly Meadows might be looking out of one of the little windows.

She felt Polly hadn't had quite a fair deal with her walk. Helen would say a dog needs proper exercise, not just dragging round on a lead. Helen was brill, she'd help her. She took Polly into a field nearby and let her chase about. She had forgotten to bring her ball, she threw a stick instead, but the picture of Miss Meadows coming out of her door and collecting her milk lingered with her. She pictured herself with a syringe, full of poison, and—had she been earlier—creeping up, piercing the top of the milk bottle and squirting in the syringeful. Meadows inside, suddenly feeling ill, collapsing, dying.

She stood still in the field for a moment. Silly idea. Silly. Someone would have seen her, that wouldn't work—still, there were other ways. She called Polly, put on her lead and headed back home to make herself some breakfast. She could make toast and put on as much butter as she liked now. No Mum to say, 'You don't need to plaster on as much butter as that, Nina.' She was her own mistress now. Sixteen. She quickened her pace and, for the moment, Miss Meadows faded away, but not altogether. She remained in the back of Nina's mind, something to be dealt with later, but definitely to be dealt with. An idea would come.

Once home, she gave Polly a biscuit, changed her water and made herself the heavily buttered toast. As she sat eating it, she realised she had to get round Dad to move in with Helen, get things moving. She knew he wanted to, Helen wanted him to, but he was a bit old-fashioned, didn't seem to see that people were swapping about all the time. What difference did it make, some old church chap in a frock muttering words over you? It made no difference. If you were in love, you stayed together.

Nina telephoned Helen, said she felt better

and was coming in, and set off for the bus.
Because of Polly, she would have to travel
upstairs on top, but she rather liked that.
'Come on, Poll, we may be moving house,' she
said. Polly looked slightly surprised at getting a
second walk, but walks were great so her tail
wagged as Nina slammed the front door.

Nina remembered back to when she was
four. She often tried, but couldn't go further
back than that. She remembered waiting and
watching for her Daddy to come home. They
lived in a smaller house then, in a row, not as
nice as this one. 'Daddy, Daddy, what have you
brought me?' She remembered always saying
that, shouting it, and Daddy always had
something for her. A doll in a box one day. She
had hated that doll because of its blue eyes
and flaxen hair. Sometimes it was only a
packet of sweets and she would stamp her feet
and sulk and Daddy would say, 'I didn't have
time. Daddy was busy working.' But she had
sulked. She remembered another day—about
a year later. Yes, she was at school then.
Daddy had come home with no present. He
had said he was sorry and after their meal he
had gone into the garden and made a bonfire.
'It's her bedtime, Henry,' Mum had said. 'But
let her stay up just to see the bonfire.' She had.
It was lovely. The flames were orange and red
and the sticks crackled and smoked. She had
run upstairs and brought down the flaxen-
haired blue-eyed doll and thrown it right in the

middle of the bonfire. Daddy hadn't minded much but he had been a bit cross. 'What did you do that for, darling? That cost Daddy money.' She had watched the doll burn. First its frock, then its hair, then the face had blackened and cracked. The blue eyes dropped out. She had watched it, fascinated. She could remember it now, like a picture in her head. Mum had come out and Daddy had said, 'She burned her doll!' Mum had looked at what was left of the doll. She said, 'Well, it's the sort of thing she would do, isn't it?' and walked away.

As she got older, ten, twelve, she had learnt to handle Daddy. She had only to wheedle, sulk a little, but not too much, give him a kiss or hug. 'Please, Daddy, I want it.' He would get it. Mum, she was different. You could get very little out of Mum. She was about thirteen before she came to know that Mum didn't like her. Oh, she acted the 'Mummy' bit, called for her from school, talked to the other mothers, but she was different from them. Nina was quick to notice it. When she got into Mum's car, there was no quick kiss or greeting. Usually Mum looked bored, fed up. They didn't talk much then. When she got older, fourteen, fifteen, Mum had tried to give her the sex talk. That had been a real gas. Mum talking about sex. School, parents, they were all sex mad or at least keeping their daughters off it. Nina couldn't understand why. She asked Jacko if his mum yacked on about it. He said no, but his dad did. Well, she and Jacko had sex. It was OK sometimes, sometimes not. She made him buy the condoms though—why should she?

One thing she was sure of, she'd never have a baby. She didn't like them. Someone had made her hold one once. It smelt of sour milk, a bubble came out of its mouth. When it did something in its napkin, it was awesome, the stink. Animals, now they were different. Kittens, a week old, were lovely to hold. Pups or grown-up dogs, cats, horses. That's why Helen was so brilliant. She loved animals so much she had given her life to them. To see her operating on a dog or a cat, or a snake even, was fab. She'd never messed with babies. Dad had got to move in with her. Her house was lovely, untidy but great. The dogs were allowed on the chairs, and the cats. Tonight she would talk to Dad, make him see the sense of moving.

She quite suddenly had an idea. Why not go and see Miss Meadows, give her a last chance, ask her to talk to the new head? Maybe she was a friend of hers. Try and get back to school after the holidays. Act up a bit, tell her she wanted to be a veterinary nurse. (Well, that was true enough.) Say she would be a model pupil, apologise for all her rudeness, not that Butchy Meadows hadn't deserved it, but forget that. Nina began to plan the interview. She'd say that Daddy had advised her to come.

213

Nothing to lose and if old Meadows could get her back, she would work now Helen had given her something to work for. It would be a bad pill to swallow, but worth it. Should she tell Dad before she went? No. Meadows had been beastly, but that didn't matter, not now. Tomorrow, she would try tomorrow. Not take Polly, not wear a short skirt, look really proper. A longer skirt or trousers. After all, she was a working girl now, but with no proper qualifications—and she did want those qualifications. Surely old Meadows wouldn't say no. She loved that dog, so she loved animals perhaps.

Nina began to feel quite excited. She felt she could move Miss Meadows, tell her about Helen, the work that went on at the vet's. She couldn't refuse. She'd better not refuse. Even Mum would approve of this, wouldn't she? Though now she had left, started a new life, she probably couldn't care less. Nina felt tears come to her eyes. Why? She didn't care Mum had gone, but she might have said goodbye. She let the tears flow down her face. 'Cry baby', she said aloud and Polly jumped up and licked her face. This made it worse. She started to sob. She couldn't understand her feelings. Polly leant against her, looking at her face. 'Oh Polly,' she said at last when she could speak. 'Why wasn't Helen my mother?' In spite of the outbreak of crying, Nina's determination to go and throw herself on Miss

Meadows' mercy persisted. She would go tomorrow morning. About ten or ten thirty.

She was nervous, hated asking favours of anyone, but she was going to try. Tell her about Mum leaving, Dad's plans too. She was at the centre of a double broken marriage and she wasn't going to spare either of her parents. If that didn't move Meadows, nothing would.

*   *   *

Henry brought home a Chinese takeaway. He knew it was a favourite meal of Nina's, but she would have stayed in anyway. He brought it into the kitchen and called, 'Nina!' Not 'Neeny'. 'You know your mother has gone? For good, I mean?'

Nina came into the kitchen. 'I guessed, Dad,' she said.

He put the Chinese packs in the microwave and shut its door. 'Which setting do I press, Neeny?' he asked.

Nina turned the microwave on. 'We can't go on like this, can we, Dad?' she said. He shook his head, but otherwise did not speak. 'Mum's only jumped the gun a bit, Dad. We don't have to stay here, you know.' He walked out of the kitchen.

Dad had to be talked to, persuaded, made to see that they couldn't live like this, and that Helen wanted both of them. Why not? She'd have to push his morals out of the window.

Morals! What did they do for anyone, except stop them doing things they wanted to do? She said as much after they had eaten and were having coffee in the sitting-room.

'Well, Neeny, I don't think you can be the judge of what I ought to do, you're only fifteen.'

'Sixteen, Dad,' Nina corrected him. 'You needn't sleep with Helen. If we move in with her there's enough rooms in that house for you to have separate bedrooms. For goodness' sake, Dad, grow up!'

He looked at her in surprise. 'Don't speak to me like that, Neeny,' he said.

Nina realised her mistake. 'Sorry, Dad, but you love Helen and I can't see why you should be apart, that's all.'

Henry looked at his daughter. He said nothing. Obviously he was thinking—about what she had said, Nina hoped.

'I'll go and wash up, Daddy.' She used the little-girl word 'Daddy' instead of the more grown-up 'Dad'. He still did not speak. She washed the dishes and put them away, then peeped back into the sitting-room. 'I'll just take Polly for her run,' she said.

Henry looked up. She noticed he had not put the news on, unusual. 'Right, I'll just make a telephone call,' he said.

I wonder who to, she thought as she put Polly's lead on. It was Polly's short night walk and in twenty minutes, she was back. For a change, she shut the front door very quietly. Henry was still on the telephone. She shot the bolt in the front door and went into the kitchen, fed Polly and filled her water bowl. She watched the little dog eat her meal, drink some water, then she went across the hall, up the stairs. She called out, 'Good-night, Daddy,' on the way. No answer, her father was still on the phone—please to Helen! she thought.

She started work tomorrow with a weekly wage. Helen had promised her that, at sixteen, but tomorrow she would be a little late. She had to go and see Miss Meadows. In the morning she would ring Helen too. Perhaps Helen would tell her that Henry and she were going to live together, that he had rung her the night before. Polly jumped on the bed. She turned to her, put her fingers to her lips and said, 'Sssh, Polly, stay.' She crept to the top of the stairs. Her father had taken the cordless telephone into the sitting-room. The door was open.

She could just see him sitting on the sofa talking earnestly, she hoped to Helen. It would be against her father's principles, she knew. Living in sin, he would call it. But Mum leaving may have made his principles wobble a little. She remembered a saying someone had said at school, some teacher or other, not Miss Meadows, someone else. 'Circumstances alter cases.' Well, whoever had said it was right. She said it out loud to Polly who wagged her tail vigorously and rolled on her back. She loved to be talked to. 'Circumstances alter cases, Polly!' she said and Polly obviously agreed.

If her father was making arrangements to move into Helen's it would be perfect and tomorrow, if she could persuade Miss Meadows to take her back, so much would be better. Funny, she thought, most girls would be crying their eyes out if their mother walked out on them, but apart from that one weep, she didn't care at all. But then there would be Helen. She knew that Margaret had rows by the score with her parents, about clothes and make-up and hair-dos and boys, but she still loved them, loved them to death she said, and Nina believed her. Why wasn't she the same? She looked at the dog, still lying upside down on her duvet. If anything happened to Polly, she daren't even think about it. Why did she love animals so much more than humans? Was it how she was made, was it her fault? It was too big a question even to think about.

That night she dreamed of a gingerbread cottage with a witch who opened the door to her and then beckoned her inside with a long-nailed claw-like hand. She woke with a start, but there was only Polly and her familiar room.

*　　　*　　　*

Nina woke at seven, unusually early for her, but the determination to go and see Miss

Meadows was as strong as ever. She lay for some time, rehearsing what she would say. She would have to eat humble pie, a thing Nina hated probably more than anything in the world. She would knock on the door, or ring the bell, whatever. Then when it was opened, if the old bitch was in—well, if she wasn't, she would try again, but she hoped, having screwed up her courage to do the deed, she would be there. Nina was surprised at the fear she felt. After all, she was sixteen now and considered herself an adult. But she was asking for something that meant so much to her. She visualised going to Helen and saying, 'I've persuaded them, the school I mean, not to expel me, just say I was suspended for the rest of the term, then I was due to leave anyway.' Then Helen would fix something up for her, was it 'one day release'? She couldn't remember because she had never showed up at the careers meeting, now she wished she had but she would study and learn. Oh, it would be wonderful. Sometimes she knew the animals and their illnesses would upset her. One or two who had had to be put down had made her feel as if her heart would break, their eyes looking at her, anxious, pleading, yet totally trusting, almost as if they knew the end of their little life was coming. She could cry, even now, at the thought of it. Her heart seemed to reach out to them.

In the shower, she thought of her father and

his talk with Helen. Had he decided to move in with her? After all, Nina had made it pretty clear she wasn't going to cook and clean, that was for sure. You couldn't live on Chinese and Indian takeaways for ever! Nina put on her white school blouse and black school skirt, taking care that the skirt looked as long as she could possibly make it. Trainers—coloured ones? No, black ankle boots with white socks. She made a face as she put the white socks on. She thought she could never bear to wear them again, but she wanted to look young, young and pathetic. She intended to use the fact that Mum had taken off and was living with her boyfriend part of the story.

Henry had gone by the time she went downstairs. She made herself coffee and inspected the bread. She noticed it was going a bit mouldy at the edges. Mum usually kept a spare loaf in the freezer. She looked. No bread. She settled for Ryvita. She buttered it and scooped on marmalade. She wondered what her father had had for breakfast. There was not a soiled cup and saucer or plate. Then, as she munched, she remembered that his secretary would rush to get him coffee and toast if he told her he had not had breakfast.

She took Polly for her short morning walk then gave her a very small breakfast, a meal she was not really allowed. But Nina would have to shut her up in the house while she made the now dreaded visit to Miss Meadows, so the little treat was well deserved and as Polly gobbled it up, much appreciated. Nina refilled the dog's dish with fresh water and looked at the kitchen clock. Twenty past ten, time to go. 'Won't be long, Polly,' she said. The little dog, recognising from her tone that she was not included in this 'walkies', went and sat in her basket, head on one side, eyes wide.

She took a quick look at herself in the hall mirror as she went out. She had on no mascara, only a very pale lipstick, nothing else. Her hair looked neat, shiny and clean. 'Oh Lord,' she said aloud. Whenever had she felt this anxious about how she looked, what she would say, how she would say it? Never before, she was certain, but a lot was at stake.

She shut the front door quietly behind her and started off. It was not a long walk to the cottage but she found herself wishing it were a good deal longer, and when she arrived at the turning into the cul de sac at the end of which was the little thatched cottage her heart was beating so fast it made her feel as if she was choking. She arrived at the cottage door, lifted the well-polished brass knocker and 'tap tap'. Nothing happened and relief flooded over Nina. No one was in, she would have to try again another day. But she was wrong. There was a short sharp bark, a voice said, 'Quiet,' and Miss Meadows opened the door.

'Yes?' she said, obviously not at first recognising Nina. Then she stood back a little, making no effort to ask her in. 'It's Nina, Nina Mason, isn't it?'

'Yes, Miss Meadows, and I would be so grateful if I could have a word with you.'

'What could you possibly want to speak to me about, Nina? I said everything I had to say at school.'

'Please, Miss Meadows!' Nina hated pleading, especially with the woman whom she hated.

'Very well, though I can't imagine . . .'

Miss Meadows led the way through to what Nina imagined to be her sitting-room. The cottage was rather dark, the windows small. 'Sit down.' She motioned towards a chair and sat down herself.

'How is your dog, Miss Meadows?'

'Very well, Nina.' Miss Meadows was sitting exactly as she had done in school, her back straight and not touching the back of the chair. Nina tried to do the same, kept her feet together and her skirt pulled down to almost cover her knees. Then she spoke her piece, about her mother leaving, apologised for her behaviour at school, her not trying to learn, her truancy, everything. As she poured all this out and watched Miss Meadows' face, she was only too conscious of a sense of failure. The woman's grim expression did not alter, nor did she relax in any way. She listened without comment, not even a nod of the head, and then Nina at last stopped her pleading.

There was a silence that seemed to last for ages. This silence was broken by a noise behind what Nina judged to be the kitchen door. 'That's my dog, I must see to him, but first . . . I am pleased that you have at last decided on a course but sorry that you have jeopardised your chances so flagrantly. I am at a loss to see how you think I can do anything to make up for your behaviour or help you in any way.'

Nina could see everything she had said was hopeless, pointless. 'I wanted you to tell someone, perhaps the new headmistress, and make it that I was not expelled only suspended and was leaving at the end of term anyway.'

Miss Meadows stood up. 'Nina, it is very unfortunate that you made it necessary for us to expel you. This, however, must stand. It is not possible to rescind it and anyway, I feel the use of drugs is not an offence that can be tolerated nor can the punishment for such behaviour be changed.'

Nina lost her temper, burst into tears. 'You don't care, do you! I could do so much good as a veterinary nurse, you know I could. It's not fair, it's not fair, and you could help if you wanted to but you don't. You've always hated me and I hate you!'

'You had better leave, Nina. I can see that your attitude has not changed at all.'

Miss Meadows walked up the little dark passage ahead of Nina and opened the front door. The sunshine and the scent of flowers and cut lawn flooded in. She shut the door behind Nina and the soft sound of it closing seemed to release a rage in her. She walked down the path. When she got to the gate, she banged it so hard the latch broke and fell to the ground. She looked down at the broken piece and kicked it back under the gate and on to the gravel path. The man in the house next door was in the garden using a hoe. He looked up when he heard the bang of the gate, then resumed his work.

Nina walked home in a cloud of rage. When she got home, the rage had gone and a sort of despair had set in. Who would have her now, even if Dad and Helen did try to get her into a private school? The fact that she had been expelled would mean, she was sure, that no school would have her, particularly if they approached Bloody Meadows for an 'assessment' as they call it. What was the use of going to the vet's? If they paid her it would only be for doing the menial work. She would never be allowed to learn to put up drips, help with the anaesthetics. She would be a 'nothing', that's what she would be, a 'nothing'.

Later Helen telephoned. 'You didn't come in. I was worried, are you all right, dear?'

Nina suppressed her longing to cry, which had replaced her rage. 'No, I wasn't feeling very well, Helen.'

'You don't sound very well, Nina.'

224

Nina was afraid Helen would come and see her. She was caring enough. 'I'm better now, it was just a tummy upset, I think.' She hated lying to Helen.

'Well, I've good news for you—at least I hope it's good news, Nina.'

'What is it?'

There was a short pause then Helen said, her voice very soft, 'I can't tell you about it on the telephone, darling.' She sounded shy. She put the telephone down.

Nina did burst into tears then, she was not sure why. Maybe it was Helen's caring tone, her soft gentle way of speaking.

Dad had telephoned Helen last night. Maybe—well, it sounded maybe—he had decided they would move in with her. He would tell Nina tonight when he came home. But she knew, through her tears of rage and frustration, that even if or even when they moved in, she wouldn't be able to get into another school, any school or any training course. Not with her record, her CV. She would have to have GCSEs and A levels or some such shit and it was all that bitch's fault.

As she waited for her father to come home, while she was walking Polly, feeding Polly, her mind was boiling with hate. What could she do to hurt Meadows, to make her pay for wrecking her chances of doing something that she really wanted to do, longed to do?

When Henry came home, he was obviously

225

in a wobbly mood. Nina said, 'What's up, Daddy?'

He hesitated, smiled, coughed and before he told her what she already guessed, poured himself a whisky. 'Helen's coming for us and we're going out to dinner.' Nina waited for more information but he only said, 'We are going to the Silver Knight. Do you want to change, Neeny?'

Nina was disappointed. No mention of going to Helen's to live, but that might come later. Perhaps Helen wanted to be there—after all, she had said she had good news for her. She decided to let it rest and not ask Dad, but wait till they were having dinner at the Silver Knight, wherever and whatever that was.

She and Polly rushed upstairs. Polly dived on to the unmade bed, thinking it was bedtime. Nina dressed in her best miniskirt, tank top and high-heeled boots. Plenty of make-up, after all she was sixteen now.

Downstairs her father was just having a second drink. 'Dutch courage,' he said, smiling.

'You look nice, Dad.' Nina was quite sincere. He did look nice, quite handsome in fact. Best suit. His figure wasn't bad for his age either. 'Good tie,' she added. She had noticed that he was looking at her tank top, but her praise for his appearance successfully put him off making any remark about the shortness of her miniskirt or the showing of her midriff. He hadn't seen her new boots before because she had taken the money Mum kept in a tin in the kitchen for paying the gardener or the window cleaner. They were black and shiny and the heels were really something, so high, made her look taller.

Helen called for them and they went straight out to the car. As they passed the turning at the end of which lay Miss Meadows' thatched cottage, Nina pictured the humiliating morning, the straight-backed, straight-lipped woman, refusing her any help of any kind. Suddenly what she would do to pay the old hag out burst into her mind. It was as if something was already settled, and just as suddenly she knew she could now enjoy the coming evening. She felt good about herself again. She knew now exactly what she had to do and somehow she would do it.

When they arrived at the Silver Knight Hotel they sat in the bar, Helen and Nina on the rather hard settee and Dad on a chair. The furniture was all red velvet and to Nina's eyes rather posh. Helen looked great. A long green silky-looking dress made her look very slinky though her face and rather severely pulled back hair-do—a bit like, Nina thought, Princess Anne's—belied the sexy dress.

'Nina,' Helen said, putting a hand over Nina's, 'your father has decided it would be better for all of us if we lived in my house. Do you agree?'

227

Nina didn't merely agree, she was delighted. Dad came back with a glass of white wine for Helen and one for her and a whisky for himself. He looked from Helen to Nina.

'I've told her, Henry, she approves.' Helen looked at Nina, smiling.

'Oh, yes, Dad, I do!'

'Well, you will act as our chaperone,' Dad said, really meaning it, Nina could see.

'Dad, don't be such an old fuddy-duddy. I shan't notice if you sleep together.'

He looked across at Helen and they both laughed. 'Teenagers!' he said, but nothing more was said about their sleeping arrangements.

The rest of the time together was mostly taken up with talk about the move. Helen told Nina that she was to have the blue bedroom. Nina was delighted. It was much larger than her own with much more room for her new computer with all its bits and pieces. Except for the verterinary nurse subject, which was not mentioned, Nina felt she had never had a happier evening. Why, she wondered, hadn't it always been like this? Or maybe, was it she who had changed? She looked at Helen and Dad sitting there, loving each other, holding hands occasionally although they were both oldies. Whey hadn't Helen married Dad and Mum married her boyfriend? Life was weird.

The dinner was gorgeous. Prawn cocktail, Nina's favourite. Roast duck. Dad let her have a second glass of white wine with her duck. 'Now you're sixteen,' he said. 'But I hope you won't make a habit of it.' He looked sincere but obviously Helen being there comforted and reassured him. Nina said nothing about her visit to Miss Meadows, and the business of her future career was not mentioned. Helen did say, 'It will be lovely to have you both with me. It's yours and Nina's home now, Henry.'

The sweet trolley was wheeled round full of luscious goodies. Nina was just going to have raspberry gâteau when something happened at the next table that thrilled her so much she ordered nothing, just sat, her eyes on the dish they were having. Crêpes Suzette. The waiter set fire to the brandy and the flames leapt round the little pancakes, blue and tipped with orange. Nina was fascinated. She watched as the flames died away and the waiter served the dish. Her eyes were wide, the pupils dilated.

'Can I have that, Daddy? she said.

Henry waved the idea away. 'No, no, Nina, it's only a little pancake filled with orange—isn't it orange, Helen?'

She nodded, 'Yes, usually, Henry.' Helen looked at Nina's face, still lit up with an expression of pure delight.

'It's a very expensive dish, Nina, and not really worth the money.'

'Never mind, Henry, if Nina would like it, I would be delighted to let her have it.'

Helen summoned the waiter and ordered

Crêpes Suzette for Nina. When it came Nina looked at the silver serving dish. 'It's the flames, they're so beautiful,' she said. Maybe the waiter put a little more spirit on the pancakes, but the flames were higher and more colourful than they had been at the next table. Nina seemed transfixed. She watched the fire lick round the plate and seemed almost sad when it died down and the waiter served the pancakes, still flaming a tiny bit. She looked up at Helen. 'Flames are beautiful, aren't they, Helen, more beautiful than flowers or anything.'

Helen smiled, but looked a tiny bit surprised at Nina's reaction. 'As long as they are under control, Nina, and not in control,' she said lightly.

Nina ate the sweet and admitted she found it a bit disappointing. 'I knew you would, Neeny,' her father said. 'But you wouldn't listen.'

Helen broke in. 'But how are you to know, Henry, until you try? You can't always act on other people's opinion.'

Nina was still seeing in her mind's eye those beautiful flames. She kept looking round the room in case anyone else was having something that needed setting fire to before or as it was served, but no one did. 'What do you ask for when you want a dish on fire?' she asked Helen.

'Flambé,' she answered, telling Nina how to

230

spell it.

'Don't they do it to Christmas puddings?' she asked.

'Yes, sometimes.'

'We never did.' Nina looked at her father, almost accusingly.

'I always thought it a great waste of brandy,' he said.

'Oh, Henry, no. Wait till Christmas and we will do it, Nina.'

Nina's eyes lit up. 'I love to see it burning,' she said.

'Well, we can have a big bonfire on Guy Fawkes night, you'll like that. No fireworks though—so many animals spend a terrified evening because of the bangs.'

That night, before she got into bed, she added two more flames to the ones that framed Miss Meadows' face, only these were not only red and orange, they had blue streaks in them like the ones in the restaurant. She smiled as she used the crayons. She felt so happy. 'We're going to move, Polly,' she said. Helen and Dad seemed to think they would move in about a week. Helen had said, 'What rubbish, Henry dear. You can't live on takeaways. Lock up the house and move in tomorrow.' Dad had tried to delay. Nina could tell he was frightened by change.

Mum gone, a new house, a new woman, a new way of life. After Helen had gone home, they had had a talk together about the move.

This time Nina felt she was supporting him. She told him how lucky he was to have found a woman like Helen who admired and loved him. 'It's all so quick, Neeny,' he had said about four times. 'Why wait, Dad, you and Helen aren't young, why waste time?' She wondered how Mum would feel if she could hear her darling daughter (darling! Some hopes!) talking to Dad. She supposed she would be very surprised. Nina had always got her way with Dad but this time really it was for his own good, and hers of course. She made his Ovaltine and when at last she got into bed, she felt worn out with persuading him that what he was doing was not immoral or wrong in any way!

Grown-ups! When would they learn, she thought. She pushed Polly a little bit further down the bed to make room for her feet. She was just about to switch the light off, then changed her mind, slipped out of bed, picked up the crayons and did two more orange, red and blue flames. She hadn't noticed when she did the others, but these last two just completed the frame. Miss Meadows was now surrounded on all sides by flames. 'Flambé' she said and got back into bed beside Polly.

Once cuddled down in bed she couldn't sleep. Perhaps it was the large meal, or the two glasses of wine, or those lovely, lovely flames which kept blazing up before her eyes the moment she closed them. There was a programme on television she loved, at least the beginning and end of it. Was it called *London's Burning* . . .? She couldn't remember because after the wonderful roaring, devouring flames on the screen at the beginning of the film, it got stupid and was all about the love lives of the firemen. Once the flames had gone she didn't want to see any more of it. Once they showed a house on fire and the men climbing in, trying to rescue someone, but that hadn't been real, not really as a blazing house would be, not like tonight—those amazing coloured flames were like no others she had ever seen. Not like the newly lit rather smoky smelly flames when she and Jacko had torched the school. They had roared a bit at first. It had been fun but not like those lovely dancing flames at the dinner with Helen and Dad. Flames were beautiful, beautiful.

CHAPTER TWELVE

The move went very smoothly, though of course it was not really much of a move. Nina took down her posters, the ones she wanted to keep. Their gardener packed up into their original boxes Nina's computer, printer and all the other paraphernalia and carried them to the car. She packed up all her clothes, make-up and special treasures, including her school books 'just in case'. When she unpacked in her new home, it was wonderful—a large table for her computer, a lovely bed with super covers. The dressing-table had four little drawers for make-up, a slightly bigger one for tissues, hair brushes and things. A chest of drawers and a bed for Polly. Helen had thought of everything, even a small bookcase for her. Nina made a face, unpacked her school books and put them on the top shelf, no others. Nina wasn't much of a reader, but cassettes, and her music player, this was a lovely shelf for the cassettes. There was simply nothing Helen had not thought of, her own telephone too. She hoped Dad was as happy as she was, but he was not moving in till this evening when he came home from work.

There was a light tap on the door.

'Come in.'

It was Helen. She had that rather shy look on her face that Nina loved. Somehow it made her, Nina, feel older and made her want to take care of Helen. Funny feeling considering Helen was a veterinary surgeon full of knowledge and wisdom in charge of so much.

'Everything all right, Nina?'

'Wonderful, Helen, thank you so much for making it so—perfect.'

'Come and see what else I've done.'

They moved out of Nina's room and along the upstairs hall. She opened the door of the room next to Nina's. 'Your bathroom, Nina.'

Another door: 'My bedroom then a bathroom,' then another: 'Henry's bedroom.'

Nina laughed—no, she giggled. Helen turned on her sharply.

'Don't laugh at your father, Nina, he is doing what he believes is right. I admire him for it. If he believes he and I should not be together until he is free, well, I support him, and so should you.'

Nina looked at her. 'Dad's lucky to have you, Helen,' she said.

Helen smiled. 'You can start work in the kennels on Monday, Nina.'

Nina nodded. 'That's all I'll ever be, isn't it, a kennel maid?'

'We shall see, Nina. Now go and ring your mother. Be tactful, dear, be tactful.'

Helen went downstairs and collected her things to go out again. Nina knew she was going back to the surgery. Such kindness, Nina thought, but it didn't alter the fact that she was a kennel maid and all Helen could say about that was 'We shall see.'

Dad came 'home' that evening. The sitting-room was bigger and different, but he seemed at home and the two golden retrievers greeted him with enthusiasm. Polly had met them before and got on well with them. Dad was watching the news when Nina came in. Helen was not yet home. Nina poured a whisky and added soda, how she knew her father liked it.

'Nina!' He looked astonished by her action.

'Dad, dear,' she said, 'this is her home and your home. I'm the lodger but one day I'll get a flat of my own.' He sipped the drink. 'You're partners now, you and Helen, you're an item, a couple, see? All right, you don't think you should have sex yet, till you and Mum are separated, divorced, legally parted, that's up to you, Dad.'

'I know I'm an old fuddy-duddy, Neeny.'

'No, you're Dad, you're a young fuddy-duddy.' She looked at her wrist-watch. 'Helen won't be home for a bit, come up and see my room.'

Helen came home about twenty minutes later and they had dinner together. Nina left them sitting very close together on the settee. Once in her room, she telephoned Elizabeth.

'Nina, where are you, how are you? How is Henry?'

'We've moved in. I've got a lovely room. Dad and Helen have got separate rooms.' Despite Helen's admonishments she giggled.

'Don't laugh at your father, it's the way he is.'

Nina giggled again. 'I bet he will soon be creeping along to Helen's room, Mum,' she said.

'Nina, it's not your business.' Mum sounded so like Mum.

'How's Stanley?'

'He's fine, and so am I, Nina.'

'You could have talked to me about him

more, Mum.'

Elizabeth agreed. 'I know, Nina, I know. But it's nice of you to phone me.'

'Goodbye, Mum, see you soon.'

She put the telephone down. It had been weird to speak to Mum from another house, another home.

Nina had started to keep a diary. She sat cross-legged on the bed. Polly pattered around the room, ignoring her new bed. She leapt on to Nina's. 'Poll,' Nina said to the dog, 'we are the victims of a broken home.' She wrote that in her new diary. She didn't feel sad about it, only excited.

She had brought the fiery picture of Miss Meadows with her. She had been glad that it wasn't on the door or on the wall when Helen had come in. Now she got it out, and drawing-pinned it on her door again. She knew what she intended to do to pay her out, but she would need help. She dialled Jacko. He sounded very thrilled to hear her, she hadn't seen him for some days. She outlined her plan to him. She knew she had only to ask, push him a bit perhaps, and he would do anything for her. She supposed he was in love with her. They had had sex a few times but she wasn't in love with him. Sex was all right, but she wasn't mad on it. It did make men, boys, do what you wanted them to.

There was silence for a time on the other end of the telephone after she spoke. She told him her plans again.

'Nina, we can't!' he said. He sounded shocked to death.

'Well, if you don't want to help me, just say so,' she said.

'No, no, Nina, I'll help you, I'll help you, sure.'

'OK. I'll ring you.' She put the phone down and switched on her television. News. Why was it always news, or a repeat funny programme? She stretched out on the bed, Polly beside her, looked at Miss Meadows, and then back to the television. In a way she felt a bit redundant here with Helen and Dad. She must make more use of Jacko and his bike. Should she ask Dad, or Mum, or Stanley (perhaps it might be a good thing to have two sets of parents), should she ask one of them, or two of them, for a moped? Why not? 'Yes, Polly, when we're a bit more settled in, we'll ask Dad for a moped. Oh, he'll carry on about safety and I'm too young to be out at night alone on a bike.' She got off the bed and opened her window, pulled back the curtains. The daylight had not quite gone and she could see across the fields. The town, not far away, made a pink glow in the sky.

There, somewhere under that pink glow, was their house where she had lived for sixteen years. From her window she could only see a farmhouse, way across the fields in the trees. So different from the road they had lived in with its symmetrical lines of flowering cherry trees and neatly cut lawns. The air seemed fresher too and smelled quite different. She looked up at the sky, at the clouds, white and feathery. 'Please make me a veterinary nurse,' she said aloud, then went downstairs to fetch Polly a bowl of the little crunchy biscuits she was mad about.

She crept by the sitting-room. The door was shut and there was no sound of television. She hoped they were kissing and cuddling, or even making love. She filled Polly's food bowl, poured herself a glass of milk and carefully, trying not to make a sound, opened the biscuit tin and took out two biscuits, one for herself and one as a treat for Polly for being in a new strange bedroom. Nina felt very safe, very much at home, no creeping out after she had pretended she was going to bed. No need to tell lies to deceive Helen. She thought again of Jacko. She could never have taken him home, that is, in the old home. He had one ear-ring, one through his nose, and unseen, one through his tongue. He was barking really, but Nina liked him, and sex was OK with him. Mum was quick, she would have guessed about the sex, and Dad would have gone spare about the piercings. But anyway, she must make a date, tell him to call for her and then she'd tell him what she wanted, needed him to do for her.

When she got back to her room she gave Polly her biscuit, then she rang Jacko again.

239

They arranged a meet, Jacko to pick her up on his bike. 'Bring my lid, Jacko,' she said.

'I will.' There was a little pause, then he said, 'I love you, Nina, I truly do. There'll never be anyone else, Nina.'

'Jacko, we are too young to be in love, permanent. I want to have a good time before I settle down—don't you? You're only seventeen.'

'I know, I know, I want to have a good time too, but I want it to be with you, Nina.'

Nina's lower lip stuck out, a commitment to anyone wasn't her idea in life at all, but she didn't want to put him off, so she said, 'You're sweet, Jacko,' and put the phone down.

He'd do what she wanted him to, she was certain. He'd tell her about bikes too. Jacko would look down on the kind of bike she was hoping to get. She planned what she would do—meet Jacko, ask him to tell her what kind of bike to get, make him feel as if he was the expert, that always pleased boys. She had always found that, since she started being aware of her sexual attraction when she was about thirteen. She could see why Mum and Dad had split up, or thought she could. Mum always seemed to put Dad down, so Dad had sort of withdrawn into himself. Nina thought that was why he loved her better than Mum, his daughter better than his wife. She buttered him up just like she did Jacko. She wondered, did Mum look up to her new man and make him feel clever, gifted? Perhaps she did, and did Helen make Dad feel more important? Yes, she decided she did. Dad seemed different, more relaxed, more like a man in love.

OK, he'd worry and fuss about the divorce, the money and the house, but Helen could wait, be patient. Nina had never admired anyone before in her life. Mostly she disliked people, but she did admire Helen, really admired her. Mum she wrote off with not much of a thought. She had always been good to Polly, that was a plus, but she was not, and never could be, like Helen. The thing Nina wanted to be was as much like Helen as she possibly could, but not until she had done what she had to do. Maybe she had lost the chance for ever to be exactly like Helen, a real professional, and the one who had made her lose it must be punished. One more look at the picture on the door, and Nina switched out the light and went to sleep, this time without horrible dreams.

Polly woke her in the night. She looked at her bedside clock: 2.15 a.m. Polly wanted a wee, she supposed. She put on her lead, half asleep, went downstairs very quietly. In the kitchen the two big retrievers were in their large beds. They hardly stirred. One opened his eyes, looked at her and his tail wagged slowly. She opened the back door, took Polly out. Nina was right, she wanted a wee and the smell round the new garden was a must. Dogs were conscious of change. Nina thought it must seem very different to Polly. The larger room, the new dog bed. She wished she had brought her blanket, she would go back to the old house and get it, ask Dad for the key. Then she had a bright idea. She hadn't got to work till Monday, she would telephone Jacko, say meet her there, they would have the place to themselves.

Dad and Helen would be at work. What a good idea! No one to disturb them, they could talk, make coffee. She could soften Jacko up with a bit of snogging and a talk about the bike she hoped to get. Then the real plans could be made. Jacko worked in his father's garage, a bit of a wreck of a place. He could get time off when he wanted. Nina sometimes thought his father didn't much care if he were there or not, but he got free petrol for his motor bike and anything else he needed for it. He was quite a good mechanic too, so he said, so that would be no problem. Free petrol too, that was useful!

Polly decided she would come in now. Nina hoped she wouldn't do this every night. They crept through the kitchen and upstairs. All the doors upstairs were shut. Nina was glad she hadn't met Dad creeping along to Helen's room. What a bummer that would have been. Back in her room, she took off Polly's lead, put her firmly in her new bed. 'Stay,' she said. Polly looked at her. 'Stay,' she said again. Polly was sometimes obedient—sometimes! This time she curled up as if she intended to stay. Nina got back into bed. The idea of using their house had been a good one, and all thanks to Polly and the garden 'walkies'. This time she lay awake thinking.

*   *   *

Nina sat opposite Jacko in what she thought of now as the 'old house'. Though they had only left it a few hours ago, the place already felt curiously deserted, and for some reason she could not explain she did not attempt to go into, or even look into, her old room. That part of Nina she felt was over, finished, changed. She was not sure if it were a nice feeling or a nasty one but one thing she did feel, it was scary, weird, her favourite word.

They snogged for a while and Jacko suggested they went upstairs, but her 'No' was dominant and forceful. He only suggested it once, but was curious. 'You said they wouldn't be back, your mum and dad, why not? We've got the place to ourselves.'

Nina shook her head. 'You wouldn't understand,' she said.

Jacko looked hurt. 'Oh yes, I would, if you explained why you don't want to when I do.'

Nina frowned. 'I'll make some coffee,' she said. At the door she turned. 'It's here, you

243

know, in Mum and Dad's house, with them gone, splitting up and everything, I just couldn't.'

Jacko shrugged, looked at her puzzled. Nina noticed his eyelashes were long and black, in fact he was good-looking. Nina had not really noticed him before. She let him have sex with her when she wanted something. He had often done her homework for her, studied up and made notes for her. He was very good at copying people's handwriting and had written notes, quite a few times, to the school saying, 'My daughter has a very bad cold and I think it is wise to keep her at home.' The last one Nina thought up was, 'Her Auntie has broken her hip and my daughter is helping her in the house for a few days.'

Nina brought in the coffee and some biscuits she had found in the biscuit tin. 'It's like the *Marie Celeste*—you know, that story of the boat they found with no crew on it and cups of tea on the table still warm.'

Jacko shook his head. 'I never knew that.' Jacko wasn't a great reader either.

'Now, Jacko, there's something I want to do and I want you to help me.'

Jacko took his coffee and looked up at her. 'Yes, so you said but—'

Nina put her hand gently over his mouth. 'Listen to me, I only want to frighten her, give her a real scare.'

Jacko took her hand away from his mouth.

'Yes, but how can we, like you say, make a little fire, how do we know it won't take over the whole cottage?'

'Course it won't! Don't be so silly, Jacko, we're only going to use a tiny bit of petrol, not like we did at the school.'

Jacko continued to look worried. 'I know, but Nina, she's an old lady, you know, she might have a heart attack or something.'

'Oh, come on. It's other people she makes have heart attacks, what about expelling me?'

Jacko rolled his eyes, drank his coffee and didn't answer.

'Well, if you don't want to help me, just say so and I'll find someone else.'

Jacko immediately reacted just as Nina knew he would. He came closer to her, put his arms round her. Nina turned her face away. 'Oh, Nina, I'll help you. It's only a bit of fun, isn't it, and the old girl deserves it—come to that she wasn't too nice to me when I was there.'

They started really planning Nina's revenge. She was beginning to look forward to it. They planned to go out together on Tuesday, say they were going to the pictures. That evening they would collect together the items they wanted for their—as Jacko put it, quoting his dad—little jape. Jacko was going to get the petrol needed. He would get it from the same place as they got it for the school. His dad's garden shed, where a full petrol can was usually left for the lawn mower. If by any chance the can was empty then they would have to think again. Once Nina was geared up to do something, she wanted to get on with it. Then the other thing was a ladder, only a little one. Night time. It was going to be exciting. Dark and silent. That little road would be deserted at about three in the morning. They'd have to be quiet though, not make a noise and have some nervous old biddy peep round her net curtains and peer out, probably hoping something was happening, anything to relieve the long long night. They mustn't be seen or heard.

'Say Thursday then, after we've got the stuff.'

Jacko nodded. 'All right, but it's a big thing to do, we'll have to be very careful.'

'Do it properly,' Nina said crisply. 'Do it properly and be really professional.'

'Professional! That's a queer way of putting it.'

Nina felt suddenly a surge of sexual desire. It wasn't Jacko who had brought this sudden feeling on. It was, Nina knew, the thought of fire, flames. 'Come on then, let's go upstairs.'

Jacko's face lit up. 'Yeah, let's do that!'

Upstairs Jacko looked at the closed doors: 'Which?'

Nina felt the same feeling about her own room. 'In there.' She made for her parents' room.

'Is this where your mum and dad . . . you know?' Jacko looked around the room. They both climbed into one bed. Nina had undressed in her usual businesslike way. Jacko had often tried to make their love-making more romantic. To her, love-making was exciting, but need not take too much time. Afterwards they lay, side by side, smoking. Nina's mind was totally preoccupied with her own thoughts. Jacko fondled her breast.

'I love you, Nina, so much, I would do anything in the world for you.'

Nina stubbed her cigarette out in the little Crown Derby ornament on the bedside table. The sound of Jacko's voice brought her back from her thoughts. 'What?' she said.

'What were you thinking about, Nina?'

Nina frowned. 'This thing we had at the meal Dad took us to, they lit the brandy.'

'It sounds daft.'

'Oh, Jacko, shut up.' She got out of bed and pulled her woolly over her head. 'You don't understand, you just don't.' When her face surfaced through the neck of the sweater, it looked quite different, sulky, cross, cold. 'Come on, I want to go home.' The mood was gone, sex now was nothing, the means to an end.

'I'll see you Tuesday then.' Jacko dragged on his trousers.

'Tuesday, oh yes. We'll hide the ladder in the garden outside.' She went to the bedroom window and pointed to the big mass of hydrangeas at the bottom of the path. 'There, look, hide it behind there.' She was impatient now, tired of Jacko, tired of the subject. 'Let's go,' she said and Jacko followed her out.

CHAPTER THIRTEEN

Monday, she started at the kennels, sweeping up, cleaning out the dogs' mess, doing the cats' trays. These were the animals who were 'staying in hospital', as Nina put it. She felt so sorry for them, the cats hated the cages, some had got plastic collars on so that they couldn't get at their stitches. One cat had a drip put up that morning because he had come in with a high temperature and was very dehydrated which meant he needed water, fluid, put back in his body. He was quite ill, but Nina, supervised by the nurse, managed to get him to eat a little. 'You're good with animals, Nina,' the nurse had said. Not in a patronising way but really sounding as if she meant what she was saying. Nina blossomed under praise.

The first day went well. Everyone, including Helen, seemed pleased with her. Nina felt in her right place, doing what she wanted to do. The waiting-room too was interesting, so many different animals: Dogs, cats, budgies, a snake, an iguana. How did Helen and the other vets know so much about every animal? By night time, or at least closing time for the surgery, she was tired out, emotionally and physically, but happy. Helen ran her home, asked if she was going out tonight. No word about if so, be in by ten thirty, or who with? When Nina answered no, she was staying in, but going out with Jacko tomorrow evening, Helen seemed pleased. 'Good, we can all three have dinner together then, which will be nice.' It was all so very different, so much less tense. Tomorrow would be different. She had kept the key of the old house and Dad had not asked for it back, so tomorrow they could store away the petrol and the ladder. Nina felt a little thrill at the thought of it.

Tuesday was not quite such a nice or exciting day as Monday. It was a sweeping up and cleaning day for Nina. The senior veterinary nurse was back. She had had an extra day on her holiday. On Monday, the other two nurses had been helpful and accepted Nina as one of them. Coffee together, cup of tea at tea time with them. All very comfortable. The senior nurse was older and obviously a protocol plus type. 'Wash the table down, sweep up all this fur. Come along, you're here to clean up after the nurses, not dawdle about trying to watch the vet carry out the operations.' The practice consisted of three veterinary surgeons and dealt only with small animals: cats, dogs, rabbits and all types of pets. Helen was the head of the practice, and she was trusted and liked. People brought their kittens and puppies for neutering or if they were ill. The reception area was quite sumptuous, at least to Nina, who had no idea what any other vets' reception areas were like. She tried to get experience but now Mrs Erskine, the senior nurse, was back, she was kept to her more menial tasks. Helen had several house calls so she was not there to stick up for her. The evening was a little on Nina's mind. She hoped that Jacko's father would have filled that wretched can and that he would be able to get a ladder or a pair of steps. Also that Jacko's father wouldn't miss the petrol or the can.

Thursday was the day. She would be so pleased to give the old bitch a real fright. That would pay her out for the very thing that was happening here in this very surgery today. All Miss Meadows' fault. She wondered how many of the pupils and teachers had the occasional smoke. Cannabis was common nearly everywhere, Nina believed. One boy at school had told her that if ever she felt like a weed, there was an usherette at the cinema that carried. 'Only grass though, nothing stronger,' he had warned. Nina hadn't bothered, she could do without it, and the couple of roaches Miss Meadows had caught her with had been given to her in the playground by a kid who had wanted to do an exchange for notes on a class he had missed. She couldn't—no, wouldn't—drop him in it, so she'd just kept shtum and said nothing, but look what it had done to her. Old Meadows had chosen to make an example of her, Nina, because she had always disliked her, picked on her, that's why she had fallen out with Mum. She wouldn't listen to her about Miss Meadows, again and again she had said she didn't want to go to school on this beastly teacher's day. Mum never said, 'What does she do?' or 'Why does she dislike you so much?' No, parents didn't listen. Margaret's parents didn't, they were both in jobs, out all day, tired out when they came home in the evening, too tired to listen to Margaret, so she, like Nina, gave up trying. Helen would be different, of that Nina was certain. She would make time, even though her life was full of work and tension and she worried about her patients too. She would always listen. She was that kind of person. How lucky Dad was to have found her.

Tuesday evening Jacko called for her after Helen, Dad and she had had a meal. Helen had been quietly insistent. 'You only have a sandwich at the surgery, dear,' she said to Nina. 'You must have one good meal, and I feel I must insist on that.' Her tone was gentle and Nina felt that she quite approved of Jacko, though she had never met him.

Dad of course had to put his oar in. 'I'm not sure she and this Jacko are a good thing,' he said.

Helen looked at Nina. 'Well, from what I've seen of Nina so far, I think she is sensible and when you're sixteen, you've got to judge characters, make your own decisions, make mistakes sometimes.'

'Jacko's OK, Helen, he really is.' She could not look Helen in the eye as she said it. What would her future stepmother have to say if she told her the truth, said Jacko had helped her burn down part of the school, and at this moment was probably stealing petrol from his father's garden shed to start another one? But this was something that had to be done and even Helen could not have stopped her.

After the meal Nina changed into jeans and a light top; the days were getting warmer now and the nights shorter. Jacko called for her. When she heard the bike, Helen went through the hall and opened the front door. 'Come in, Jacko, Nina won't be long.' Nina was horrified. Dad would now see Jacko's ear-ring, he might have his nose ring in too, a recent adornment. As Nina came down the stairs she heard them going into the sitting-room and Helen saying, 'Henry, this is Nina's friend Jacko.'

She followed them in. Dad had stood up, switched off the inevitable news and was looking at Jacko as if he were some rare species from another kingdom—and yes, of course, he had put in his nose ring to impress his girlfriend. Helen looked completely

252

relaxed and at ease. 'Coffee, Jacko?' she said.

Dad, thoroughly put out, said, 'If you can drink it with that nose thing in.' His remark was meant to be sarcastic but Helen turned it cleverly.

'Oh, I don't think nose rings stop you drinking coffee, do they, Jacko?'

He refused the coffee, but looked appealingly at Nina.

'We must go, Helen,' she said.

Helen smiled at Jacko. 'I think they're rather smart, your rings. Did it hurt to have them done, particularly the nose one?'

Jacko shook his head. 'Not much—a bit though, but only when they, you know, made a hole.'

Helen nodded and put a hand up to her ear. 'I was terrified when I went to have my ears pierced, but all my friends were having it done. They laughed at me, and in the end I got up enough courage to have it done.'

Jacko smiled. 'You're a vet, aren't you?' Helen nodded. 'Qualified and all that?' Again she nodded. 'That's a job worth doing, I reckon.'

'Come on, Jacko,' Nina said.

'Good-night, Mr Mason.' He looked uncertainly at Helen.

'Helen,' she said.

Jacko smiled back at her. Nina had never seen her boyfriend as relaxed with adults before. They made for the door.

'Don't keep her out too late, Jacko,' Helen said.

As they crossed the hall to the front door they heard Dad say, 'Why do they want to put those rings and things in themselves, it's barbaric, uncivilised,' and Helen's much quieter tone: 'Well, dear, it will disappear in time, we all do things when we're young. Didn't you?'

When they got outside Jacko handed Nina her helmet. 'She's all right, your Dad's new girlfriend. She's real cool, isn't she, real cool!'

He had got the petrol but not the ladder. 'Can't get a ladder, but I found a pretty tall pair of steps. Why do we want them, though?'

Nina explained her plan. 'We'll wait till it's really dark and there's no one about, then we'll take the steps and the can to the back of the cottage. You've arranged to borrow your dad's car?'

Jacko hesitated and looked a bit sheepish. 'Well, not exactly asked, but I took his spare set of keys.'

'Won't he hear us drive away?'

'Dad? You must be joking. He keeps the car outside in the road. We haven't got a posh house like you.'

Nina nodded. 'And he won't wake up?'

'Dad, no, he's usually got too much beer in his belly, sleeps like a log, or hog, whichever word you want to use.'

Jacko's mother had taken off some time

254

ago, he mostly fended for himself. His garage job didn't pay much, but he never moaned about it, just picked up a bit more money where he could, cleaning a car, mowing a lawn. Nina rather admired him for that. She bought him a jumper once, she wheedled the bread out of Dad, but Jacko hadn't been pleased. He liked the jumper all right, but said he didn't like her buying it for him. They had had quite a row, nearly split up over it. But they made it up in the end and he'd taken the jumper and worn it too. But it taught Nina that some people are sensitive about being poor, and didn't like presents. Some, like Una, a girl at school, would grab anything she could, though she certainly wasn't as poor as Jacko's dad.

These were the things about people that Nina would have liked to talk over with Mum but Mum seemed not to be bothered about such problems and Nina's troubles, and Dad was always too busy. He would give her a present if she was miserable about something, it wasn't always buttering him up for something she wanted. Mum thought it was, but sometimes it was just to try and make Dad listen to her, give her a bit of advice, tell her why people behaved as they did.

Why did Miss Meadows hate her so? At first they had got on all right, then irritation had grown between them. Nina became rude and insulting, Miss Meadows turned more and more against her, and now it had all ended like this. Would she have changed if she had known what it would result in? No, she thought, I couldn't be bothered, the lack of support was all too much to put up with. The burning, the lovely burning of the school had helped more than anything, only Jacko knew this. He had been nervous but she hadn't.

There was little more Nina wanted to say to him. All she wanted was him to get the ladder, steps or whatever, and Thursday was the night. Wednesday, tomorrow, was no good as Helen had asked someone to dinner and wanted Nina to be there. She said good-night to Jacko in a rather offhand way. He looked hurt, so she made up to him by one of their special kisses. 'See you on Thursday,' he said. 'What time?'

'About ten?' Nina suggested.

'Yes, that's OK, if that's what you want.'

They parted, but neither realised that a lot was to happen before they would meet again.

*   *   *

Wednesday passed much as usual at the surgery. A dog was brought in who looked exactly like Polly. She had a large lump on her neck which was to be removed under general anaesthetic. Because she looked so much like Polly Nina could not resist going to her little cage where she sat in a corner in a plastic dog bed. The owner had brought in a blanket.

Many owners did this to make the dog feel more at home. The Jack Russell looked at Nina with big, brown bewildered eyes every time she came near. She had to speak to the dog. Her name was Betsy. She had to try and reassure the little creature that everyone was on her side, wanting the best for her. No need to be frightened. She was standing in front of the little wire kennel talking. 'Everyone here is clever and will make you better.'

One of the nurses came by and laughed at her. 'You'd be surprised if she answered you and said, "Thanks, but I'd rather go home, thank you."'

Nina flared up. 'Don't speak to me like that. They should be talked to! They understand all we say to them.'

The nurse looked surprised at Nina's tone and obvious rage. 'I was only teasing, of course. We don't really think they understand exactly what we say, but they like to be talked to, as you say.'

Nina scowled at her. 'Well, don't mock me then!'

'Sorry'. The nurse moved off, surprised.

After work Nina went home, had a bath, and dressed for the dinner guest. She didn't know who was coming and had forgotten to ask, though she presumed it would be an oldie. She was wrong. It was 'young Harper', the one Dad had so resented and Mum had been going to ask for dinner. It had never come off because the split was looming. Dad seemed quite relaxed with the young man, largely due, Nina felt, to the way Helen handled the situation. The dinner was nicely served and Helen hardly had to leave the room because she employed someone who came in and did the meal, and all the washing up.

Nina felt a slight compassion towards Mum, who, if she had gone ahead with the invite, would have had to do all the work herself. Money helped, Nina thought, but then Helen and Dad both earned. Mum didn't. She should have found a job, trained for one, not just taken up painting, which brought in nothing in the way of bread.

'You're very quiet, Nina,' Dad said suddenly.

'Was I, Dad? I was thinking.'

'I won't ask what about,' Dad said laughing.

'Oh, I don't mind, I was just thinking how much easier it would be for me to get around if I had a moped.'

Nina could sense that, in spite of the guest, Dad was gathering his forces to object but 'young Harper' broke in.

'Good idea, my sister has got one. It's a great saving on Dad's car, he says. She used to borrow mine when I was at home, now I've got a car, an old banger though.'

Dad mumbled on about dangerous roads, too young, but 'young Harper' went on: 'My sister is just seventeen, but she's had it some months now, loves it.'

'Well, we'll see,' Dad said.

Nina looked at Helen, who gave her a sly wink as if to say 'Leave it for the moment' so Nina let it drop, well pleased with the guest Dad had so disliked when he had talked about him to Mum at the 'old house'. Perhaps being in love with Helen had already made him more tolerant about everyone.

After they had had coffee, Nina made her escape and went to her room to listen to music, look at television or play computer games, all of which she felt would be a good deal less boring than the conversation downstairs.

Jacko rang while she was in her room. 'Everything ready?' she asked him.

'Yep, well, I got those steps, not as good as a ladder, but I couldn't—'

Nina cut him off. 'Don't worry, what I'm thinking about is the petrol. I suddenly remembered, in the shed at home, I mean when Dad and Mum were together, there was a syringe thing for spraying the roses. It was quite big, it would hold quite a bit of petrol. We can spray the thatch with it, then chuck up a match and whew, up she goes!' She giggled a bit, but there was no answering giggle from the other end of the telephone.

'I don't know, Nina, I don't like the idea all that much, I told you that.'

Nina sighed noisily into the receiver. 'Jacko,

it's only a joke, just to pay her out, give her a fright, try and be a bit laid back about it, for goodness' sake. I know what I'm doing.'

Nina opened a drawer and scrambled round in it to find her cigarettes. Strictly contraband. She knew Helen would be against her smoking just as much as her Dad, but she didn't care. Jacko was being such a pain about it all. She lit the cigarette.

'You smoking?' Jacko asked.

'Yes, and don't start going on about that!'

He just said, 'Thatch burns pretty quickly, you have to pay masses to get it insured.'

'Yeah, yeah, but we're not going to do enough damage to make her want to be worried about insurance, just a tiny bit of the thatching. Nothing way out, I promise.'

Jacko went on a bit more but he ended, 'I'll do anything for you, Nina, you know that.'

Nina wasn't impressed, but she didn't want to put him off completely. She hadn't anyone else to help her, and she was a bit scared of being out alone at two or three in the morning, so she didn't snap his head off as she would have liked to do.

'I know you would, Jacko, it's just that you worry too much.' She managed a 'darling' at the end of the sentence, with some difficulty. She hated being put off, argued with, when she had made up her mind to do something. She put the receiver down gently after the 'darling', not banging it back on its stand as she felt like doing. She was pleased, though, about remembering the garden syringe thing, it would do the job perfectly, spread a fine spray of petrol, just enough to make a small amount of smoke, maybe a flame or two. Then all they had to do was bang on a couple of doors, shout 'Fire' and scarper before anyone had the chance to recognise them. It was risky, but that's what made it a thrill. One thing would put her off, rain! The forecast had been OK so she could only hope for the best. When tomorrow night was over, the school would be behind her, she would have paid them out— the school, Miss Meadows, the whole poxy lot who hadn't even managed to leave her in the end with a single qualification to become what she wanted to be most in the world: someone who was able to cure and look after animals.

The thought of the flames made her see another picture: fire, out of control, licking all over the thatched roof like a huge torch. It would be a wonderful sight. But no, she dismissed the thought from her mind with some difficulty. She truly didn't want to get Jacko involved in anything as big and dangerous as that. The school fire had been different.

Nina watched TV for a time but soon got bored with it. She looked at her bedside clock—twenty to eleven. She felt tired. She put on Polly's collar, snapped on her expanding nylon lead and took her downstairs, through the kitchen and into the back garden. This garden was much larger than theirs had been. Polly was not yet used to it and might go sniffing around for ages before she decided to come in. Helen's two were much more obedient than Polly and would come in when called, but Nina didn't take the risk. The garden smelt of jasmine, and the tobacco plants near the back door gleamed white in the darkness and gave out a lovely scent. Polly went to the length of the lead, squatting down now and again. Nina inhaled the air and a curious feeling came over her.

She felt calm, happy. Perhaps, she thought, contented would be a better word to explain her feelings as she stood there in the dark garden. Yet she hadn't got what she wanted. There were lots of things she needed in order to qualify as a veterinary nurse. She also wanted a moped. Dad wouldn't go for that, though—well, not easily. Mrs Erskine, the senior nurse, to cope with . . . She wondered too how Mum and Stanley were getting on. She shrugged her shoulders. How little it meant to her. Funny, that—after all, Mum had been Mum for sixteen years of her life. Now she was someone else.

The calmness persisted. Nina took one more long breath, inhaling the perfume of the white flowers beside her, then she reeled in Polly's lead and they went upstairs together. Polly curled up in her new bed, eyes brown and sleepy but still open as she watched Nina getting ready for bed.

As she got into bed, she heard the front door close and then a car start up and drive away. The guest going. 'Young Harper' had departed. There was silence for a while. Nina hoped that Helen and Dad were at least having a snog. She was just going to put out her bedside light when there was a light tap on the door and Helen's equally quiet voice said, 'May I come in?'

Nina, genuinely pleased, answered 'Yes, of course.'

Helen came in, looked over at Polly. 'She's really taken to her beddy, hasn't she?' she said. She came over and sat on Nina's bed. 'How's work going, Nina?'

'Great, great. I love it. The nurses have always been nice to me, Helen.'

'Good.' Helen looked pleased.

'Mrs Erskine. She came back from her hols. Strict, isn't she?' Nina made a little face.

Helen laughed. 'Strict? She's strict with me, Nina! A real sergeant major! But she is wonderful with animals.'

'Wonderful?'

'They trust her, she's got such good hands with them.'

'Good hands?'

Helen nodded. 'Cats, dogs, budgies, snakes. They seem to know, to feel the confidence, the kindness in her hands when she holds them.

Even for an injection. Don't mind her strictness, as you call it. She's a born teacher anyway.'

'She'll never have to teach me, Helen. I've blown it.'

Helen put out a hand and covered Nina's. 'I have, dear, with your father's help, got in touch with a private school.'

Nina's face lit up. 'Oh, thank you, Helen.'

Helen shook her head. 'We had to tell them everything, Nina.'

'Why, why?' Nina asked.

'Because honesty is the only way, darling!'

'What did they say?' Nina felt almost sick with fear. The answer was what she feared. Helen shook her head.

'I'm afraid they wouldn't even consider you as a pupil, Nina.'

Nina burst into tears. Helen put her arms around her. 'We have contacted another school. They may feel differently.' She hugged Nina tightly.

'They won't, they won't.' Nina sobbed.

'They may. We will try. You did a silly thoughtless thing. I know children in school think "weed" is nothing, just a bit of fun, Nina. But it's not, dear. It can lead to so much trouble.'

Nina mopped her eyes with tissues. 'Well, it's led me into—it's ruined my chances of doing what I want to do.'

Helen shook her head. 'As long as you learn

that cannabis is not legal, cigarettes are harmful, that's something.'

Nina thought guiltily of the pack in her drawer. 'I'll never do any of it again if I can get another start, Helen!'

Helen got up, went over and gave the now sleeping Polly a pat on her head. 'Good-night, Polly.' The dog opened one brown eye and looked up at her, then closed it again. Helen came back to the bed, bent down and kissed Nina's cheek. 'Sleep well, dear, and remember, everyone is on your side.'

Nina watched her leave the room. Luckily Helen had left the door almost wide open when she came in, also Nina's dressing-gown was hanging on the door, so she did not see the picture of Miss Meadows now with the completed ring of flames right round her. Nina slipped out of bed, took the cigarette pack. There were about fifteen left. One by one she broke each cigarette in half and dropped it down the lavatory. She pulled the flush and threw the pack in her waste-paper basket. 'No more fags and no more weed.' Only one thing she would not give up. She wanted to see Miss Meadows rushing from her cottage, screaming, 'Fire, fire!' Then she'd be, not happy, but feel she had paid a debt, got rid of a resentment, a hatred.

Nina knew, and it kept her awake for some time, that Helen would not only disapprove of what she was doing, she would be horrified,

horrified too that she was involving another person, Jacko. It was strange, she had known Helen a very short time in her sixteen years yet she wanted to please her more than anyone in the world. She didn't even feel that for Mum, yet she felt that Mum didn't feel it for her either. Was that wrong? Nina had always felt slightly muddled about herself and Mum. Dad was fonder of her, she supposed. That was why he spoiled her. Was it to make up for Mum? Mum had said little about the fact that she had had her later in life. She had always been sharper with her than Dad and Nina searched her memory as far back as she could. She couldn't remember Mum ever hugging her like Helen had done that night.

Nina felt no animosity to Elizabeth, just a puzzlement as to why it had been so. Was she different with Stanley? As Dad was with Helen. She thought of an oldie, a song she must have heard when she was young. Mum sang it when—who was it? Sinatra?—sang it. 'Change partners and dance, you may never have to change partners again . . .' Perhaps it was from a film, she couldn't remember, but it fitted Mum and Dad perfectly, perhaps their new partners would last and they would never have to change partners again.

Nina looked at the clock: nearly midnight. She'd better get to sleep. Tomorrow night would be a long one. She tried not to think too much about it. She wondered how Jacko was feeling. Should she call him? It wouldn't wake his dad, according to Jacko. She tapped his number.

'Yes?' He sounded sleepy.

'Sorry, it's Nina, you all right?'

'Yes.'

Nina spoke quietly. 'I've made new arrangements for tomorrow night.'

'Yes, what?'

Nina felt cross with him for not sounding more wide awake. 'Well, get your head together. Let's meet at our house, I've still got the key, earlier than I said. I've looked, it's dark by nine thirty. Let's meet at the house at seven, or eight. Go round to the cottage about eleven. We can try out the syringe with water in the garden, we want it right.'

Jacko sounded more awake now. 'I think that's good, why wait till later, no point. I've got the matches.'

'Good, see you at the house, then—say eight?'

'Yeah, say eight. I love you, Nina.'

Nina put the telephone down and sighed. 'I've got the matches.' Big deal, she thought. It was difficult to get to sleep with tomorrow night on her mind, but at last she slept, accompanied by a short rhythmic snore from Polly's basket.

CHAPTER FOURTEEN

Nina woke with a start. She sat up and looked over at Polly. She was sound asleep, still making her little noise. What had wakened her? Nina looked at the bedside clock. Ten past five—why had she wakened so early? The birds were twittering outside in the trees. It was not fully light and the birds themselves sounded as if they were not yet fully awake.

Nina stretched, then pulled the duvet close around her neck and tried to settle down again. Go to sleep until a more reasonable hour! She started thinking, tried not to. Wanted to feel drowsy, sleepy. What day was it? Thursday. Yes of course. Her day off. The rota this week gave her Thursday off, but that meant she worked on Sunday. Of course it was Thursday. As she let her thoughts rob her of the wished-for drowsy comfort, she snuggled under the duvet. The light had grown a little stronger and she could see Miss Meadows staring at her from the the door—no dressing-gown there now, as there had been when Helen had come in to say good-night. That was thrown over a chair. Miss Meadows with her ring of flames was visible, looking more realistic, more threatening than Nina could remember the picture had ever done before.

Well, Thursday would mean a lot to Miss

Meadows. Fear? No. Terror, Nina hoped, would be part of her day today. She thought of Jacko and his continual 'I love you, Nina.' She wished he would shut up. She didn't like to say, 'Cool it, Jacko. I don't love you, never will,' not while she wanted his help anyway.

The light grew stronger still; the birds' twittering burst into full song. The picture on the door grew clearer. Six fifteen. Nina certainly did not intend to get up. She could hear stirrings in the house, though. Helen was a very early riser. She liked to have plenty of time to have breakfast, get dressed and clean the cats' trays if they had used them. She never asked the daily to do that. Nina thought of last night, that lovely hug, that kiss. She knew Helen would do everything she could to get her a place somewhere where she could get the grades she needed but Nina was not convinced. No one would take her on after the record 'Miss Butchy Meadows' had given her.

At last she managed a morning doze and when she woke it was nine o'clock. Dad must have gone to the office, Helen to the surgery. She almost wished she was there to while away the long day, till she could talk to Jacko and carry out their little plan. She could hear the daily working in the kitchen, then the hoover started up. Nina decided to have her bath and dress. After giving Polly her usual few biscuits and making herself some toast, Nina got ready for Polly's walk. She could hear the daily working upstairs now. Helen's routine was, Nina thought, marvellous. The daily came in six mornings a week, then, at about five, the cook came in to do the evening meal. Dad was usually on time. Nina remembered how much 'overtime' he used to do when Mum and he were splitting up.

Helen was sometimes a little late, sometimes quite late, if an emergency operation or illness had detained her. Normally they dined together, but tonight since her new arrangement to do their 'deed' at an earlier time she had had to tell Helen that she would not be in for the evening meal. Helen had asked no questions, just offered to leave something out for when she got in. She expected Dad would say, 'Where's she gone and who with?' But he did much less of that kind of questioning these days.

Polly galloped about at the end of her long extending lead. Nina would not let her off in case she couldn't find her way back to her new home. The other two dogs went to work with Helen—had done so, she told Nina, since they came to her as puppies. Nina had never thought of her father as particularly a dog lover. He was nice to Polly, but never played with her or took much notice of her. Nina had wondered how he would cope with a horse, two big dogs, plus a little one and two cats. He seemed to love them and, in consequence, Polly got more attention from him as well.

Nina thought with a little giggle that if Helen had kept alligators Dad, she was sure, would have become an 'Alligator Man'. Such was love, she thought. As for herself and Jacko, that wasn't love. Never would be, that was for sure. She wondered whether she would ever feel like Dad did about Helen and Helen about Dad. Never. She decided it wasn't for her. Mum and Dad had had the feeling, loved each other at one time. But that was all over now. They had both found someone else. But supposing one of them hadn't, just been left on their own? Nasty!

No, she decided, reeling Polly's lead in. Not for her. But—what for her? Nothing now. That's why she and Jacko were putting their torch tonight. The depressing thought made her feel like crying or breaking something. She thought of the snug little thatched cottage and the old witch inside it. She would love to see it burn to the ground, old witch and all, but in her heart she knew she couldn't do that.

She made herself some lunch, cold chicken and salad; there was always something to make a meal with in Helen's house. She fed Polly too. She felt so restless when she had finished her meal. She could not stay here. She needed, for some reason, to be in the 'old house'. She needed to go and look at the cottage. She had told Jacko last night to meet her at eight. That was hours away! She could ring him at the garage and ask him to come earlier. He could work at any time. It was hardly a garage. His dad's drinking had reduced it to a 'mend a banger' place really. Jacko would have liked to move on, to a bigger, better garage. But he didn't like to leave his dad.

Nina decided not to telephone Jacko. She wanted to be alone. She didn't know why. She gave Polly another walk. Right across the field this time. She had decided to leave and get the three thirty bus. She gave her little dog a meal. Polly went contentedly to bed. Nina locked the back door, left the house and walked to the bus stop. She felt cold, as if she were going somewhere with no reason. There was really no reason for the bus. She had only to ring Jacko. He would fetch her, or take her to any place she wanted to go. She only had to ask and he'd be there, at her bidding, no questions.

But she wanted to go to the old house, stay a while and think, without even Polly. The bus came, she boarded it, paid the driver and sat. She hardly noticed the route they were taking. She had travelled this way enough when she first went to the vet's as a sort of volunteer before. Now she really had a job there! She didn't even look out of the bus windows and almost passed her stop.

Once off, she walked briskly to what had so recently been her home. She let herself in, closed the door behind her and went up to her old room to see if there was anything she had left behind she would now like to keep. She opened the few drawers, found in one a roach. She smelled it, collected it between her finger and thumb. She took it along to the loo, dropped it in and pulled the chain. What had made her do that? She might just as well have smoked it, help pass the time. But she didn't want it.

She looked at her watch. She would walk round and peep at the thatched cottage, just look at it. Jacko wouldn't be here for ages. She started along another familiar road where she often walked Polly. At the road edge of the cul de sac she peered down. There was the cottage. In front of it two fire engines! The flaming roof, the blackened top windows did not entrance her now. She raced nearer, around the engines, before anybody could stop her.

The man she had seen before, mowing his lawn, was standing, one hand over his mouth. He hurried to her, seemed to recognise her.

'I lit a bonfire, then the wind started to blow the sparks about a bit. I went in—tea was ready.' He almost broke down.

'Where's Miss Meadows?'

'Who? Oh, the lady. She wasn't very well yesterday. The doctor said she had a little stroke. I and the wife went in this morning. You know, neighbourly. She said she'd go to bed, said she was giddy.' Nina felt giddy herself at the enormity of what had happened.

Now an ambulance arrived. Smoke began billowing out of the lower window on the left-hand side of the door, the room where Nina had sat with Miss Meadows, her 'tormenter' as she called her then. The smoke from the other lower window caused the firemen to shift about four of the hoses to that side and water gushed from their great nozzles into the lower room.

'She'd be dead. That smoke!' the man said, almost wringing his hands.

Suddenly Nina clutched his arm. 'The dog!' she said.

'What?' The man looked at her without understanding.

Nina ran round through his garden, over the low wall and into the cottage garden. She peered into the kitchen. There was the labrador, the puppy. He was barking. Smoke was already coming under the kitchen door. Nina looked round in desperation, picked up a large lump of rock from a small rockery, smashed the glass of the back door. She cut her arms on the glass as she hurtled into the kitchen. She grabbed the dog—he was coughing but alive. He seemed to weigh a ton, but she carried him round to the front of the house.

She could hear the next-door man shouting at the fireman above the roar of the burning thatch. 'She's gone in there to try and get her out. She's gone in there!'

'Who has?'

'The girl, she ran up the road, just as you moved to the other window, said something to me then ran through my garden and . . . here she is, look!'

Nina staggered up to the fireman.

'Bring her into my house, and the dog. That's Miss Meadows' dog. Is he alive?'

The fireman was not so kind. 'What the hell did you think you were doing? We've had two men with breathing apparatus trying to get to her. Part of the roof's fallen in, you could have been killed!'

The fire chief came up. 'They're bringing her out now—looks like we're too late.' And as the limp, smoke-blackened body of Miss Meadows was laid gently on the ambulance trolley, Nina burst into tears.

*   *   *

Jim, as she now knew he was called, took Nina and the dog into the house next door. Nina felt herself shaking.

'It's my fault, Lil. All my fault. I should never have made that bonfire, but we've done it before, haven't we, and it's been all right?'

Lil, a fat motherly woman, tried to comfort him. 'Of course we have, dear. You couldn't know how it would catch, not that far away.' She turned to Nina. 'You were a brave girl, a very brave girl, to try to save her. Did you know her?'

'She was deputy head at my school. I've left . . .' She stopped. 'How is the dog?' she asked. As if in answer the puppy sidled up to her, still coughing over and over again.

'I expect the puppy needs water and I'll get you a cup of tea. Nothing like it when you've had a shock.' She waddled out to the kitchen. Jim still sat, his heads in his hands. Nina did not know what to say to him. She got up and went into the kitchen.

'May I use your telephone, Mrs . . . ?'

'Skinner, but everyone calls me Lil.' She motioned to the hall. 'Yes, of course you can.'

Nina went into the hall. She rang the surgery. 'Is Helen there?' she asked.

'Yes. It's Nina, isn't it?'

Nina was thankful the receptionist recognised her voice. 'Yes,' she said.

'I'll get her, hold on.'

There was a sound of footsteps as the receptionist crossed the floor. Then Helen spoke. 'Yes, what is it, Nina?'

Nina burst into tears. 'Please come, Helen. I'm in the house next door to Miss Meadows' cottage.' She gave the address and the number of the house supplied by Lil Skinner. She put the telephone receiver down after Helen's immediate 'I'll come at once.'

Lil put an arm round her waist. 'Come and have a cup of tea, dear. Is that your mother you phoned?'

Nina wiped her eyes. 'Yes, sort of. In a way,' she said.

*   *   *

Jacko loved Nina, there had never been anyone else since she was thirteen. Her brown eyes, her full pouty lips, her determination, her natural rebellion against the oldies. She loved setting fire to things just like he did. They had some laughs, not burning anything serious, but setting fire to skips, dustbins, pouring on a bit of petrol first. It was great. Once, though, he had suggested setting fire to a chicken house up on the allotments. When Nina found out that there were chickens in it, she went ape. 'It would hurt them, they'd catch fire, suffer,' she had yelled. He had tried to make a joke of it. 'Well, roast chicken is OK!' he had said. Nina hadn't spoken to him for a week.

Nina was clever. Her parents wanted her in by ten, ten thirty, till she was sixteen, they said. She got out whenever she wanted to, on to the flat roof and down and away. They went to discos. Nina wasn't keen, rowed with other girls or boys sometimes.

When she had planned to burn the school, he had been a bit shocked. That was to get back at Miss Meadows. Nina hated her. Jacko drew her a picture—well, a cartoon of Miss Meadows. She had been his teacher too. Nina had put it on her bedroom door, so she said, and drawn little flames all around it with orange and red crayons. He liked drawing and was good at posters. Nina's mum had been livid when she saw it but Nina wouldn't take it down. When he'd got the bike, that had been brill too. They could go where they wanted, sometimes stay out late, or early morning. They had sex. Nina told him what to do, not that he didn't know but what she wanted him to do, how she wanted it. Condoms were a must with Nina.

Burning the school had been brilliant too, more than anything else. He had pinched an old can from his father's shed, back from the days when his father used to mow the lawn. Now he was never sober enough to use the petrol mower. Since Mum took off years ago, he just drank and gambled. They had poured the petrol, Nina and he, on the wood post of the bike shed. The flames leaped up. Nina had gone quite wild, dancing about saying, 'More, more!'

It had got a bit out of hand, spread to one of the classrooms. They had ended up in the field at the back, having sex. They'd scarpered then. The fuzz had come, questioned everyone, but Nina had been in bed at half-ten according to her father. He wasn't trying to get her off the hook, he really thought she was. Anyway, the fuzz never fixed it on anyone.

Then Nina got expelled. She was gutted. She had wanted to take some course or other, now she couldn't. She blamed it all on Meadows. Threatened she was going to frighten her, a little petrol on the old girl's thatched roof—just a little. A bit of a fire, make her run out screaming. Jacko worried about this, worried a lot. Everyone at the school, and probably outside the school too, knew Nina hated Miss Meadows. She had even boasted she'd get back at her.

Jacko wanted to protect her, that's why he had decided to come to the cottage earlier, spray the petrol, set it alight and watch Miss Meadows rush out then go and tell Nina he had done it. He longed to do it to pay her out for being so rotten to his Nina. He'd tell Nina afterwards he'd done it just for her.

God, it had all turned out so awful, awful! He'd turned up early in the afternoon. Not a soul about. Only the man in the house next door trying to make a bonfire and not making much of a success of it. Jacko had gone round to the back of the cottage, looking for twitching curtains. Nothing. He worked quickly, chucking a plastic bag of petrol, only a small amount, up on to the thatch. Then he lit a bundle of matches and threw them up after it. At first the flames had been small, just licking the straw. Then they had got bigger, bigger, higher and higher and much wider.

He had run, torn across the field behind the cottage, hid amongst the trees and tangled shrubs, which they would be clearing soon to build more houses. Thank goodness the greenery was still there. Hidden, he had watched. He could see very little of what was going on in front of the cottage. A red car drew up and a man got out and went into the bonfire man's house. Then a fire engine arrived, lights flashing, siren going, then another. Then an ambulance.

Thank God, Jacko thought. She's alive. Relief surged through him. At least he hadn't killed her! The roof of the cottage collapsed. Had they got her out yet? He must see more. Carefully he made his way nearer and nearer. Another fire engine rattled down towards the cottage. He must risk it, he must see! Oh God, what had he done?

Then he saw Nina running towards him round the side of the cottage, momentarily deserted by the firemen who were concentrating on the front. 'The dog, the dog!' she was yelling. He was not even sure if she saw him, although they almost collided. He slowed down and joined the crowd, watching, but held back by the police. A grey-haired woman spoke to him, holding a white handbag clutched to her chest. 'They reckon it was the bonfire that started it,' she said. 'That's what they say. They reckon she must be dead in there—ill in bed, she was. Must have died of the smoke. They're still trying to get her out. What a terrible thing. So quick. You don't expect it, do you?' She wiped her eyes.

As the woman spoke Jacko saw Nina coming round the side of the cottage carrying a dog. She went round the bonfire, now doused by the firemen. She was talking to them. It looked as if she was crying. He heard her say, 'I did think I could reach the sitting-room, I thought she'd be there.' In that instant Jacko knew she was lying. Nina was good at lying. She would risk her life for the dog, but not for Miss Meadows. He knew it, she knew it, but no one else did, or ever would. He saw a last glimpse of her talking to the fireman, then he moved off, away from the crowd and away from the terrible smell of smoke.

*   *   *

After she had telephoned Helen, Nina's mind seemed to stop working. She drank the heavily sugared tea. The only thing that seemed warm and real was the dog—he was hardly more than a puppy. He leant against her legs, still trembling, coughing now and again. She put her hand on the dog's back and rubbed it to and fro. She noticed his collar and disc but, for some reason, she did not want to read the name on it. Through the big double-glazed window she could see the the scene outside. The roar of the burning thatch was now silenced. It was just a blackened, dripping tangle. Smoke had blackened the windows. Nina could only see one fire engine now. From that engine a steady stream of water was still being poured on to the roof and wall in case, she supposed, there was more fire. Flames still liable to sneak up again. The smoke was still rising, black and smelling acrid.

The crowd was thinning now, but there were still people there watching. Policemen too. Jim had gone outside to talk to them. There must have been flames, Nina thought, to really make a fire. But now she knew that she never wanted to see another fire or flame again, never, never, never! She could not forget the blanket-covered body on the ambulance trolley—Miss Meadows. The hated Miss Meadows! Well, there was no Miss Meadows now to hate or blame. She was gone.

Nina could not take her eyes off the scene outside the window. She could only stroke the dog's warm back. Without the dog Nina felt she might easily have had to run screaming into the road outside. Someone rang the door bell. Lil said, 'I'll go,' got up and opened the door. 'Oh, yes, do come in. She's right here. It's the local paper, dear. A reporter.'

A young man came in. He looked both apprehensive and apologetic. He carried a camera. Nina looked at him. He asked her a question. She did not, could not answer him. The question seemed to mean nothing. The reporter looked at Lil, 'The young lady, I believe . . . she risked her life to . . .'

'Yes, she did. She's a real heroine. She got

in and she knew the firemen were trying to get into the room where Miss Meadows was. She was trying to save her, see?'

The reporter turned to Nina. 'Did you know the lady who has . . .' He hesitated. '. . . who has died in the fire, miss?'

Nina nodded then answered in a husky voice, an almost inaudible one: 'She was deputy head at my school.' She couldn't say any more. A light flashed which made Nina jump, another flash and the reporter thanked them. For what? Nina wondered. The door bell rang again. This time it was Helen. The door bell, the noise outside, the reporter and his camera—it was all too much.

Nina felt she had never in her life been so pleased to see anyone. Helen took her in her arms. 'What has happened, what are you doing here?' Helen had just brushed past the departing reporter. She was greeted by a tumble of words from Lil who was plying Nina with tea.

'That was the reporter from the local paper, they get on to things so quickly now, don't they? No wonder though, your daughter has been so brave. She went into the house from the back, you see. This is Miss Meadows' dog, but she was already dead, the lady. She had a stroke, you see, not a bad one but she was upstairs in bed and—', Lil paused, '—My husband blames himself. "It was all my fault," he said. He lit this bonfire and one of the sparks must have blown over. It got a bit windy. Oh, God. He's very upset. We've had bonfires before and it's been all right, and your daughter—'

Helen had to stop her as she would have prattled on for ever. Nina said, 'Can we go home, and take the dog? It hasn't got anyone now.' She was still shaking and the dog at her feet coughed now and again.

'Let me just go and have a word with the fireman and the police, dear.' Helen got up and went out and Nina could see her first talking, then listening to a fireman, the one who seemed to be in charge. He talked at length to Helen, then Nina saw her have a word with the policeman who seemed to be taking particulars from Helen. The big hose with its shiny arc of water was still playing on the cottage.

Helen came back into the house, thanked them for all they had done for the girl they still referred to as 'your daughter'. The dog followed Nina. He was limping a little. Helen put him in the back of the Land Rover and helped Nina into the passenger seat. 'You were very brave and a bit foolish to risk your life like that. The chief said you only got in because you slipped round the back of the crowd just as they were moving their hoses to another part of the building.'

Once home Helen insisted Nina went to bed. 'I'll take the dog to the surgery and go over him. Poor thing, he doesn't know what's happening.' She was about to come upstairs with Nina, but then went to the kitchen. Nina knew she must get the picture off her door and tear it into a thousand pieces before Helen saw it. There was so much to do, so many thoughts and so much remorse. Once upstairs she phoned Jacko on his mobile. There was no answer and she had to put the telephone down at last, but she felt she wanted to talk about it to someone.

She telephoned Elizabeth. She already knew. Helen had rung her while Nina had been on the phone trying to speak to Jacko. Next the picture. She tore it off the door, then ripped it into smaller and smaller bits before it went into her waste-paper basket. It brought back memories of burning the clothes in front of her mother—it seemed ages ago. Elizabeth had been quite distressed on the telephone. 'Poor Miss Meadows,' she had said. Nina, all her hatred gone, could see herself as she had been, particularly to the dead woman. She hated herself. She could not think of the teacher with love, even liking, only sorrow, regret.

Everything changed for Nina that day and the next. The local paper gave her a front page headline: BRAVE SCHOOLGIRL ATTEMPTS TO SAVE HEAD. Then the story occupying half the front page. Mostly told by Lil, and mostly inaccurate. Still, what did it all matter? Miss

Meadows would never be able to enjoy her cottage, her retirement, her dog. Nina grew up that day, saw herself as she really was, selfish, stupid, not worth thinking about, but capable, she knew, of making a fresh start.

A few days later, Elizabeth rang to say the school had asked her to bring her daughter to see the new headmistress, what for, she did not know. It was weird joining up with Elizabeth again. The new head met them at the school front door and led them up to her office. They sat down. Nina felt her heart racing—what now?

'We cannot overlook, Mrs Mason, your daughter's great bravery and selflessness in trying to save poor Miss Meadows. So we feel that, while we cannot approve of the misdemeanour, we would like to rescind the suspension and subsequent expulsion. It will not be on her records if she wishes to come back to school or pass on to any other course.'

Before Elizabeth could speak, Nina thanked the new head. 'I want to be a veterinary nurse more than anything in the world,' she said.

The head nodded. 'Well, if you work hard for your GCSEs and A levels, you should have no trouble with that.' She even smiled quite warmly. 'If you wish to come back here at the start of next term.'

As they walked from the school, Nina looked at her mother with new clarity. 'Are you happy now, Mum?' she asked.

286

Elizabeth put an arm round her daughter's shoulders and kissed her on the cheek. 'So happy, Nina—and Henry, is he happy, do you think?'

'Wonderfully,' then with rare tact Nina added, 'Helen is just as perfect as your Stanley, I expect. And I'm the victim of a broken home, but not so badly off.'

Elizabeth laughed and, for the first time, they felt a bonding.

'One day you will find a boy you really love and you will want to give up your work just to look after and love him.'

Nina looked her in the eye. 'As I said long ago and hurt your feelings, Mum, "Dream on!"'